Switching Hands

Sipping her drink, Melanie walked over to investigate Jason's photos. They featured a clan of college boys in various situations: lifting tankards of beer at an outdoor bar, wearing football uniforms at a sunny park, dressed in formal tuxedos on the marble steps of a Georgian mansion. In every shot the fellows were physically close, arms draped around each others' shoulders, hips and thighs pressed close together. Each member of the gang was better-looking than the last, from the blond with the cruel sneer and floppy hair to the tanned bodybuilder with the military crewcut. Together they formed a smorgasbord of cute boys, and they all shared Jason's sultry, jaded expression.

What a bunch of spoilt brats! Melanie said to herself. The pictures filled her head with homoerotic scenes as she imagined the young men nude, sweaty, engaged in wrestling matches in a grassy meadow à la D.H. Lawrence. Better yet, she pictured all of them – more than twenty-five altogether – overpowering her and taking her like a band of marauders. By the time Jason reappeared, the potent blend of alcohol and her imagination had made her more th— little ho

Other books by the author:

Hard Blue Midnight

Switching Hands
Alaine Hood

BLACK LACE

Black Lace books contain sexual fantasies.
In real life, always practise safe sex.

First published in 2004 by
Black Lace
Thames Wharf Studios
Rainville Road
London W6 9HA

Design by Smith & Gilmour, London
Printed and bound by Mackays of Chatham PLC

ISBN 0 352 33896 2

Contents

1 Winter Affairs

Summer flings get a lot of attention for their emotional drama, but winter affairs are really more important, Melanie thought as she walked down Harbor Street one frosty morning in November. Raw weather demanded raw lust, especially in a climate where snow could fall for seven months of the year, but she also had to find a lover whose moods were stable enough to put up with long dark evenings indoors. Her criteria were tough. He should be well read, funny, and good at card games, but not so cerebral or competitive that he bored her after the first weekend. He should be able to cook, or at least not be stingy about paying to have meals delivered from exotic restaurants, and he should be highly creative and experimental, because nothing was more exciting than a few hours of kinky roleplay on a snowbound afternoon.

Not that Melanie would have any afternoons to spare in the coming season. She had just taken over as the manager of Chimera, the vintage boutique where she had worked since she was a teenager. Under her influence, the shop's inventory had grown increasingly daring, with more emphasis on lingerie and sexy outfits. Last month she had made one of her fantasies come true, adding a selection of sex toys and classic erotica to the shop. Since then, sales had been skyrocketing. The place was making twice as much money as it used to, but Melanie was working three times as hard just to keep her head above water.

As soon as Chimera's customers heard about her new business interests, the edgy ones among them began clamouring for fetish clothes. They wanted to mix and match leather corsets and PVC halter tops with vintage skirts, gloves and jewellery. More often than not, Melanie could find the article in question on the Internet, but her dream was to be able to offer a wider variety of clothes and toys, objects that people could stroke and hold and try on in front of her mirrors. There was something so intimate and exciting about shopping in the flesh, touching things that you'd seen only in your dreams, and being able to take them home that same day.

Thinking about corsets and halters made Melanie shiver. Her nipples were turning into icy nubs under her sweater – a pale-pink, beaded cashmere cardigan that she wore over skin-tight black trousers. The outfit was too thin for the grim weather, but Melanie couldn't bear to ruin its effect with an overcoat, not when the old house next door to her shop was swarming with carpenters and restoration experts.

The house was being converted into a local-history museum, and the crew was working overtime to get the bulk of the work done before the severe snowstorms set in. A stream of men was flowing down the sidewalk right now, each one more divine than the last, all of them tall and muscular and gorgeous. They wore their own unofficial uniform: faded jeans and freshly laundered white T-shirts under flannels and denim jackets, work boots, and a plain gold earring or a tattoo here and there. They smelled of freshly laundered cotton and shaving cream and mint toothpaste. Some had neat beards, others were clean-shaven. All of them gaped at Melanie as if she were a young Jane Russell, stepping out of an old movie.

'Good morning, boys,' she trilled, waving and giving them a mock pout that turned into a radiant smile. The men stumbled and collided like a herd of startled bulls. Any one of those juicy hunks, maybe all of them, would be ideal for a weekend of carnal gymnastics, Melanie thought, but her mind was still fixed on her imaginary winter lover. She wanted someone to settle down with until spring came.

She unlocked the door to the shop, savouring the early morning silence. By noon the place would be packed. Weekdays brought out the housewives who came from surrounding towns and cities to shop for lingerie and toys to spice up their private lives. Along with the vintage clothing, Chimera was now offering brand-new day and evening wear for women who didn't have the money for older designer clothing, the time to care for them, or the space to store them. It was a shame that the pace of modern life didn't leave more time for collecting couture, and that closets in modern houses were built so small that they couldn't hold enough clothing for a single season, much less four. But as a practical businesswoman, Melanie knew that she had to tailor her inventory to her customers' lifestyles.

Three weeks ago, Melanie had taken the liberty of redecorating the shop's interior. She had had the back wall and one of its adjacent walls painted a dramatic shade of plum, giving the room the impression of being informally divided into departments. Large mirrors created a sense of space, and one of Melanie's salesgirls had splattered the edges with metallic paint to make eclectic borders. In the purple section were displayed the new lingerie, evening wear and toys, which were hidden in an area called the Alcove. In the first days of its existence, Melanie had hung a sarong over the Alcove, but since then she had replaced it with a curtain of shimmering opalescent beads, aiming to be a little less coy.

The remaining walls were antique white, sponge-painted with dusky lilac. Here vintage gowns, linens and accessories were arranged, and wreaths of dried roses hung above the antique mirrors. Customers could try on a pair of jeans or a slinky Spandex dress in the plum section, then go over to the lilac section to accessorise the outfit with sequined sweaters, elbow gloves, or rhinestone clip-on earrings. The overall effect made the shop seem larger, but illusions created by paint and mirrors didn't solve the basic problem: she was running out of space. The Alcove alone demanded its own room, a more open area where people could browse freely, without having to worry about literally bumping into their neighbours.

Every time she looked around the shop and saw the vivid, colourful results of her imagination, Melanie had a mental orgasm. Still, a day never passed that she didn't think about Lori Marwick, her best friend, business partner, and the owner of the old Victorian house that was home to Chimera. Lori was living out her own fantasies in Europe, travelling from one country to another with her sexy new husband Gavin and writing a book about erotic photography. But Lori couldn't live in Europe forever ... could she? Some day she would come back to reclaim her house, her shop, and find that her upstart business partner had thoroughly transformed it.

The telephone rang, giving her an excuse to push guilty thoughts about Lori out of her head.

'Melanie? Harrison Blake here.'

'Harrison! You couldn't have called at a better time.'

Harrison's family had been overseeing the town's oldest bank for over a hundred years, and he chaired the architectural planning commission.

'I have good news for you,' he said in a voice loaded with importance. Everything Harrison said was loaded with importance, but he sounded especially full of it today. 'You're on the docket for December's planning meeting. I can't guarantee the outcome, but just between you and me, your proposal looks very promising.'

Melanie let out a whoop of triumph. For the past few weeks she had been sweating over her request to add a wing onto the side of the house, a space that she would allocate to new clothing. The Alcove would be moved to one of the upstairs bedrooms, which would solve two problems: the lack of space, and the growing curiosity of the under-eighteen crowd. In the late afternoons Melanie often spent most of her time gatekeeping; it was so hard to keep the younger customers away from the erotica. If Morne Bay weren't so uptight about the slightest modification to any architectural structure that was more than fifty years old, she would be knocking a wall out of the house this very second.

'That's terrific, Harrison. I can't wait.'

'I'm especially pleased with your idea about working in partnership with the new museum. If you increase your inventory of antique clothing, it should dovetail perfectly with their mission.'

'Well, it only makes sense that a visit to the museum would whet the tourists' appetite to buy vintage clothes. We purchase most of our stuff in this county. You can't get a much better example of local history than the clothing that people used to wear around here.'

'Quite right. I think your expansion could benefit both enterprises. I want to arrange for you to meet the new curator of the museum, Nathaniel Wentworth. He's a fine scholar and an innovative thinker. We were at Harvard together.'

'I'd be thrilled,' Melanie said politely, although the thought of meeting one of Harrison's college cronies sounded about as thrilling as scrubbing her bathroom floor with a toothbrush. She lowered her voice and turned away from her salesgirl, Luna, who was eavesdropping from the other side of the room. 'I hope you don't think that this news is going to get you off the hook, Harrison.'

'Oh no, I'd never think that,' he replied, allowing the conversation to move into the power dynamic where Melanie had the upper hand.

'I know you have mixed feelings about wearing that butt plug at an official occasion, but trust me, you'll love the end result. It takes courage to live out your fantasies.'

Melanie smiled as she thought back to the strange afternoon a couple of weeks previously. Harrison had come into the shop during a quiet period looking for an anniversary present for his wife. Melanie had helped him pick out a bird's-nest brooch made of rubies interwoven with pearls but, as she wrapped it for him, Harrison had confessed through a bout of nervous coughs that he also wanted to choose a gift from the Alcove for himself. Once behind the beaded curtain, he quietly confessed his guilty secret. For many years he had harboured a fantasy of being trained by a dominant woman to wear an anal plug. She would help him gradually get used to the sensation of the foreign object until he reached the point of being able to wear it in public.

Harrison was very handsome, if you liked the strait-laced mortgage-banker type, but Melanie had always thought he had the erotic appeal of a telephone pole. She had been thrilled to learn that he had such a kinky dream. Harrison's dainty wife didn't exactly fit the role of the authoritarian butt-plug instructor, so Melanie had agreed to play that part for him. First she had given him a private tutorial in inserting the plug into his squeaky clean, tightly clenched hole. Then she gave him assignments that involved wearing it a little bit longer each day, and in situations that involved increased risks of exposure. He had progressed from wearing the plug around the house by himself, to wearing it at dinner with his wife. Now he was able to take an evening stroll through his neighbourhood or shop at the grocery store with the plug nestled against his prostate, giving him the most delicious sensations he'd ever dreamed of.

'You know, Harrison,' Melanie said, 'I think it would be the perfect finale to your training if you wore it at the

sandstone: hard, warm and slightly rough to the touch. Melanie imagined what it would feel like to have them scooping her breasts, massaging her thighs. Like a lot of his crew, he wore a single gold earring. Without the hardhat and denim jacket, he would look like a grown-up bad boy.

Melanie sighed and moistened her lips while Dean stared at her, looking her up and down unashamedly. She had to speak or she would lunge at him in a most uncivilised fashion.

'I want to say how much I admire the work you're doing here. That's what I came over to talk to you about,' she said nervously. 'I'm planning to expand my shop in the spring. I wondered if you and your crew might be available.'

'Your shop is in that old house next door, right?'

'Right.'

'And you want to add on to it?'

'Exactly.'

Dean shook his head. 'Good luck.'

'What are you saying? Don't you want to help me?'

'Show me a permit, then we'll talk,' he said dismissively. 'With this museum going up, every building on the block is going to turn into an historical landmark. Six months from now you won't be able to put up so much as a fencepost without a notarised certificate of approval.'

'It just so happens that I'm meeting with the town's architectural planning commission next month. I fully expect them to approve my proposal.'

'Don't hold your breath.'

'What's that supposed to mean?'

'Look, Melanie, from what I hear, you're a popular lady right now. But I grew up in a fishing village down the coast, and I know what small towns are like. A woman who's upfront about the kind of things you are gets labelled as a bad girl, and bad girls don't get ahead.'

Stung, Melanie took a step backwards and almost tripped over a paint can. 'I know this community a lot better than you do, and these people aren't half as narrow-minded as you think. They're my customers, after all. They've been starving for a shop like mine.'

Dean laughed. 'Oh, don't get me wrong, people are always interested in sex. But deep down, towns like this haven't changed much since the 1950s. Or even the 1850s.'

'You don't know what you're talking about,' she huffed.

Dean smiled and turned back to his work, indicating that he saw no point in continuing the conversation. As he leaned over to pick up a power drill, his jacket and T-shirt rode up his back. Melanie got a good look at the hard panels of his olive-skinned muscles. Tattooed along the beads of his spine was a cruelly intricate dagger. Though the sight of it made the breath catch in Melanie's throat, his cocky, dismissive smile annoyed the hell out of her.

'You'd better adjust your attitude, Dean. You're going to be working for *me* in six months.'

Dean responded with a long dirty look. His moustache and goatee framed a mouth that was full, ripe and sensual – prime kissing material.

'Why wait six months? I could be working for you tonight,' he said.

Melanie's first impulse was to blast him with a withering refusal. But she had a weakness for arrogant men, and she thought she saw some potential for rehabilitation in this one. He stepped past her as if to get back to work, but when his body brushed against hers she knew the contact wasn't accidental. With his flesh pulling her like a magnet, she followed him through the minefield of paint buckets and stacks of cement.

'What time tonight?' she called after him, as he disappeared behind one of the hanging plastic sheets.

He pulled the sheet aside. 'I'm off at six. Then I have to go home and get a shower.'

'Six is fine,' Melanie said. 'Don't bother with the shower.'

As she left the male chaos and returned to the feminine sanctuary of her shop, she was grinning like a fiend. She hoped Dean didn't go home and wash; she could already taste the sweat of a hard day's work on her tongue.

For the rest of the day, Melanie rode a hurricane of emotions. One moment she was high on anticipation and self-confidence, thinking about the planning commission meeting. If she didn't have a fighting chance, she wouldn't have gotten so far as to get a place on their agenda. Ten minutes later, she would remember Dean's condescending smile as he assured her that he knew what small towns were like, and her excitement would curdle into anger. If he could see how Melanie's customers changed when they came into her shop, how their faces glowed when they touched the silk of the vintage gowns and pictured themselves looking like the sensual visions of their dreams, he might catch a glimpse of the transformations she witnessed every day.

That jerk, Melanie thought to herself, pacing back and forth behind the counter. She was so upset that she didn't notice the curious looks that her salesgirls were giving her. He has no idea what he's talking about.

Whenever she needed reassurance that her business ideas were sound, Melanie didn't have to look any further than her Alcove. She walked over to the nook and pulled back the curtain of beads, feeling the rush of pride that always greeted her when she introduced a customer to her magical cavern. Its shelves were stocked with vibrators, plugs, paddles and ticklers in all the colours of the rainbow. The materials ranged from functional to exotic

– from wood and silicone and stainless steel to fur and feathers and iridescent ribbon glass – but the objects shared one purpose: to deliver pleasure. Melanie thought of them as jewels brought up from the sea of the subconscious; and she was the mermaid who guarded the treasure trove.

Dean DeSilva didn't know what it was like to sell a conservative banker his first anal plug, or help a lesbian couple choose the perfect double dildo. He might know who these people were in their public lives, but Melanie knew who they were when they were daydreaming, masturbating, or making love. She wasn't so naive as to think that these public and private selves would ever be fully reconciled, but she refused to give up hope.

Besides, she wasn't simply tolerated in this town; she was all but worshipped. Between the time she got back to the shop that morning and the time she closed down the cash register, she had received two phone calls from local men – one an offer of prolonged sodomy, another an invitation for pizza and ice-skating. In her e-mail she found an offer from a software engineer in Boston to fly her to the Bahamas for Christmas, and several grammatically incorrect declarations of love from teenage admirers with nicknames like HawtDawg and SkaateRat.

Best of all, Bridget Locke, the style editor of the local newspaper phoned to ask if she wanted to be interviewed for a Sunday feature, complete with a two-page spread on Chimera and a full-colour photo of its new manager.

'Are you kidding?' Melanie laughed into the telephone. 'Listen, Bridget, there are three things I never turn down: hot sex, hot clothing, and free publicity.'

She made arrangements to meet Bridget at Chimera for the interview, and when six o'clock rolled around, Melanie's optimism was restored. By springtime she would have an expert contractor and a crew of merry men working for her. She would have to find a more flattering hardhat, however. White plastic didn't look so bad on a stud dressed in jeans and a tight cotton T-shirt, but it was unthinkable on a woman with an addiction to classic couture.

Six o'clock passed, then six-thirty. Melanie sat at her computer in Chimera's tiny back office, fine-tuning the spreadsheet that showed the projections for her business expansion. There was so much to think about. Once she got permission to expand the house, she would need to get a loan from the bank to cover the cost. She was counting on Harrison Blake to help her in that area, but he was a tight-fisted lender. She would have to convince him that the expansion would be profitable enough to pay back the loan. Absorbed in her calculations, Melanie didn't check the time until her stomach rumbled, reminding her that she had been expecting some Grade A beefcake to come by that night.

Melanie scowled at her watch. Cocky bastard. She should have known he would stand her up. She thought about calling the man who had asked her out for pizza and ice-skating; maybe the offer was still good. But she wasn't in the mood for holding hands at a skating rink. She had spent the whole day on a mood-swing roller coaster, and she was primed for some hard, dirty fun.

At seven o'clock she decided to lock up, walk home, and give herself a good workout with a new vibrator that she'd just received in the mail as a tryout product. This iridescent green invention, called the Mermaid, was designed to tickle a woman's clitoris with two tiny fins while hammering away at her G-spot with its tail flipper. You could always count on a Japanese engineer for some ingenious gratification.

Climbing the narrow staircase to her apartment in the old Victorian house where she had lived for years, Melanie saw a folded sheet of paper taped to her door. It was a note from her landlady, reminding her that her lease was up at the end of the month, and asking if she had set a date for moving out.

Moving out? She sank down onto the steps to re-read the note by the flickering illumination of the safety lamp:

Though you've been a perfectly adequate tenant over the years, I've decided not to renew your lease. My sister has been in poor health for months now. She will be moving into the apartment so that I can take care of her while she recovers from a long illness.

'Perfectly adequate?' Incredulous, Melanie repeated the words out loud. This apartment was her home; she had invested not only her time, but her creativity, her imagination, and a lot of money in turning the place into a shrine of Gothic sensuality. Her landlady had been leaving messages on her answering machine for days, asking to speak to her about the lease, but Melanie had assumed that she just wanted to notify her of a rent increase. Never in her worst nightmares had she imagined that she would be pushed out of the place.

Slowly Melanie tore the note into pieces, then tossed them over the railing and watched them float into the darkness. The story about the landlady's sister was an outright lie. Melanie happened to know that her landlady had no siblings, chronically ill or otherwise.

She stood up and hurried down the stairs. She wasn't going to abandon her home that easily. As she turned down the shadowed pathway that led to her landlady's front door, a man-shaped mass emerged from behind a holly hedge. Melanie shrieked. The mass laughed.

'What's the matter? Did you forget we had a date?'

'I didn't forget,' Melanie choked. She recognised Dean DeSilva, but her heart was still in her throat. 'You did!'

'Not likely. I've been hanging around for half an hour. I was just ready to leave when you came up the sidewalk.'

'I thought you were going to meet me at the shop.'

'I went by the shop at six-thirty. The place was dark, so I assumed you'd gone home.'

'How did you know where I live?'

'Sweetheart, everyone within a twenty-mile radius of this town knows where you live. You're a celebrity.'

'This celebrity won't be living here much longer. I just received notice that my lease won't be renewed.'

'That's too bad,' Dean said, looking up at the elaborate Victorian facade. 'This is a great old house. I'd love to get my hands on a classic like this one. What happened with your lease?'

'My landlady cooked up a story about an ailing sister so she'd have an excuse to get rid of me. I'm thinking about consulting a lawyer, but first I'm going to have a talk with that bitch.'

'There's not much you can do, Melanie. She has a right to do whatever she wants with her property.'

'What about me? I have rights as a tenant. And you don't sound very surprised about all this.'

'I'm not surprised, to tell you the truth. You're a controversial item around here.'

'So you think she has a right to kick me out because she doesn't like what I do for a living?' she asked indignantly.

'I'm having a hard time thinking at all, with you standing there looking so gorgeous.'

'Don't patronise me.'

'I'm not patronising you. I'm admiring you.'

Dean's dark eyes gleamed in the light of a full moon. His mouth, wreathed in the smoke that his breath left in the cold air, was a tempting mystery.

'I guess I could talk to my landlady tomorrow,' Melanie sighed.

'I could talk to her, if you'd like. Maybe a little muscle would help to convince her that she's making a mistake.'

'I'd try anything at this point.'

'Anything?'

Dean took hold of Melanie's shoulders then snaked a hand around her waist. She smelled the cowhide of his jacket, heard the creak of the leather, felt the firm pressure of his lips and fingers. He planted a small kiss, little more than a peck, on her neck and it was so packed with sensations that Melanie's libido roared back to life.

'Let's go upstairs,' Melanie said.

'What, no dinner first? I've been labouring all day – I'm starving,' he whinged.

'Oh, you'll eat. Don't worry about that.'

Melanie took Dean's hand and led him up the stairs. Between her distress over the lease and her lust for the horny workman she had forgotten that her apartment was in disarray. She took him straight to her bedroom, where she lit a bank of beeswax candles, counting on their gentle light to hide the clutter. She hadn't washed her sheets for over a week, and they reeked of eau de Melanie.

'I haven't had a lot of time for housekeeping lately,' Melanie confessed.

'Well, you make a very sexy mess,' said Dean. 'This place is a dirty old man's dream.'

Dean plucked a grey silk stocking and a lace bra off the unmade bed. The garments looked like cobwebs in his large, well-carved fingers. He handed the lingerie to Melanie and took off his leather jacket. Underneath he wore a loose white cotton shirt with an open collar and a black leather vest over black jeans and boots. His earring glittered against his shiny black hair. The candlelight turned his skin to Mediterranean honey. He looked as if he had just stepped out of her wildest pirate abduction fantasy.

'Oh dear,' Melanie said.

'What's wrong?'

'I didn't expect you to look so damn good.'

'Anything wrong with a man looking good?'

'Nothing at all. But it makes me wonder what it will be like to be your boss. We haven't even started working together yet, and I'm already committing sexual harassment.'

Dean grinned. 'Be my guest.'

Melanie placed her hands on Dean's chest. His heart thrummed under her palm. He had disobeyed her request that he not take a shower, but his skin emitted a cinnamon musk that was almost as good as work sweat. She ran her fingers along the ledges of his chest, then down to his abdomen, which was equally hard. When she reached his silver belt buckle, he caught her wrists.

'Call me old-fashioned,' he said, 'but I like to have at least five minutes of fully clothed foreplay before I get down to serious business.'

'Why?' Melanie pouted.

'Once my dick makes an appearance, it's all over.'

'Just as I thought. You *are* a cocky bastard.'

Melanie had trouble getting the words out, because Dean was sucking her fingertips like a man trying to get the last savoury shreds of meat off a barbecued rib. Melanie gasped.

'You like this?' he asked around a mouthful of fingers.

'You should have a licence for those lips,' she teased.

'I'm just getting started. Wait till you see what's next.'

All of a sudden Melanie was sailing through the air, Dean's hands grasping her around the waist. She landed on her back with a thud, her legs draped over the edge of the bed. Dean knelt between her thighs and pulled off her shoes, then he began to apply the same delectable sucking to her toes. Pins and needles of pleasure shot through her feet all the way up to between her legs. Before she could get used to these sensations, he abandoned her feet and peeled off her pants. He pulled her further down the bed so that her bottom touched the edge of the mattress, then he spread her thighs and went to work on her pussy.

Never in her life had Melanie been eaten out so voraciously. Dean took her whole vulva into his mouth as if it were a sun-ripened strawberry and sucked her flesh with such relish that it might as well be edible. He sucked in a slow, pulsating rhythm that had her going wild. The intensity increased, but before Melanie could give herself over completely to a climax, Dean pushed her legs back and shifted his attention to her bottomhole. As he teased her anus with his tongue, he fondled her slit with his fingers, avoiding direct pressure with her overly sensitive clit.

Melanie pushed up her sweater and bra and milked her nipples in time to the motion of Dean's tongue. She heard herself moaning, but her voice sounded alien, like a she-wolf's howl. Through her pleasure she was hazily aware that Dean was watching her. When she looked down to meet his dark, gloating eyes, he pushed his thumb all the way into her cunt, then pulled it out and smothered her clit with juice. Then in, then out, then over her clit again and again, looking her in the eyes all the while. She responded with an orgasm that soaked his hand to the wrist. His face rose up from her thighs, his black goatee glistening with her cream. His mouth was berry red from its efforts, and his lips were parted in a smile of wicked pride.

'I never knew that a pirate could be so good at oral sex,' Melanie slurred, drunk on post-orgasmic bliss.

'So you think I look like a pirate?' Dean laughed. He stood up and removed his vest, then unbuttoned his white shirt. His chest and stomach were glorious, ripped and cut in all the right places, but his torso had the lean toughness of a man who keeps fit by working, not just by working out.

'You're the closest thing I've ever seen to one,' Melanie said.

'I hate to disappoint you, but I come from a long line of law-abiding Portuguese fishermen.'

He unbuckled his belt and unbuttoned the fly of his black jeans. His circumcised cock was as long and lethal as the dagger tattoo on his back. In the flickering shadows, the shaft looked like burnished copper.

'That looks like a pirate's cock to me,' Melanie teased. 'Are you sure I can trust you?'

'You can trust me to please you. That's a start.'

Dean sheathed his huge erection with a condom and slid into her. He thrust his hips slowly, pumping into her with the determination of a man thoroughly enjoying his job. After ramming into her to near orgasm he turned her over and planted her on top of him, facing her, looking her in the eyes while he drove himself to his peak. When he came, he gritted his teeth and threw back his head, revealing his golden, corded throat.

'You're one of the hottest men I've ever had under me,' Melanie said, stroking the silky black fur on his chest as he came back to consciousness. 'It's going to be a constant temptation to have you working around the shop.'

'You really are confident about that addition, aren't you?'

'I don't see why I shouldn't be,' she replied, rolling off Dean's body and nestling under his arm. 'We should start sketching out the plans tomorrow.'

'Melanie, I can tell that you're a strong woman. You go for what you want; I have to give you credit for that.'

'But?'

'But I'm a realist. I'm not going to do any planning until I see a permit.'

'When you see that piece of paper in my hand, will you change your mind about the people in this town?'

'Probably not, but I'll draw up your plans for you.'

'Won't you at least come and look at my shop?'

'Until you get that permit, there's no point.'

'Cocky *and* stubborn,' Melanie said sadly. 'Where's your sense of adventure?'

'Adventure doesn't pay the bills, darling. Not for an ordinary guy like me.'

Melanie sighed. The problem with the men around here was that there were too many fishermen among them, and not enough pirates.

As soon as she heard her landlady puttering around downstairs the next morning, Melanie climbed out of bed and steeled herself for a confrontation. The other side of the mattress was empty; Dean had crept away early, without leaving so much as a note. The guy was sexy beyond reason, and he was a terrific lover, but he had quickly shown his true colours, and they were suspicious shades of 'hypocrite' and 'coward'.

Melanie showered, then dressed in a tailored 1940s pantsuit that would have done Joan Crawford proud. She strapped her feet into a pair of three-inch heels, giving herself plenty of extra height, then went downstairs to face Paulette Winters, who she knew would be in her kitchen right now, sipping her first cup of coffee of the day.

Far from being an 'old bat', as Melanie had called her, Paulette was an attractive woman in her early fifties. Fifteen or twenty years ago she had been a stunning raven-haired bombshell, and her son Neil had inherited her good looks. Melanie had had a blistering affair with Neil a few months ago, which had ended after he went away to college. He had left Morne Bay swearing undying love to her, but she hadn't been surprised when his e-mails and phone calls petered out after six weeks. Neil's mother was probably still stewing over that affair. Maybe she was giving Melanie the boot out of sheer vindictiveness.

On any other day, Melanie would have walked up to Paulette's kitchen door and knocked like a friendly tenant. Today she went to the front door and rapped on the wood like a government official. She expected her to come to the door, bleary-eyed and confused at having an early visitor, but even after knocking three times, no one answered. Melanie gave up and decided to go around to the kitchen. Paulette, who had a weakness for country-cute decor, had hung a pair of blue gingham curtains over the window of her back door. The curtains were tied back with crisp white bows and, through the opening between them, Melanie saw her landlady.

In all the years she had lived in that house, Melanie had never seen or heard any evidence that Paulette had a sex drive. As far as she knew, no midnight visitors had come through her door, no anonymous brown paper packages had been delivered to her house; if Paulette Winters was a prude, at least she wasn't a hypocrite. Now, as she watched the most amazing view of her landlady that she had ever seen, Melanie knew that she had underestimated the older woman by a long shot.

A row of antique copper-bottomed pots and pans had always hung on hooks above the kitchen counter. This morning one of those hooks was occupied by something far more interesting than a pot – it was Paulette Winters herself. With her wrists wrapped in a dishtowel and tied around the hook, she sat on the kitchen counter. Her quilted white bathrobe had been pushed aside to reveal a pair of small, dark-tipped breasts, quite firm and high for a woman in her fifties. With her arms elevated above her head and her hands bound to the hook, those breasts stood at full attention. The dusky nipples had been coaxed into points by a very talented tongue ... the same tongue, in fact, that had been wandering through the hills and dales of Melanie's private parts the previous night.

Dean DeSilva was on his knees lapping away at Paulette's crotch, which was wide open for his enjoyment. Paulette's thighs were in a full straddle, her ankles criss-crossed over his back. Dean had stripped down to the waist. Through Paulette's sparkling glass, Melanie could see the dagger tattoo at the base of his spine; it was wiggling as he enjoyed a breakfast of well-seasoned cunt. From the way Paulette's head was thrown back, her long salt-and-pepper hair falling all the way down to the Formica counter, Melanie could tell that Dean was performing just as well with her as he had with herself – maybe better.

She didn't know whether to scream, laugh or open the door and join them. This couldn't be the first time that Paulette Winters had used one of those pot hooks for sex. She probably watched Martha Stewart faithfully, taking down notes on all the alternative kinky uses for various household gadgets and appliances. Then she had the gall to act as if Melanie wasn't good enough to live under her roof!

Melanie threw open the door and burst into the room. She stood spread-legged in the middle of the quaint kitchen like a sheriff in a spaghetti Western. Paulette, in the midst of a howling, full-blown orgasm, didn't even register the fact that her tenant was watching her climax, and Dean, happily munching away, didn't notice a thing. It wasn't until Melanie stomped her foot that Dean whipped around and saw her. His lips and beard were glazed with the landlady's juices, and his eyes had the sullen, guilty look of a dog that's been caught with his nose buried in a freshly baked pie.

'It looks like you *did* have that talk with Mrs Winters about my lease, Dean,' Melanie said. 'Did you persuade her not to evict me, or does she still think I'm more of a slut than she is?'

Paulette, now coming back to reality, was flopping about on the hook, trying to free herself. Her skin was still awash with the flush of her pleasure, the colour now heightened by embarrassment. But good old Dean, with his fisherman background and carpentry skills, had tied her knots with such expertise that she wasn't going anywhere. Dean stood up and pulled on his shirt. He began to fasten the buttons at a leisurely pace. By the sneer on his face, Melanie guessed that he was enjoying himself immensely.

'Just taking care of business, Melanie,' Dean said. 'There are a lot of women in town who need my tools. Don't be jealous if I share the love, babe.'

'Jealous?' Melanie snorted. 'Are you kidding? I don't care if you apply your "tools" to every woman on the East Coast, Dean. I'm just astonished that you have such a broad palate. Three or four hours ago, you were eating me out like a starving man who's just sunk his teeth into a filet mignon. What happened, did you wake up with a craving for some beef jerky?'

Paulette gave a wounded moan, and Melanie wished she hadn't made such a cruel joke. She couldn't blame the woman for being seduced by Dean, who didn't even have the courtesy to untie her at this mortifying moment. Melanie stood up tall and planted her hands on her hips.

'Actually, you've both done me a huge favour this morning,' she said. 'Paulette, you've made it easy for me to leave this house, which has been my home for years now. I don't want to pay rent to a hypocrite, so I'll be happy to move out when my lease is up. And Dean, you've saved me from wasting any more of my energy on you. Within twenty-four hours, you've proven that you're untrustworthy, unreliable and disrespectful to women. You're the last man on earth that I'd want to have working for me.'

With that, she turned on her spiked heel and left Paulette's kitchen for the last time. New beginnings were always exhilarating, even if they were launched by another woman's orgasm.

2 Sexual History

Nathan Wentworth never had a problem getting sex, but he found it all but impossible to get the kind of sex he wanted. While living in Boston he had met plenty of women who were happy to be spanked or dominated, but most of them were professional submissives who expected money in exchange for the privilege. He had discovered a lot of natural subs online or at clubs, but while their meekness pumped up his ego, it didn't do much for his libido. In his fantasies, he dominated harems full of eager-to-please slavegirls; in reality, he found himself seeking out rough edges, complications, resistance.

Dana McGillis might be such a woman, if the ebb and flow of blood through his groin were anything to go by. He had been working with her for the past three months, and his powers of concentration were starting to slacken whenever he was around her. Dana was an historian from Beardsley College, an assistant professor whose wardrobe bore a troubling resemblance to a Catholic schoolgirl's: Black Watch plaid skirt, crisp white tailored blouse, even a navy-blue headband in her bobbed auburn hair. Her figure boasted a feature that was usually described as a flaw in women's magazines – a round, muscular bottom that jutted out from her frame, making her look as if she were wearing an old-fashioned bustle. Her skirts were so tight that he suspected she knew that her ass, far from being a flaw, was a temptation to anyone who was lucky enough to brush against it.

Unfortunately, conditions weren't right for pursuing

her. Dana was helping Nathan plan the installation depicting the major local industries of the nineteenth century, and since his interests tended more towards early colonial days, he needed her professional input more than he needed to turn her over his knee and burnish her bum with his palm. But as she gave him a tour of a similar installation she had built at the Beardsley College museum, his thoughts kept being drawn to that part of her anatomy like iron filings to a magnet.

'. . . and I'm particularly proud of this reproduction of a textile mill,' Dana was saying, gesturing gracefully as she showed off the life-size reproduction she had designed. The display included an arrangement of mechanical looms with three female mannequins toiling over them. Shreds of wool had been strewn around the floor, to give the impression that labour was in progress. 'This is one of our most popular displays. The area is full of the descendants of French mill workers, and they love to come here and see what their ancestors' lives were like. It was backbreaking work, largely done by women.'

'Amazing.'

Though Nathan was truly impressed by the exhibit, he couldn't stop thinking about Dana bent over one of the looms, her skirt hiked up around her waist, cheeks in the air, taunting him, begging for his hand. He wondered what kind of panties she wore. He guessed that she would either prefer sensible, waist-high white knickers, or a simple black thong. Nathan himself couldn't decide which image aroused him more: her bum modestly covered in cotton, which he would tear off as soon as her skin began to redden, or the twin globes bare from the beginning, separated by the thin line of a G-string that nestled into her slit.

Something hard was filling Nathan's trousers, and it wasn't the pocket paddle that he carried with him at all times.

'Have you mapped out all your installations for the Morne Bay Museum?' she asked.

'Oh. Well. No, not completely,' Nathan stammered, dragging his thoughts back to his latest project. 'I've had a lot of catching up to do. My area of expertise is colonial America. Morne Bay didn't start to flourish until the nineteenth century.'

'So why did you leave a good job in Boston for this?'

'I'm fascinated by some of the bandits who made the town a success. I've gotten tired of the austerity of the colonists. I wanted to spend some time with a few debauched shipping pirates.'

'You're planning to depict Morne Bay's founding fathers as pirates?' Dana laughed. 'I don't think the town's bigwigs will be too crazy about that.'

'Don't worry. I'm not going to risk a public hanging by trashing anyone's ancestors. But the fact is, the first shipping magnates of Morne Bay – Josiah Price, Sylvan Colwell, and of course Darius Morne – were ruthless, acquisitive, decadent sons of bitches. They came to Morne Bay because it offered a quiet, sheltered seaport, but once they arrived, the area didn't stay quiet for long. Morne and his buddies imported exotic objects from all over the world, turned a backwater into a thriving international bazaar. Darius Morne and his wife Amélie lived life to the hilt. Their homes were packed with luxurious objects from Europe and Asia, and, according to historical rumour, their sexual tastes were pretty exotic, as well.'

'For example?'

'Well, Amélie was an exotic import, herself. Darius spent a lot of time in Europe, and when he came back with a wife, he introduced her as the daughter of a Parisian banker. Turns out she did know a Parisian banker, but he wasn't her father. He was her lover, and she was one of the most celebrated cancan dancers in the city.'

'Let me guess ... she knew a lot more tricks than the cancan.'

'Oh, yes. Darius got one look at Amélie, decided that he wanted her for himself, and stole her out from under the banker's nose. He dressed her up in the finest clothes that his money could buy, and brought her back to Morne Bay, where she proceeded to shock the whole town with her extravagant parties and wild extramarital affairs. She was also a sharp businesswoman, with an instinct for purchasing things that suited people's desires.'

'Sounds fascinating. Much juicier than my textile mill.'

'Your textile mill is a work of art. I only hope I can do half as well.'

'I love recreating these historical scenes,' said Dana. 'I only wish that we could make them even more realistic. If I had my way, I'd use live actors instead of these costumed mannequins, and I'd let people go in and interact with the displays. Get the full sensual experience: sights, smells, textures, sounds.'

'I agree. I've dreamed of doing exactly the same thing.'

Dana's words reminded Nathan of an idea he had entertained since he was an undergraduate. He had fantasised about having a museum dedicated to the history of American eroticism, from colonial times to the present. The exhibits would portray history at its most natural, complete with reconstructions of down-to-earth intimate encounters, with nude or nearly nude models playing the roles of historical lovers. The displays would not simply be curiosities preserved behind glass, but full-blown representations of American sexuality, with all its double standards and excesses, glories and hypocrisies.

'Have you?'

'To tell you the truth, Dana,' Nathan ventured, 'I've always wanted to have a museum devoted to the history of sex in the States.'

Dana's green eyes grew huge behind her black-framed,

cat's-eye glasses. At first he thought his comment might have gone over the limit, then Dana gave him a come-on smile that he couldn't possibly misinterpret. Before he could press the moment any further, the campus bell broke the promising silence.

'Oh, damn! Is it ten o'clock already?' Dana grabbed her bookbag and hitched it over her shoulder. 'I have a class to teach.'

Nathan followed her out of the building. 'Should I meet you here next week?'

'Definitely.' Dana's smile had reached a dazzling level. 'I'll have some sketches to show you. And listen, there's a woman in Morne Bay you should meet – Melanie Paxton. She runs a shop called Chimera. She's an expert in vintage clothing, and she specialises in the sexy stuff. Most of it is early twentieth century, but she might have a few genuine antiques. Plus, she's a knockout. You have to see her to believe her.'

Dana winked, waved, and rushed off to her class. Her buttocks and thighs pumped efficiently under her skirt as she power-walked across the campus square. Nathan stood watching her, his cock thickening again, until she was swallowed by a crowd of students. He loved smart, sexy women, especially when they were generous enough to refer him to other smart, sexy women. Nathan had heard about Melanie Paxton and her shop, but with his new house and the museum project he'd been too busy to meet her. With nothing on his agenda until a meeting at three o'clock, he had a clear stretch of time to drive back to Morne Bay and pay her a visit.

Morne Bay was abuzz with gossip about Melanie Paxton, but Nathan hadn't paid much attention. She was the kind of phenomenon that he preferred to investigate for himself. Most of what Nathan had heard about Melanie and Chimera had been positive, but he'd sensed a current of envy, possibly even suspicion, in the river of talk.

People were so contradictory, he thought, as he drove back to the coast. They craved change and novelty, but just when life began to get interesting, they often scurried back into their burrows and turned their backs on innovation.

The narrow streets outside of Chimera were lined with cars; Nathan had to circle the block several times just to find a space large enough for his pick-up truck. Parking was going to pose a problem once the museum opened. The museum would have its own lot, but Nathan could already predict that Melanie's customers would encroach on it. A sign on the shop's display window advertised a pre-holiday sale, and the place was crowded with customers trying to get an edge on their seasonal shopping. Nathan felt out of place among the clusters of women and teenage girls. He could see why they flocked here. The shop was a small paradise of sensual delights, filled with a variety of textures, colours, and styles that merged into a single sensual vision.

The creator of that vision stepped out from behind the curtain of opalescent beads that hid her cavern of sex toys. She was followed by a pregnant woman whose face was radiant with something other than maternal joy. Nathan edged through the shoppers, ducking behind a rack of clothing so that he could eavesdrop.

'I never realised that pregnancy made you so horny,' Melanie was saying.

'It's unbelievable. My husband can't keep up. He tries, but I think he's afraid he's going to hurt me or the baby. Meanwhile, I'm going crazy. I need at least six orgasms a day.'

'With the Mermaid, you can have six orgasms in an hour, if you want to.'

'I come so hard these days that it's kind of scary.' The woman looked around furtively, as if her husband might be lurking in a corner. 'I get so wet, I flood the sheets.

And I scream like an animal,' she added in a near whisper.

'Let him watch you using the vibrator, or better yet, ask him to help. Then he'll see that there's nothing to worry about. A few screaming orgasms won't hurt your baby.'

'The baby seems to like it when I come. The kicking gets so wild sometimes that I almost get knocked out of bed.'

Melanie laughed as she led her customer over to the cash register to ring up her purchase. Everything about Melanie, from her black cashmere sweater trimmed with ostrich feathers to her rhinestone pendant earrings, screamed 'high maintenance', but she had a rich, dirty laugh that would sound perfectly at home in any working-class bar. Though she looked like a woman who loved to be pampered, Nathan guessed that she probably took care of that pampering herself. When she wasn't smiling at her customers, her face wore a look of stubborn self-reliance that made Nathan's cock go as hard as concrete. Under her professional acumen was the spirit of a rebel.

And the rebel in Melanie was making the disciplinarian in Nathan go mad. As he watched her close the cash drawer and strut across the room on her high-heeled alligator pumps, legs flashing through the deep slit in her long black skirt, Nathan was already visualising the things he wanted to make for her in his woodshop. An oak spanking horse, elegant but serviceable, with dainty spooled legs and a dainty pommel to hold Melanie in the perfect paddling position. He might even have the pommel covered in black velvet, because it would make such a striking contrast with her ivory bottom. For that bottom he would craft a paddle out of bloodwood, an exotic, nearly crimson wood that he would have to order just for her. He would cover half of the paddle's face with white rabbit's fur, for soothing and stimulating her tender skin.

But the service end of that paddle would see the most use.

Melanie caught Nathan staring at her. She smiled graciously, like a woman who was used to being stared at by slack-jawed men, and made her way towards him.

'Looking for something special?' she asked, glancing at the lingerie rack he had chosen as his observatory post. 'Or are you just a friendly neighbourhood pervert?'

'Yes, and yes.'

Melanie responded with that raunchy laugh. Nathan felt every throaty note running the length of his spine, from the back of his neck all the way down. Up close, he could see how soft and plush her lips were. She smelled of something fantastically rare, yet soothing and familiar at the same time, like rare tropical fruit seasoned with cinnamon. He shifted his weight and turned his body so that, if she looked down, she wouldn't see how aroused he was.

'Can I help you find something?'

'I've already found it. I was looking for you.'

'Oh?'

'I thought it was time we met. I'm the curator of the new museum that's going up next door.'

Melanie seemed to hesitate. 'You're Nathaniel Wentworth?'

'I'm known as Nathan to everyone but my father.'

'I'll call you Nathan, then. And I'm Melanie Paxton.'

'I know. I've heard a lot about you.'

'Anything you can repeat?' She tilted her head and looked up at him. Her tongue flickered out at the corner of her mouth – just a flash of pink, but it was enough to send a jolt of heat through Nathan's groin. It was way too soon to go into his disciplinarian mode, but Nathan wasn't thinking with his brain.

'From what I've heard, you're a notorious bad girl.'

Melanie's flirtatious smile vanished. Her posture stiffened, and her attitude cooled by about twenty degrees.

'I'm a bad girl under certain circumstances, but I'm also a very good businesswoman.'

'Isn't it possible to be both at the same time?'

Melanie didn't answer right away. For a few moments she appeared to be considering Nathan's question, then she held out her hand at a formal angle, as if she and Nathan were a couple of dignitaries at a fundraising dinner.

'Nathan, it's been a pleasure to meet you, but I have to take care of my customers. Let's get together sometime when I'm not so busy.'

'I'd love to. Do you have a free evening this week?'

'I can't tell without checking my calendar. We'll have to settle for goodbye for now.'

Nathan felt no warmth in Melanie's handshake, nor in her polite farewell. He left the shop feeling embarrassed and confused. Five minutes ago, he could have sworn that Melanie was attracted to him. He had pushed his luck too far by trying to dominate her before she was ready. Her outright sex appeal, combined with her self-possession, made him feel like a sixteen-year-old boy again, clumsy and out of control. That awkwardness made him all the more determined to get her where he wanted her: bent over his knee.

Darius Morne must have been hit the same way, over a hundred and fifty years ago, when he saw the French dancer who would become his partner in lust and business. A frequenter of lowlife establishments and a lover of loose women, he had seen his soul mate dancing onstage at a seedy cabaret, and from that moment on the hardcore pervert had belonged to her, cock and soul. Melanie Paxton was having approximately the same effect on Nathan. She even looked a bit like an old daguerreotype he had seen of Amélie, with her glossy dark bangs, smoldering eyes, and oh-so-fuckable hourglass figure.

From what Nathan had learned in his research, Amélie had had her own collection of toys, including a set of obscene Chinese figures carved in ivory, an ebony dildo, and a horsewhip that had never been used on any four-legged creature. Nathan would kill to get his hands on those objects; he would love nothing more than to display them in the Morne Bay Museum. But as far as he knew, Amélie's collection had been lost long ago, and he had found no concrete proof that it ever existed.

Outside, a light snow was falling, blown off the bay by a cold, salty wind. The seaside air, so bracing after the fragrant warmth of Melanie's shop, brought Nathan back to his senses. When it came to women, Nathan loved nothing more than a challenge. He would bide his time, prepare Melanie gradually, wait until she was ripe for discipline. When the time came, he would pluck her like a bright scarlet berry and squeeze every last drop of juice out of her. Over and over again, until she was ready to swear that she had never been so satisfied.

After Nathan left, Melanie tried to help out with the preholiday activities, but her thoughts wouldn't stay in one place.

'I have to get out of here for a couple of hours,' she told Pagan. 'There's an estate sale in Colchester that I don't want to miss. Can you and Luna handle this mob?'

'Sure we can,' Pagan said breezily.

Melanie wasn't half as confident that the two girls could keep up with the customers, but she had to have some time alone to clear her head. 'Then I'll leave the shop in your hands. Just remember the ground rules, OK?'

'No bargaining on the vintage stuff,' Pagan said, 'unless you're on the premises.'

'Keep the jewellery case and the cash register locked,' Luna chimed in.

'And?'

'Don't let anyone under eighteen into the Alcove,' the girls chorused.

'Excellent. I've trained you well.'

Colchester was a town about twenty miles from Morne Bay. It had once been the site of a minimum-security prison, and the estate sale was being held at the mansion of the former chief prison warden. The warden had passed away years ago, and his widow had lived in the house up until her recent death. Now her children were selling the contents of the mansion. Melanie had high hopes for this sale. A person would have to be kinky to be a prison warden, and the items for sale would be bound to include a few restraints – a straitjacket or two, maybe some handcuffs or manacles.

Visions of restraints brought her mind back to Nathan Wentworth. When she first saw him, she had assumed he was a farmer who had come in to buy a present for his wife. In his mud-crusted boots, faded jeans and sheepskin coat, he looked like a man who would spend his spare time restoring old rusty ploughs or driving out to the boondocks to guzzle beer at high school wrestling matches. He didn't match Melanie's image of a museum curator. When Harrison had talked about the new curator, she had envisioned a lean, dark sophisticate, not a stocky blond brute.

Though Nathan Wentworth was undeniably attractive in a rustic way, he had a serious demeanour that hadn't been softened by Melanie's charms. On top of that he was too big for Melanie's taste, so tall and broad-shouldered that she had felt uncomfortably small in comparison. His thighs had been thicker than her waist, and as for what was between them ... well, his package did bear some thought. He was probably hung like a Clydesdale horse, but that didn't make up for what he had said. Melanie was still smarting from Dean DeSilva's remarks about bad girls. Then Nathan had come in and repeated that condescending phrase, as if there were some conspiracy going on among the town's males.

'Fuck you all,' Melanie declared, though there was no one to hear her inside her Volkswagen. 'Or better yet, go beg another woman to fuck you.'

Melanie didn't find any handcuffs or manacles at the estate sale (the widow's children had probably squirrelled away those goodies for themselves), but she did dig up a few treasures: a black silk mourning shawl trimmed with jet beads, a crushed straw bonnet that she estimated to be over a hundred years old, three pairs of the elegant elbow-length evening gloves that her customers were always begging for, and best of all, a pair of men's riding breeches.

Oh yes. As soon as she touched the breeches, Melanie felt that heart-stopping thrill that told her she'd unearthed a gem. Those fawn breeches would fit the wearer like a second skin. Just holding them got Melanie's juices flowing, especially when she examined the crotch and imagined how it would look filled out by a nice cock and a set of firm balls. As she fondled the pants, she had a flashback to an erotic fantasy that she had all but forgotten.

She tucked the fantasy into a mental pocket for future exploration, paid for the items and drove back to Morne Bay. She found Luna and Pagan closing up the shop, gloating over the money from the sale as if they had earned every cent themselves.

'Well done, ladies,' Melanie said. 'This calls for a celebration. Anyone in the mood for pizza?'

Luna had a date, but Pagan stayed to share a pepperoni pie with double cheese. Melanie found a bottle of spumante in the mini-fridge in the office, and she and Pagan washed down their pizza with the sweet fizzy wine.

'Isn't it nice to have an evening without men?' Melanie asked. 'I get so fed up with them sometimes. They spend most of their waking hours thinking about sex, but when they find a woman who wants it as much as they do, they stuff her in a mental pigeonhole labelled "slut" and never let her out.'

'I know what you mean,' agreed Pagan, who had graduated from high school the previous year. 'If you don't want to have sex, you turn into a social outcast. If you like having sex, you end up with your name and phone number scribbled all over the bathroom stalls.'

'Things haven't changed much, then. I once had my name spray-painted all along the fence outside the football field.'

'You're kidding.'

'No. Someone wrote "Melanie sucks" in purple Day-Glo paint. The letters were three feet high. I saw it when I was walking to school one morning.'

'That's awful. What did you do?'

'I felt terrible at first, but when I thought about it, I realised that it was true. I loved giving blow jobs, and I gave quite a few of them. But the next day, someone else added "Melanie bites". That made me furious. I was a damn good cocksucker, and not one of those boys ever felt my teeth. So I went to the principal's office and told them to paint over it by the end of the day, or I'd hire an attorney. Of course, that was all a bluff; I had about ten dollars to my name. But it worked.'

Pagan laughed and put down her half-eaten slice of pizza. 'I can't eat another bite. Will you show me the stuff you bought today?'

Melanie brought out the items. Pagan, who had little interest in collecting clothes for their historical value, wasn't impressed by the moth-eaten shawl or tattered straw bonnet. But when she saw the men's riding pants, her eyes lit up.

'These are perfect!'

'You want to wear them?' Melanie asked dubiously, comparing the long breeches to Pagan's stocky figure.

'Oh no, not me. My brother Jason. He belongs to some secret club at Beardsley College, and they love to dress up in things like this.'

'Really?' said Melanie. 'I wish there were more men around here who wanted to wear vintage. We get so many glamorous suits and trousers. And those old fedoras, like something Humphrey Bogart would have worn. Your brother and his friends must have a great sense of style. Is it a fashion club?'

'Well, not exactly.' Pagan, a dedicated political activist who wore combat boots and spiked leather wristlets as basic accessories, was blushing like a virgin spinster.

'What kind of club is it?' Melanie pressed. 'Now you have to tell me.'

'I can't really describe it. My brother might not want me to say anything.'

'Well, all right. But if he wants these breeches, he's going to have to talk.'

'He'd probably love to tell you about his club, but if he thought I'd said anything, he'd kill me.'

'I understand. Why don't you give me his phone number?'

Pagan scrawled a number on the back of a napkin. 'Don't say I mentioned the club,' she pleaded.

'I won't. I definitely won't.'

Melanie took the napkin and folded it carefully. She had never seen the spunky Pagan act so ruffled. Jason was definitely going to get a phone call. A college boy who belonged to a top-secret club and loved tight riding pants was way too good to miss.

After Pagan left, Melanie got ready to lock up for the night. She was giving the toys in her Alcove one last loving glance when the bells above the shop door jingled.

'I'm sorry, we're closed,' Melanie said, trying to keep the impatience out of her voice. Her irritation fled when she saw who her customer was.

'Don't you have time for one more exchange?' laughed the blue-eyed, sandy-haired man. In his hands he held a brown paper bag.

'Only if it's an exchange of body fluids,' she joked. 'God, it's good to see you, Ted.' Melanie threw herself at her former high school teacher, flinging her arms around his waist. 'The men around here have been driving me insane.'

'I think it's the other way around, isn't it? From what I hear, you're the most popular girl in town these days. You don't even have time for your old drama coach.'

'Oh, please. You're not old; you're well seasoned. And it's you that hasn't had time lately,' Melanie said accusingly. 'Ever since you left the country for that theatre tour, I haven't seen you at all. What have you been doing with yourself? Anything daring and adventurous?'

Melanie tightened her hold on Ted, grinding her hips against his. Behind his wire-rimmed glasses, his blue eyes had a come-on gleam, but for once, his posture felt stiffer than his cock.

'Well, as a matter of fact, I did do something daring, for once in my life.'

'Tell me!'

'I got married.'

'You did what?' Melanie leaped away as if Ted's sweater had spontaneously combusted.

Ted laughed. 'Don't look so shocked. I got married. People still do that, you know.'

'Who's the lucky woman? Do I know her?'

Melanie hadn't meant to sound jealous, but her question

was tinged with venom. Maybe she really was envious. In high school, she had had a massive crush on Ted Dupre. He had been the subject of more masturbation fantasies than she could count, but it wasn't until years later that she finally had her chance to live out those fantasies. One day Ted happened to walk by the shop while Melanie was arranging a display in the storefront. She had lured him inside, where she told him about her plans to add a selection of erotic merchandise to the shop's inventory. She ended up showing him some of that merchandise, specifically, a riding crop, which he tried out on her bottom. They gave up the crop in favour of an old-fashioned over-the-knee spanking, which Melanie had enjoyed more than she ever would have expected.

Pain and humiliation had never been Melanie's cup of tea, but the resounding smack of Ted's hand on her bare ass and the shame of crying in front of him had given her a gut-wrenching orgasm. Any woman who could look forward to that kind of treatment every night was way beyond lucky, as far as Melanie was concerned.

'As a matter of fact, you do know her. You remember Hannah Morse, don't you?'

'Hannah? From the drama club?'

'Exactly.' Ted beamed with pride.

Melanie did remember. In her mind's eye she saw a plump girl, pretty in a clean-scrubbed, home-grown way, with apple cheeks and brown eyes. Hannah used to wear her long carrot-red hair in two prairie-girl braids, and there was never a touch of make-up on her face, only a spattering of cinnamon freckles. Wracking her memory, Melanie couldn't recall the slightest hint of attraction between the drama instructor and his chunky, freckled pupil. If anything, Hannah had been one of the few students who wasn't chasing after Ted, whose clean-cut Ivy League looks and double-edged wit had made him the wet dream of every female in the school, and quite a few of the males as well. Hannah had been a good, solid actress, but her mild manner and sweet round face had confined her to supporting roles. Hannah had played the nurse in *Romeo and Juliet*; Melanie had played Juliet.

'This must have happened very suddenly,' Melanie said.

'It did,' Ted admitted. 'We only met – or met again, I should say – a few months ago. That's the daring part.'

'A whirlwind wedding. How romantic. Listen, Ted, I'm very happy for you, but I have to close up now.'

Melanie turned away. She wished Ted would leave, so she could go home, crack open a pint of mint-chocolate-chip ice cream, and enjoy a long spell of self-pity. Melanie hated weddings – hated attending them, hated hearing about them. She especially hated hearing about weddings that happened between other women and men she wanted for herself.

'Not so fast. I brought you a present.'

'You mean you wanted to give me a consolation prize?'

'No, not at all. This is from Hannah.'

Ted held out the paper bag. Melanie accepted it cautiously. She felt a familiar build-up of anticipation as she unrolled the bag, but she wasn't prepared for what she saw inside. A spear of joy pierced her heart as she lifted a pair of red satin pumps – circa 1950, she guessed, judging by the stiletto heels and pointy toes – out of the bag. With their gold spikes and red sequins, they looked like a sexy, grown-up version of Dorothy's ruby slippers from *The Wizard of Oz*.

'Well? What do you think, Melanie?'

Holding the shoes in her hands, Melanie found herself speechless. These were the kind of shoes that become the centrepiece of an outfit, the kind of shoes that people talk about for years after you've made your first appearance in them. Melanie saw herself wearing them at a Christmas party, at dinner at a fancy restaurant in New

York. She saw herself wearing them with nothing else, for drunken sex after a New Year's Eve bash, or a naked fashion show with her new winter lover.

'They're your size, aren't they?' Ted asked.

'They're exactly my size. Where did you get them?'

She had trouble getting the words out; it was all she could do to keep breathing. What were the chances that someone would walk into her shop and hand her such a treasure? She had devoted her life to vintage retail because of miracles like this. In this business you could find treasures in mouldy steamer trunks, cardboard boxes, and even the occasional brown paper bag.

'Hannah's grandmother sold her farm last month and moved to a retirement home in Florida,' Ted explained. 'She gave Hannah some of her things, things that were too nice for a rummage sale. Hannah took one look at these and thought of you.'

'She thought of me? After all this time?'

'Hannah had quite a crush on you in high school,' Ted laughed. 'I don't think she's ever stopped fantasising about you.'

'Hannah Morse had a crush on *me*? I think I need to sit down. I've had too many surprises for one evening.'

'While you're sitting, try the shoes on.'

Melanie didn't need any encouragement. She sat down in a formal Queen Anne chair in front of the three-way mirror, kicked off her shoes and replaced them with the pumps. The red shoes slipped onto her feet with glorious ease. The insteps made her arches exquisitely high. Her slender legs looked like they were tipped with gems.

'Beautiful,' Ted said. 'Now take off everything else.'

Melanie looked up at her former instructor. Ted had a firm, authoritative tone in his voice, the tone he had always used when directing Melanie onstage. Her throat went dry, and her heartbeat speeded up.

'Go ahead. Get undressed,' Ted insisted. 'I have to get

home to my wife soon. Hannah is waiting to hear about this.'

'You mean you're going to watch me take my clothes off, then tell your brand-new bride all about it?' Melanie said in disbelief.

'No, I'm going to watch you take your clothes off, then I'm going to fuck you senseless, and then I'm going to go home and tell her about it. Now, hurry. I'm too hard to wait much longer.'

Melanie stood up and slipped out of her skirt. Underneath, she was wearing only a black garter belt and stockings. As she pulled her sweater over her head, she could feel Ted's gaze roaming up the length of her slim calves and thighs, focusing on the trimmed thicket that covered her mound. She had decided not to wear a bra today, because she liked the feeling of the cashmere sweater against her nipples. She started to unsnap the garter belt, but Ted stopped her.

'No, no. Leave that on.' His voice was thick and hoarse. 'I love the way the lace frames your bush. Now, I want you to turn around facing the mirrors. Straddle the chair, and sit down.'

Wearing nothing but the red shoes, her stockings and garters, and her dangling rhinestone earrings, Melanie followed his instructions. She rested her hands on the back of the chair and lowered herself until her bum was resting on the upholstered seat. While Ted undressed, she watched him in the three-way mirror. He had a fine body, trim and tanned, his muscles as firm as a much younger man's. His prick, dark pink and visibly pulsing, jutted out from a thatch of straw-coloured curls.

'Lift your arms, and clasp your hands behind your neck,' he said.

Melanie obeyed. Ted stood behind her and ran his fingers down the sensitive planes of her inner arms. Melanie didn't realise that she had been holding her breath until his hands gripped her breasts, and the air whooshed from her lungs. Ted squeezed her nipples, milking moans from her lips, until the nubs were so stimulated that they were almost painful. Ted lowered himself onto the chair behind her and kissed the nape of Melanie's neck. His erection was hot, even through the latex of a condom, so hot that she imagined the rod of flesh leaving a mark like a brand in the small of her back.

'Play with yourself, Melanie. Make yourself come. I want you to watch yourself come.'

After all the attention that Ted had paid to her nipples, Melanie was so aroused that it didn't take long for her to finger herself to an orgasm. When she came, Ted sank his teeth into the base of her neck where her throat curved into her shoulder, and the pain doubled the intensity of her pleasure. The woman she saw in the mirror didn't look at all like the Melanie who managed a shop – she was wild, crazed, her eyes burning, her cheeks the same bright scarlet as the shoes that she wore. Before the last spasms had died away, Ted was lifting her feverish body off of the chair. He sat down with his back to the mirrors and eased her onto his cock. She gripped the back of the chair, digging her gold-spiked heels into the floor to stabilise herself as he drove himself into her, up and up into her cunt, until he shot his load, gave a deep groan, and shuddered to a standstill.

They sat quietly for a while, recovering in the antique chair that had probably once graced some wealthy woman's drawing room. Ted pulled the clip out of Melanie's hair and loosened her long black locks with his fingers.

'You're incredibly beautiful,' he said. 'It's no wonder that Hannah wanted me to fuck you.'

'So the two of you must have an open marriage. I suppose that was your idea,' Melanie teased.

'Actually, it was hers. Hannah is very adventurous when it comes to sex. She told me from the beginning that she was too young to be tied down; she wanted us both to be free to explore.'

'My, my. Hannah must have grown up. That doesn't sound like the shy, awkward girl I remember. I'm going to have to see her for myself.'

'You will. How about on Saturday night? We'd love to have you over for dinner. It wouldn't be anything fancy, just plain home cooking.'

A home-cooked meal sounded heavenly; Melanie had been so busy lately that she hadn't had time to prepare anything more nourishing than instant noodles. She had gotten a lot of dinner invitations ever since she became the town's answer to Aphrodite, but she was tired of restaurant fare. And she had a growing desire to witness Ted and Hannah's sex life first hand.

'I'd love to come,' Melanie said.

'You already did, you greedy girl,' Ted replied, giving her a sharp swat on the ass.

'How about a little more of that? I've been feeling very undisciplined lately,' Melanie said, wriggling suggestively on Ted's lap.

'Later,' Ted said, kissing her on the cheek. 'If you show up on Saturday night, you'll get all the discipline you need.'

Once Ted was gone, Melanie stayed to unpack some new merchandise that had arrived that afternoon. Pushing the boundaries of taste, she had ordered something a bit more lewd than usual, a dildo that came with its own leather harness. The artificial penis was so graphically detailed that Melanie wanted to lick it to reassure herself that it wasn't made of flesh. Now that she had it in her hands, Melanie saw that it was too obscene to display. A nine-inch silicone beast like this didn't exactly fit in with the exotic hardwood paddles, rabbit-fur mitts and ribbon-glass dildos. Best to show it to only a few select customers.

As she was carrying the dildo back to the storage closet, the strangest image leaped into Melanie's mind. With absolute clarity she envisaged Hannah wearing it. The straps of the leather harness fit snugly around her plump hips and bottom, and the phallus rose proudly from her groin, in contrast to her womanly curves. Her eyes glittering with lust, she approached a naked Ted from behind, then held her husband as she pushed the *faux* cock into the crevice between his ass cheeks.

The details of the image were so vivid – Hannah with her red hair hanging in crimped waves, her pale breasts flattened against Ted's back, Hannah's hand reaching around to grip Ted's very real cock while she fucked him with the artificial one – that Melanie had to stop for a second to collect herself before she went back out into the shop. She had no way to tell what Hannah, or Ted for that matter, was capable of, unless she observed them in their natural habitat.

Melanie couldn't stop thinking about Hannah that night. How did a girl who had looked as wholesome as Rebecca of Sunnybrook Farm transform herself into a bisexual free spirit living in an open marriage? It was funny how your assumptions could limit your idea of a person's sexuality, the way the contents of a steamer trunk could crush the lines of an old silk gown. It wasn't until you cleaned the garment thoroughly, reshaped it, and draped it on a living body that you saw the original intention of the design, the lovely fluidity of the fabric.

3 Dinner, Dessert and Discipline

Ted and Hannah lived in a rambling eighteenth-century house, complete with an ell connecting the main structure to the building that used to serve as a kitchen. On Saturday night Hannah gave Melanie a tour of the place before leading her into the roomy library, which was clearly the heart of the home. A motley gang of dogs dozed on the Persian rug in front of a crackling fire, and a fat orange tabby cat was lying in a bookshelf, stretched out across three volumes of Shakespeare. Hannah shooed the whole furry menagerie out of the room and invited Melanie to sit down in one of the battered armchairs that surrounded the fireplace.

'I can't resist animals,' Hannah explained. 'I work in a veterinary clinic. People abandon their pets all the time, and I bring at least half of them home. Ted keeps threatening to set a limit, but he can't complain when we've got so much extra room.'

'If you're in the market for a roommate, I'd be happy to move in,' Melanie ventured. 'I just found out that I'm being kicked out of my apartment. I've got to find a place to live by the end of the month, or I'll be sleeping at Chimera.'

'There must be lots of extra room in that lovely old house,' said Hannah.

'Yes, there is. But I need a place to get away at night. I could never live over the shop the way Lori did. It would feel like I was at work twenty-four hours a day.'

'I see what you mean.' Hannah had an intent, thoughtful look on her face. 'You know, Ted and I have been talking . . .'

'About what?'

'Oh, never mind.' Hannah began picking up the scattered dog toys that lay on the rug beside the fire. 'I should wait until he gets here to discuss it with you.'

'Where is Ted, by the way?'

'He wanted to find the perfect wine to serve you. He insisted on going all the way to Leesport to go to that fancy vintner's.'

'He shouldn't have gone to so much trouble,' Melanie said, though she couldn't help feeling flattered. 'I hope it doesn't take him too long.'

'I told him to choose a good red that would go with the rack of lamb, but that could take forever. My husband is so picky when it comes to wine.'

It was odd to hear Hannah refer to Ted Dupre as her husband. It didn't seem all that long ago that Melanie was a horny teenager masturbating to images of her drama instructor, pretending that her fingers were his tongue as she wanked herself into a frenzy in her bed after school. Unlike a lot of the other girls in her class, Melanie had never fantasised about marrying her teacher; she only wanted him to fuck her brains out. Hannah had gone the whole way, wedding and all. Melanie was dying to know how they had gotten together, but couldn't exactly start firing off questions the moment she stepped into Hannah's home.

'Seems like it's been a long time since we were in the drama club together, doesn't it?' Hannah said.

'Not long enough.' Melanie shuddered. She wasn't one to wax nostalgic about high school, a time she associated with enforced conformity, bad beer and worse sex. 'I love your house,' she said, quickly changing the subject. 'The very idea of having a library – what a luxury.'

'I love it, too. Ted grew up in this house.'

The house wasn't decorated in any particular style, but Melanie could see Ted's preference for handwoven fabrics, jewel colours, and native woods. Family heirlooms mingled with the work of local craftsmen to make a homey, unpretentious decor. Countless books filled the cases that lined the room, holding mostly well-worn dramatic works, from Euripides to Shakespeare to Ibsen, Oscar Wilde and Tennessee Williams. The overall effect was one of shabby comfort, a room filled with well-loved objects and books.

Melanie felt almost too formal in her black taffeta cocktail dress, which she had chosen to match her sequined red pumps. The dress had a wide circle skirt that flared out from a tight bodice. Under the dress Melanie wore a full tulle underskirt in the exact same shade of red as the shoes. She wore her hair, currently dyed a glossy black with Betty Page bangs, in a pile of curls on top of her head that were secured at the back of her neck with a rhinestone banana clip.

'I love your hairstyle,' Hannah remarked. 'I wish I had the nerve to try something like that. I haven't done anything more than trim the ends of my hair since I was six years old. And I've never had any fashion sense. Clothes don't look good on me.'

Melanie tilted her head to get a good look at Hannah. She was still wearing her hair in braids, but she had wound them up in a glossy crown on top of her head. Her long brown woollen dress made her figure look formless. Where on earth did she get a smock like that? Melanie wondered. Probably from one of those mail-order catalogues that featured a lot of yuppies striding through muddy fields with their Labrador retrievers.

'You know, Hannah,' Melanie said, 'maybe you don't need any clothes at all.'

'What?'

'I'm serious. You're a Lady Godiva type; all you have to do is show up naked at a party with your hair down, and everyone in the room will be at your feet.'

'I don't go to many parties naked,' Hannah laughed.

'Why not try it now?'

'Are you serious?'

'Sure. It's nice and warm here by the fire. And I've seen you naked before, in the showers at school.'

'That was eight years and twenty pounds ago.'

'Oh, come on. Start with your hair. Those braids would look great if you were a waitress at a beer garden, but I'd much rather see you as Rapunzel.'

Blushing, Hannah unpinned her braids and let them flop down to her waist. Then she loosened the ropes of hair and shook them out with her fingers. Finally her hair hung free, a crimped shawl that fell just above the crest of her hips.

'Now take off that dress,' Melanie urged. Seeing Hannah's hair, as shiny as molten metal in the firelight, made Melanie impatient with all the forms of dullness and restraint that plagued the universe. Without that frumpy dress, Hannah would be a goddess.

'I don't know, Melanie. I feel weird.'

'Maybe a little music would help. Do you have a stereo in here?'

Hannah pointed to the sound system. Melanie flipped through the rack of CDs. Ted and Hannah had an extensive collection, and Melanie was happy to see that most of their music had great seduction potential. She settled on a Nina Simone CD and inserted it into the player. Within a few seconds, the room filled with the singer's smoky voice singing 'I Love Your Lovin' Ways'.

'Now, close your eyes, Hannah. Listen to the music. It's just the two of us, nice and warm and cozy. Are you starting to feel sexy?'

'I think so.' Hannah swung her hips to the intoxicating beat. 'Yes. Yes, I am.'

'Go ahead, then.'

Hannah took a deep breath and held it as if she were about to plunge into the deep end of a swimming pool, then she yanked up the brown woollen dress and pulled it over her head. For a few moments she stood there in her white cotton bra and underpants, then she reached behind her back to work at the hooks on her bra. With her full thighs, rounded belly, and hair falling to her waist, Hannah reminded Melanie of medieval woodcuts she had seen of beautiful young witches. Her beauty was archetypal; she didn't need any embellishment. Melanie was perched on the edge of her chair, admiring Hannah in all her glory, when the door opened.

'What on earth is going on here?' Ted's voice boomed.

Naked except for her panties, Hannah snatched her dress off the floor and held it over her splendid breasts. Ted set down the bottle of wine and stood frowning at the two women as if they were a couple of delinquents caught smoking a joint in the school's boiler room. He pulled off his wire-rimmed glasses, giving Melanie the full force of his intense blue eyes. Those eyes used to turn her flesh into butter when she was in school; they were having the same effect on her now.

'Let me guess. This was your idea, Miss Paxton.'

'Yes, it was,' Melanie admitted.

'Do you always act so bold when you're a guest in someone's home?'

His voice sent a feathery thrill of fear down Melanie's spine. It had been one thing to play games with Ted at her shop, but tonight she was on his turf. Maybe she had overstepped the bounds by encouraging his wife to let her hair down and take off that hideous dress. After all, they hadn't even had cocktails yet.

'I didn't like the dress Hannah was wearing.' Melanie lifted her chin, trying to salvage a morsel of dignity. With Ted glowering down at her, that was a real challenge.

'I have to agree with you on that point. Hannah, go upstairs and change. Put on the blue velvet gown I bought you for your birthday. It's much more flattering.'

Melanie exhaled, but her relief was premature. As Hannah tried to slink away, Ted caught his wife by the arm and pulled her over to a nearby armchair. He bent her over the chair's overstuffed arm, got a grip on her hair with one hand, and delivered ten hard, fast blows to her bottom with the other. Then he pulled her upright and let her go with a final smack that rang out like a shot. Hannah heaved a big, gulping sob and rushed out of the library.

'It looks like you haven't learned much about humility since the last time I punished you, Miss Paxton,' Ted said.

Melanie stood up and smoothed the puffy folds of her taffeta skirt. 'Humility has never been my strong suit. You should remember that.'

'Believe me, I do,' Ted laughed. He had dropped some of his disciplinarian manner and was looking at Melanie with more admiration than authority. 'You were always a disruptive influence on the other students. It was all I could do to control the classroom when you were around. I wasn't exactly surprised to come home and find that you'd been working on Hannah.'

'You were just angry that we started without you.'

'Actually, I wasn't angry at all. Hannah is still self-conscious about her body, and it's good to see her letting go of her inhibitions. But we've been practicing domestic discipline, so I have to give the appearance of being the dominant one around here. I can't let you waltz in and turn my wife into a naked maniac.'

'Apparently domestic discipline isn't the only thing that you and your wife are practising these days,' Melanie said with a wink that referred to their encounter the other night. 'I heard a rumour that you're playing with other people. Is that true?'

Ted smiled. His smile was incredibly sexy, boyish and knowing at the same time. 'Why do you want to know? Are you interested in one of us?'

'I've been interested in *you* since I was jailbait,' Melanie said.

They were standing close together now, so close that Melanie could see the fine web of summer wrinkles around Ted's twinkling eyes, and smell the baby shampoo that he used. Under that clean, innocent scent was something primal, the sharp spice of sexual attraction. Whatever was cooking in Ted's imagination was a lot hotter than mere play.

'Is this better?'

Hannah stood in the doorway. A shy smile touched her face like candlelight. She had left her hair loose, and its length shimmered against the midnight-blue folds of her gown. The collar and flowing sleeves were trimmed with golden ribbon. The dress had a deep neckline that framed Hannah's cleavage, putting her breasts on full display. Only a man who loved her could have chosen a dress that suited her so perfectly.

'You look like a princess,' Melanie said. She walked over to Hannah and took both of her hands. 'You're beautiful, Hannah. You should always look like this. Every day.'

'Only special occasions, I'm afraid. This dress wouldn't do for handling newborn kittens or stitching up wounded dogs.'

'Well, you should always look this way for us,' Ted said.

He kissed Hannah on the lips. Then, to the surprise of both women, he turned to Melanie and kissed her, too. The three of them stood there for a while, considering the implications of the moment. Then Hannah hurried away to pull the rack of lamb out of the oven, Ted went off to make a pitcher of martinis, and things went back to being normal – or as normal as they could be when three people wanted to jump into bed with each other.

Melanie couldn't stop smiling throughout dinner. If that kiss were any indication, the next few months were going to yield a lot of surprises. Best of all, she had found the answer to her erotic needs for the coming winter. Why settle for one versatile, imaginative, and domestically gifted lover to spend the snowy months with, when you could have two?

After devouring Hannah's herb-crusted rack of lamb, Melanie and Ted and Hannah made their way back to the library. Once they had polished off a dessert of French vanilla ice cream drizzled with a raspberry brandy sauce, Melanie decided it was time to feed her curiosity.

'So tell me, Ted. How did the two of you get together? And how did you marry Hannah without getting strung up for retroactive impropriety?'

'It wasn't easy. We had to leave the country.'

'We fell in love on the theatre tour in England,' Hannah said. 'It was the first vacation I'd taken since I graduated from technical college. Ted was on the tour, along with a couple of other people from town, but most of them didn't know us. When we were in Europe, all the rules went out the window.'

'I hadn't seen her for years,' said Ted. 'When she showed up at the Boston airport, I couldn't believe it. I remembered Hannah as a sweet, timid kid. All of a sudden here was this luscious redhead, looking like a woman Titian would have painted. I was dying to get to know her again, but it still felt taboo. One evening we all went out to a performance of *Midsummer Night's Dream*, followed by a couple of hours of pub crawling. I walked

Hannah back to the hotel, then dropped her off at her room with a fatherly kiss. Twenty minutes later, I heard a knock on the door; it was Hannah wearing a Japanese kimono with nothing underneath. Her hair was down, and her skin seemed to glow through the silk. Once we started making love, it was like falling into a bathtub full of warm cream – I never wanted to come out. Aside from catching a couple of plays and taking some private trips out to the countryside, we spent the rest of the two weeks in bed. The tour director was disgusted with us.'

'It wasn't easy coming back to the States,' Hannah went on. 'I was terrified of what my parents would think – of what the whole town would think. You know how they can turn against you.'

'Only too well.' Melanie had never been allowed to forget the time she was arrested for shoplifting. To this day she lived in the shadow of a crime she had committed as a troubled teenager.

'We talked about living together in secret, but we knew that wouldn't work for more than a week or two. Ted thought about getting a job in another town, but he would have had to sell this house. We finally settled on a small, quiet, and extremely proper church wedding, so that everyone could see that we were doing things by the book. There was a little scuttlebutt at first, but that quieted down soon enough.'

'Morne Bay is already moving on to bigger and better scandals.' Ted sighed with satisfaction.

'Like your extramarital experiments?' Melanie suggested with a wicked smile.

'We're very discreet about that,' Ted said. 'We try not to get involved with anyone local, unless we're absolutely sure that they're as close-mouthed as we are. And we try to keep our play light, to avoid emotional complications. Right, Hannah?'

'Right.'

Melanie saw a wave of colour creep from Hannah's throat to her forehead. A redhead like Hannah would never be able to hide anything; with such transparent skin, she might as well advertise her feelings in neon. As if she sensed what Melanie was thinking, Hannah leaned down to pet the tabby, who had wandered back into the library.

'But is it really possible to avoid complications?' Melanie asked. She looked around at the hundreds of plays and novels that lined the walls. 'Look at all these stories of obsessive love, passion, jealousy. *Othello*, *Medea*. Even the gods and goddesses got jealous. You two must feel those emotions from time to time.'

'Sure we do. But we try to keep our emotions from getting out of control by being as honest as we can. We tell each other about every experience that we have – in very intimate detail.'

'Then we get to have the pleasure twice,' Hannah added. She was smiling to herself as she stroked the tabby, who had curled up on her thighs.

'Do you have something to tell us, Hannah?' Ted asked. 'You look as self-satisfied as that cat on your lap.'

'I do, as a matter of fact.'

'Then give us a complete report. If I think you're leaving anything out, I'll punish you severely in front of our guest.'

Ted was back to being a disciplinarian. How lucky Hannah was, to be able to explore her sexuality within the boundaries of such a comfortable marriage! As if that weren't enough, her husband was a natural dominant, who could give her all the sexual control she craved. Melanie sighed. If there were a flaw in this homespun libertinism, she hadn't seen it yet.

Hannah put the cat down on the floor. She got up and sat down next to her husband on the leather couch. He pushed her hair away from her face and began to pet her throat and breasts.

'Well,' Hannah began, 'I've been having fantasies about someone who just moved into town. Someone who's into spanking.'

'Who's that?'

'Nathaniel Wentworth.'

'Nathaniel Wentworth?' Melanie's jaw dropped. 'You mean that new curator is a spanko?'

Hannah gave Melanie a smirk that could have outdone the *Mona Lisa* for maddening secrecy. Melanie made a mental note to get the curator on her social calendar as soon as possible. Apparently he wasn't as dull as she'd thought. Judging from Hannah's gloating smile, whatever Nathan had to offer must be too good to share.

'I thought he looked like a disciplinarian,' Ted remarked. 'He has that stony, puritanical demeanour. I can imagine him sitting on a tribunal of colonial judges, passing judgment on wanton women like you. He probably keeps a pillory behind his house.'

'He doesn't have a pillory, as far as I know, but I've heard he makes his own spanking equipment in his woodshop. If I'm very lucky, he might try some of his equipment on me.'

'Hannah craves discipline,' Ted explained to Melanie. 'On the surface she's a good girl, full of the classical puritan virtues. She's honest, modest, a hard worker. She never does anything to deserve punishment. That only makes her want it more.'

'But what's the point of being punished if you don't misbehave in the first place?' Melanie asked, feeling put out. 'I misbehave every day of my life, but I rarely get caught, much less punished. Why should good girls get all the discipline, when they haven't done anything to deserve it?'

Ted sat up straight and stared at Melanie over the top of his glasses. 'Do you think I haven't noticed your need for discipline, Miss Paxton? Two hours ago I walked into my own home and found my wife doing a striptease while you urged her on like a sailor on shore leave. I can't have that kind of thing going on behind my back – in my library, no less. What do you think I should do about that, Hannah?'

Hannah winked at Melanie. She knew what was coming; Melanie couldn't wait to find out.

'You should punish both of us,' Hannah said.

'Damn right. You'll be first, Hannah. I'm going to correct you for your lewd behaviour, then I'll give your partner in crime the spanking she sorely needs. And if you want to be able to sit down this week, Miss Paxton, I suggest that you conduct yourself in a ladylike manner while you're waiting for your turn.'

Melanie was so excited that she thought she might burst if he made her wait too long. She sat with her hands folded, her knees pressed together, while she watched Ted turn Hannah over his knee. They made such an elegantly perverted tableau beside the fire: the boyishly handsome Ted with voluptuous Hannah draped across his lap. The folds of her blue velvet gown pooled on the floor, and Ted grasped her hair like a rope so that Melanie could watch the expression on her face as she was getting her punishment.

First Ted rolled up the sleeves of his Fair Isle sweater, baring his muscular forearms. Leaving his wife's dress in place, he ran his hand back and forth across the soft blue mounds of her cheeks. His hands, tanned and strong and lightly roped with tendons, had been one of the features that made Melanie dizzy with lust when she was a girl. Now she knew why. Ted had the gift of shifting easily between tenderness and severity, and those hands were equally adept at caressing, restraining, and spanking. When Hannah's bottom had been warmed up, he began the punishment with a few light smacks to either cheek. Then he upped the pressure and speed, getting down to the business of correction. In the aftermath of every swat, her flesh jiggled under the soft blue cloth. Hannah moaned.

Ted smacked her sharply. 'Crying already, darling? I'm just getting started.'

He pulled up her skirt, tossed its length over her thighs, and spanked her through her cotton panties. The simplicity of those panties made the scene all the more arousing; Hannah looked like a naughty girl who had been caught playing dress-up in her mother's best gown. Through the sheer white cotton, Melanie could see a delicious apple-red stain spreading across Hannah's flesh as Ted spanked harder and harder. At first Melanie tried to keep count of how many times his hand fell, but she soon lost track.

Then the panties came down, and Ted's hand made direct contact with Hannah's bottom. Melanie knew from personal experience how much that palm could sting on naked skin. She almost felt sorry for Hannah, who had dropped all pretense of dignity and was bawling like a baby. When Ted finally let his hand rest on his wife's thigh, he looked up at Melanie, who felt the electricity of that eye contact all the way down to her aching sex.

'Your turn, Miss Paxton,' he said.

Hannah crawled off Ted's lap. Whimpering, she stiffly made her way to the overstuffed armchair, where she curled up on her knees, avoiding any contact between the chair and her bottom. Melanie assumed that she was going to take Hannah's place face down across Ted's lap, but he had other plans in mind.

'Lie on your back,' he ordered.

Melanie followed his instructions, stretching out across his lap.

'Now lift your legs straight up in the air. Let's get this ridiculous skirt out of the way.'

The yards of stiff taffeta and the red crinoline under-skirt consumed a lot of space, but Melanie knew that she made an enticing picture with her long legs rising from the masses of fabric. She wore black silk stockings and black suspenders, and of course the ruby red shoes. Ted ran his fingers admiringly up and down the length of her thighs and calves. He held both of her ankles together in one hand while he pushed the fabric away from her hips and bottom.

'Just as I thought,' he said, his voice grim with disapproval, 'no panties. What kind of woman struts around without panties in the middle of November?'

Melanie thought the question was rhetorical, but when Ted applied a stinging smack to her rear end (even with the fire going, it did feel a bit chilly without underpants), she realised that he expected an answer.

'Well?' he pressed. 'What kind of woman are you? A tart? A tease?'

'Neither,' said Melanie, as defiantly as she could in that humiliating position. 'I'm a sexual adventuress. I'm discriminate in my choice of lovers, and I never, ever tease.'

'You never tease? Are you sure about that?'

'Absolutely.'

'I disagree. Based on personal experience, I think you've elevated teasing to an art form. But there comes a time for every tease to be put to the test.' He gave Melanie's bottom a brisk, stinging smack. 'Do you really crave the kind of discipline you just asked for, Melanie? Or is spanking just a novel form of titillation?'

'I want to be spanked. I really do!'

'Oh, I don't doubt that you want to be spanked at the moment, with your skirt hanging down and your bottom in the air. Your pussy is already seeping. But my question is, do you know the difference between spanking and punishment?'

'I'm sure I'll find out, if you give me what I deserve.'

'What you deserve, young lady, is some serious discipline. You play at being submissive, batting your eyes and pouting, but what you really are is a bratty, spoiled hedonist who's used to snatching whatever she wants out of life.'

'What's wrong with that?' Melanie retorted.

Her question was met with a hailstorm of tight, short swats to her buttocks and thighs. Ted lifted Melanie up by her ankles so that he could cover her entire rump. By the time he was done, she was feeling a lot less saucy. Ted must have gotten a lot of practice since the last time he spanked her, because he knew exactly how to attack her tenderest parts. She thought that the least he could do after that painful ordeal would be to finger her to a climax, but he simply lowered her legs and lifted her unceremoniously off his lap.

'That wasn't any fun.' Melanie stood up and furrowed through her voluminous skirt until she found her burning bottom. She rubbed her sore buttocks until the pain began to ebb.

'If you were looking for fun, young lady, you missed the whole point.'

Hannah and Ted exchanged knowing smiles. They had probably discussed Melanie before she came over tonight. Ted would have told his wife all about the time he spanked Melanie at her shop, and how poorly she tolerated pain. Hannah would have thrown in a few reminiscences about Melanie in high school, recalling how she preferred freedom to structure, fun to self-sacrifice.

'Hey,' Melanie said, 'I get the point. You think I'm shallow and undisciplined.' She snatched up her beaded purse.

'No, Melanie. We don't think that at all. Don't go,' Hannah pleaded. She stood up and stroked Melanie's trembling arms. 'We want you to stay. Ted, will you ask her?'

'We'd like you to consider spending some time with us, Melanie. Possibly the whole winter, if you're interested. There's plenty of space in this house, and we'd love to rent you a room.'

'What?' Ted's words came so close to what Melanie had been thinking earlier that evening that she couldn't believe what she was hearing.

'We'd like you to think about moving in for a while,' Ted repeated. He got up, and together he and Hannah led Melanie back to the leather couch. They eased her down onto her sore backside, then sat down on either side of her. Hannah smoothed her hair, while Ted nuzzled her neck. Within a few moments, Melanie was purring contentedly. This was more like it.

'We've been looking for someone to be part of our lives on a more permanent basis,' Hannah said. 'Maybe not forever, but at least long enough for us all to find out what it's like to be involved with more than one person.'

'Why me?'

'Because you're desirable, warm, and exciting,' Ted said.

'You're funny, smart, and pretty,' Hannah added.

'Anything else?' Melanie asked, basking in their compliments.

'And because you're crying out for discipline,' Ted growled. 'I've made it my mission in life to train women like you and Hannah in the ways of virtue.'

'Please say you'll try it,' Hannah said.

'I'm sure I'd love the attention, but I'm addicted to my independence. I love having my own life.'

'You'd still have your own life,' Hannah assured her. 'This house is plenty big enough for that. You might like the attic bedroom, or even the old carriage house. Those rooms are so far away that we'd never know what you were up to.'

'You and Hannah could learn a lot from each other,' Ted said. 'And I could learn a lot by spending entire days making love to both of you.'

Melanie smiled. 'I'll think about it,' she said. 'Meanwhile, you're welcome to try to convince me.'

Though she had already made up her mind, Melanie let Ted and Hannah use their combined powers of persuasion to coax her into staying the night. They took her upstairs to the master bedroom, which was dominated by a vast four-poster bed heaped with pillows and down comforters. It was a bed made for long bouts of sex on bitterly cold nights. Across from the bed stood a full-length antique mirror with panels that could be arranged at creative angles. Melanie saw infinite possibilities in those mirrors.

Ted and Hannah worked beautifully in tandem. Hannah paid court to Melanie's body, taunting and tickling her with her fingers as she whipped her long hair back and forth across Melanie's breasts and belly. When Melanie had been teased into a fit of anticipation, Ted took over and fucked her the way she had dreamed of in her adolescent reveries. He had a fit, lean body, made trim by running and swimming, and he was able to thrust effortlessly for as long as Melanie required. Hannah seemed content to watch her husband and friend make love, but Melanie insisted on giving Hannah her share of attention, laving her pussy with her tongue until her copper curls were soaking wet and Hannah begged for release. Each coupling flowed smoothly into the next, until the black sky outside the icy window panes turned blue, then lavender with dawn.

As the three of them lay slick with sweat in each other's arms, Melanie floated off to sleep with a peaceful smile on her face. She had lived for a quarter of a century without being lured into a live-in relationship with any of her lovers. This experiment in domestic stability might be her most daring adventure yet.

The next morning, while Ted and Melanie slept late, Hannah drove her truck out to the farmhouse where her grandmother used to live. The maples and copper beeches had lost their fiery autumn splendour; their branches were a gnarled tangle of witches' bones. The forbidding woods and the steely water of the bay made Hannah long for a crackling fire and a hard-bodied male. She didn't know if the new owner of the house would have a fire going at this time of the morning, but he definitely had a large, rock-solid body. Hannah smiled, thinking about the way Nathan Wentworth's chest and arms filled out a flannel shirt. The taut bulk of his ass packed in tight, faded jeans got Hannah's mouth watering every time she looked at him.

This morning Hannah had promised herself that she was going to do more than look at him, if the situation allowed. And she would make damn sure that the situation did allow it.

Carrying a dish of apple crisp that she had baked the day before, Hannah approached her grandmother's former house. It felt strange to knock on the door that she had been opening freely for her entire life. She had spent so much of her childhood here that losing access to the place was like losing her own home. Looking down the hill towards the water, she could see the tombstones of the small family plot. Her ancestors had been buried facing the water, so that they could see the bay and its beadwork of tiny islands for as long as they remained.

Her attention was distracted by Nathan's blond stallion, who was grazing in the meadow. Samson lifted his magnificent head, tossing his mane as he sniffed the brisk air. Hannah could feel his pleasure at being allowed to roam in the field, at drinking the salty breeze, at occupying a strong, healthy body. She had more of an affinity for animals than for most people; that was why she had decided to become a veterinary technician after she finished high school. Hannah had animal tastes herself, simple and basic. If she were well fed, well rested, and well fucked, she could be happy under almost any circumstances. Now here was Nathan, stepping out of the barn, hopefully to take care of at least one of those requirements for her.

Nathan looked like a human version of his horse: tall, blond, and packed with muscle. His 'mane' was tied back in a ponytail, and the sleeves of his plaid flannel shirt were rolled up, revealing his thick, veined forearms and massive hands. Hannah's throat went dry as she stared at those hands. She knew that his palms were as hard as granite, and that his fingers were covered with calluses. She felt a bit disloyal comparing those hands to her husband's, which were roughened only by summer sailing. Nathan was a farmer and a craftsman, in addition to being an expert on colonial history. Like Hannah's ancestors, he was accustomed to backbreaking work. And she would bet anything that, given the right opportunity, he would be able to deliver an old-fashioned spanking that would leave her soaking wet and whimpering like a newborn puppy.

'Hello, Hannah.' From this distance, Nathan's face looked stern and unwelcoming. 'Come to check up on the house?'

Flustered, Hannah couldn't reply. Nathan thought she had come over to pry, and in a way he was right. Maybe she was being possessive, trying to maintain some kind of claim on the property. She held out the pan of apple crisp like a white flag of surrender. 'I just came to bring you this,' she said in a tiny voice. 'It's a housewarming gift. For *your* house.'

Nathan smiled, and the stony expression became an

illusion. 'You're an angel. I haven't had breakfast yet. Care to join me?'

'Thanks, but I've already eaten.'

'Have a cup of coffee, then. I could use the company.'

Hannah was so relieved that her knees buckled as she followed Nathan into the house. Nathan had seemed so aloof when he first greeted her. When she saw how inviting the kitchen looked, she knew that she must have misinterpreted his attitude. An array of shiny stainless-steel pans dangled from hooks above the stove, and crisp yellow curtains hung from the windows. The wood stove was burning, and its fragrance mingled with the smell of freshly brewed coffee. Nathan poured a mug for Hannah.

'Let's see,' he mused, studying her with his frank blue eyes, 'you take your coffee with whole milk or real cream, no sugar. Am I right?'

'How did you know?' Hannah's face blazed like the belly of the stove.

'Lucky guess.'

Nathan winked at her. He leaned against the counter and attacked the apple crisp, eating large forkfuls right out of the dish. Hannah occupied herself by stirring cream into her coffee. The silver teaspoon rattled against the mug's rim. Her confidence was dwindling. Even from across the kitchen, Nathan's physical presence overwhelmed her. Tall and full figured, Hannah was used to being as big or bigger than the men in her life, but Nathan had at least four inches on her, and considering the bulk of his muscles he probably outweighed her by at least fifty pounds. As if his size weren't intimidating enough, he was much better educated than Hannah, with a doctorate in American history and a couple of published books under his belt. Hannah had earned a veterinary technician's certificate from a vocational college. Looking at herself through Nathan's eyes, she saw a foolish country girl with a crush as blatant as the scarlet patches on her cheeks.

Nathan scraped the dish with his fork, then set it down with a sigh of satisfaction. 'That was the best meal I've had since I moved here,' he said. 'You made that yourself, didn't you?'

'How did you know?' Hannah asked for the second time. Her conversational skills this morning made her sound about as brilliant as an old garden hoe.

'I know,' he said, approaching her, 'because you're obviously a sensual woman. You like rich, simple foods, like real cream and pure butter. You don't like refined white sugar; you sweeten your food with dark maple syrup, freshly grated nutmeg, cinnamon.'

Hannah kept her eyes on Nathan's boots as he walked across the linoleum. She didn't have the courage to look any higher. When he set his hands on her shoulders, she gnawed her lower lip and prayed that she wasn't dreaming. His hands were as hard and heavy as she had imagined them. She hadn't had a man lift her off the ground since she was eight years old, but Nathan could do it, if he wanted to. She had the strangest sense that he did want to.

'Thank you for bringing me breakfast,' he said. He kissed her cheek. 'Would you like to see what I've done with the rest of the house?'

'I'd better go,' Hannah squeaked. 'I have to get to work.'

'Work? On a Sunday?'

'Well, I don't officially work. But I told Dr Heath that I'd make a couple of house calls today.'

'At least come and see the shed. I think your grandfather would be proud of what I've done with it. I cleaned out all the old debris, cleared the ventilators, and dusted off his old equipment. I'm going to reinsulate the building soon, so it's more comfortable for winter work.'

That spacious shed, where Hannah's grandfather had had his own workshop for many years, had sealed Nathan's decision to buy the property. Nathan's hobby was building reproductions of old American furniture. His oak reproduction of a Quaker meeting table, with its simple twin benches, was evidence of his craftsmanship. Hannah had heard a rumour that he built other things, as well – implements and furniture to fulfil his love of corporal punishment. Hannah had been dying to find out if the tale was true, but she was suddenly nervous about going out to the shed. She tried to take a step away from Nathan, but she couldn't break free from those hands.

'Hannah, I want you to come to the shed with me. No talking back. Just come.'

His stern tone had returned. This time she knew she hadn't misinterpreted him. Holding her elbow in a grip that was too firm to be friendly, Nathan led her out of the kitchen door and down the stone steps into the yard. He walked two steps ahead of her, pacing his stride so that she had to stumble after him like a naughty little girl. Though she hadn't done anything wrong, Nathan's severity filled her with an intensely pleasurable shame. Her cuntlips swelled against her jeans. She had a keen urge to pee, or maybe that was just the tingle of anticipation.

They entered the chilly gloom of the shed, which smelled of wood shavings and straw and varnish, all smells that heightened Hannah's arousal. Whatever Nathan had in mind, it wasn't going to be tender or romantic. He closed the door, switched on the overhead light, then turned to Hannah and crossed his arms over his broad chest.

'It's a bit too early in the day for deceit, isn't it?' he asked.

'Deceit?' Hannah swallowed. She had no idea what he

was talking about, but his disapproval pierced her conscience. Now she knew how women must have felt back in colonial Salem, standing in front of a tribunal of judges accusing them of witchcraft.

'You came over here carrying your bait, trying your best to tempt me. Then you claimed that you didn't want to stay. I know what you came here for, but you didn't have the courage to ask for it. Am I right?'

Nathan was right. She had come out to his house to seduce him, but she'd been too much of a coward to follow through. It was a good thing that she wasn't on trial for witchcraft, because she'd be a human barbecue by now.

'Answer me, Hannah.'

Hannah lowered her head. 'Yes,' she whispered.

'You came out here to fuck me this morning, didn't you?'

'Yes.'

'Then you changed your mind, and you tried to leave me standing around like a fool with a hard on. Am I right?'

Hannah nodded.

'I told you I wanted to show you my woodshop, but that's not all I'm going to do. Take your coat off. And your boots and jeans.'

'What?'

'Your boots, coat and jeans. Take them off. And hurry; I don't have all day to correct your bad behaviour. Your parents should have done that years ago.'

Hannah slipped out of her pea coat and laid it across Nathan's workbench. She pulled off her flannel shirt, then took off her boots and wiggled out of her jeans. Finally she stood in front of Nathan in her long thermal underwear, which had been washed so many times that it was dingy grey and worn through in spots. The temperature in the shed was so low that her breath left plumes of smoke in the air. Even in her underwear, her nipples felt like knots of ice. Hannah tugged at her long braids, wishing that they were a pair of drapes that she could yank across her body. Being undressed in a man's bedroom, with her body swathed in shadows or curled up under a quilt, was one thing; standing around in your long johns was another.

Nathan's scowl softened as he gazed at Hannah's body. 'You're one big, beautiful woman. I almost hate to punish you.'

Nathan walked over to the table that held his tools and a jigsaw. He picked up a flat, lovingly carved instrument that looked like the back of an antique hairbrush. Made of varnished bird's-eye maple, the paddle glowed in the pale sunlight that seeped through the shed's dusty windows.

'Everyone knows I build traditional furniture, like tables and chairs and cabinets,' Nathan said, slapping the paddle against the heel of his hand, 'but very few people know that I make other things, as well. I make paddles, like this one. And I build furniture that can be used for multiple purposes. That's very useful in households where there's a need for discipline. Were you disciplined as a child?'

'Not really,' Hannah admitted. 'I usually did what grown-ups told me to do. Even when I disobeyed, my parents didn't spank me. They didn't believe in corporal punishment. The worst punishment I can remember is being told to go to my room and think about what I'd done wrong.'

'You should have been taught to be more honest with yourself, and with others. You have a tendency to hide your desires with silly fibs. Then you change your mind about what you want, and you tell more lies to get free of the situation.'

Nathan pushed Hannah's clothes to one side and sat

down on his work bench, his legs spread. Between the solid slabs of his thighs, an impressive bulge was rising, straining the inseam of his jeans.

'Hannah, look at me. Not at my crotch, at my face, please.'

Hannah forced herself to look Nathan in the eye, though every particle in her submissive being was telling her to stare at the floor. God, he looked incredible, sitting in that milky shaft of light. He wasn't handsome in a Hollywood way, but his features were so strong and purely cut that they gave him a look of timeless stability. He looked like a man who had infinite patience and kindness, but underlying those qualities was a flinty integrity that could be unforgiving.

'Tell me what you came here for,' he said. 'I want to hear you say it.'

'I came here because I wanted to see my grand-mother's house again.'

'And?'

'Because I wanted to see you.'

'Why?'

Hannah took a deep breath. 'I wanted to have sex with you.'

'Why didn't you tell me that in the kitchen? We could have gone upstairs to the bedroom and spent the rest of the morning fucking. I didn't ask you if you wanted to see the house so that you could admire my interior decorating skills.'

'I don't know. When you touched me, I was afraid all of a sudden. I changed my mind, and I wanted to leave.'

'Do you still want to fuck me?'

Hannah lifted her hands helplessly. 'That's the problem – I think I know what I want, but I don't know how to say it. Or I can't say it. I try, but I just ... flop. That's the only way I can describe it.'

'Well, we'll have to teach you how to express your

desires. Come over here. Stand between my legs and tell me, with complete honesty, what you want me to do to you.'

Hannah did as she was told. When he put his hands around her waist, her stomach fluttered as if it were filled with moths. Standing in the warm bracket between Nathan's enormous thighs, she felt so small that she didn't see how she could possibly know her own desires, much less voice them.

'I can't,' she said. 'I'm sorry. I can't.'

'All right, then. We'll try a firmer approach.'

Before Hannah knew what was happening, Nathan's hands were lifting her off the ground, and she was rotating through the air, coming to rest across his thighs. The change in position happened so quickly that she lost her breath. Ted often warmed her up before a spanking, massaging her cheeks with aromatic oil or brushing them with a fur mitt. Nathan didn't indulge in any preliminary ass-worship, he just set in with the palm of his hand, covering Hannah's cheeks with stinging smacks. She was grateful that he had let her keep her thermal underwear on. Though the waffled fabric didn't offer much cushioning, it was better than getting the full impact of his callused palm against her skin.

He wasn't content to stop with his hand. Once he had set her flesh on fire, Nathan let Hannah rest for a few moments. She glanced over her shoulder to see what he was doing. He picked up the polished wooden pocket paddle and held it up to the light, admiring the wood's honey-gold colour, its satiny grain. Then he unceremoniously pulled down Hannah's long underpants, exposing her skin to the frigid air, and rubbed the paddle over her rump.

'I've been wanting to try this little beauty on a broad firm bottom,' Nathan said. 'Yours is the ideal size, and your skin colours so nicely. If you hadn't stopped by this morning, I would have had to come into town to find you.'

The first swats were light, teasing blows to the undersides of her buttocks, just where the tenderest part of her thighs swelled into her cheeks. Hannah squirmed, enjoying the crisp bite of the wood after the crude blows of Nathan's hand. He responded to the movement by spanking her harder. The pretty paddle packed a vicious wallop when it was powered by a muscular arm. Hannah yelped, kicked, and tried to roll off Nathan's lap. He wrestled one of his legs over her lower body, bracing her just below the fleshy mounds.

Tears filled her eyes, but she felt so ashamed of herself that she couldn't make a sound. She had thought she was so sophisticated when she and Ted started experimenting with other lovers, but when she met a man who really attracted her, Hannah was a bumbling innocent. She couldn't even take a real spanking, apparently, because when Nathan paused to ask her what she was thinking, she begged him to stop.

'I've had enough,' she sobbed. 'I can't take any more.'

'Are you ready to tell me what you want?'

'I want you to stop.'

He lowered his hand and caressed the backs of her thighs in slow, calming strokes. He made soothing noises as he stroked her. When her sobs had died down to sniffles, he parted her legs from behind and fondled her cuntfolds, fingering her with such nimble delicacy that she couldn't believe she was being stimulated by the same hand that had just paddled her.

Hannah wiped her nose on her sleeve. Now that she wasn't being spanked, she could appreciate the dimensions of the long, thick ridge under her belly. As Nathan's fingers located her clit, the burning pain of her bottom melted into a slick, buttery pleasure that spread through her sex and radiated through her limbs. Every part of her body, from her feet to her belly to the tips of her fingers and toes, simmered with self-awareness. When she shifted her weight on Nathan's lap, she thought she could hear the liquid squeak of her lower lips skidding against each other. Being so close to him, separated from his flesh by only a few millimetres of cloth, was torture, and there was only one way to end it.

'I want you to fuck me now.'

She didn't have to ask twice. Nathan lifted Hannah off his lap as if she were no heavier than a feather pillow. He arranged her across the workbench with her bottom in the air. Then he got on his knees behind her, bracketing her hips with his thighs, and unbuttoned his jeans. As she listened to him removing a condom out of its wrapper, Hannah thought that she had never been so happy. Her senses were fully aroused, she had just received the hardest spanking of her life, and she was about to be reamed by a man she was wildly in lust with.

Ream her he did, marking the tempo of his thrusts with harsh grunts, his mass pounding hers as he held her by the shoulders and drove himself into her. He gave Hannah what she loved more than all the romantic fondling and exquisite caresses in the world: an old-fashioned fuck that ended in blunt, aching spasms that started from deep in her core and shook her whole being. In her heart of hearts, Hannah was an animal, happily domesticated, but still a beast.

4 Jason's Schooldays

Ever since the estate sale, Melanie couldn't stop thinking about fawn breeches moulded over muscular thighs and rumps. Those breeches had flooded her mind with images so old that they had all but faded from her imagination. When Melanie was a little girl, she had seen a BBC production of *Tom Brown's Schooldays* on *Masterpiece Theater*. Watching the televised drama of Tom's persecution at Rugby School, she had sown the seeds of some of her earliest erotic fantasies.

Though she was years from knowing anything about sex, much less its more exotic variations, Melanie had witnessed Tom's trials with rapt fascination. Whether he was being tormented by the wicked Flashman, harassed by a gang of older boys, or tormented by the schoolmaster, Tom's trials grew more severe with each episode. They culminated in a scene that burned itself into Melanie's memory: Tom bending over a desk, a rag stuffed between his full lips as his tightly clad bottom was caned in front of his classmates.

No wonder I'm such a pervert, Melanie thought as she coasted off to sleep. It's all Tom Brown's fault. But Flashman was really the sexy one ...

The first thing on her mind when she woke up was Pagan's brother. Though she knew that it was probably futile to telephone a college boy before noon, she couldn't wait until a decent hour. To her surprise, Jason sounded wide awake when he answered the phone at eight-thirty. Maybe he had an early morning class, but somehow she thought he sounded more mature than most young men his age.

'I'd love to own a pair of breeches like that,' Jason said, 'but I live at Beardsley, and I don't have a car. I won't be back in Morne Bay until the holidays. Can I mail you a cheque and pick them up when I'm home?'

'Well,' Melanie said, winding the telephone cord around her finger, 'if you really want them, I could bring them to you.'

'Sounds like a lot of trouble,' Jason said, but Melanie could tell by the deepening of his voice that he was hoping she would insist.

'I insist. The trip will give me an excuse to leave the shop early. Besides, your sister told me that you love vintage clothing, and I want to encourage that interest in men as much as possible.'

'What else did she tell you?'

'Not a thing. Only that you're a student at Beardsley, and you like old clothes.'

Jason gave Melanie directions to the house he shared with a group of classmates. They made plans to meet there on Friday night. Melanie thought it was odd that a college student would be willing to give up part of his Friday night for the sake of a pair of pants. Either his interest in vintage fashion bordered on mania, or he had no social life to speak of.

Or maybe he was hoping to get more than a pair of breeches out of Melanie. She preferred this alternative. Judging from Jason's voice and manner, he was the type of young male she liked best: confident to the point of arrogance, with an ironical courtly manner and a preference for 'older' women.

According to Melanie's mother, the first words she ever strung together into a statement were 'cute boy'. The story was a legend in Melanie's family. She was sitting in her high chair, dabbling in a bowl of puréed bananas, when a college freshman came to the door selling newspaper subscriptions. Melanie had peered out the open door, past her mother's back, and uttered the famous phrase. Her preoccupations hadn't changed much over the next twenty-odd years. All she thought about for the rest of the morning was meeting a houseful of well-built studs. She almost forgot that Bridget Locke was coming over to interview her for the Living Arts section of Morne Bay's newspaper, the *Foghorn*.

Bridget arrived promptly at ten, with a photographer in tow. Bridget, who happened to have a seat on the town council, hadn't spent much time at Chimera since Melanie added the Alcove, so Melanie spent their first fifteen minutes together giving her a guided tour. The photographer tagged along, taking snapshots of Melanie as she demonstrated how she had arranged the merchandise so that the new items and vintage clothing complemented each other. At the photographer's suggestion, she struck a few campy poses in front of the Alcove, holding the beaded curtain aside to display the erotic books and toys.

As Melanie chattered on about her plans to expand the shop and increase its selection of sexy merchandise, an inner voice warned her that she should be choosing her words more carefully. Bridget seemed friendly and open-minded, if a bit prim, but she was a journalist, and you could never tell how a journalist might portray you in print.

Melanie ignored the internal nagging. There wasn't enough room in the back of her mind for admonishing voices, not when all of her spare mental energy was being used to think about her meeting with Jason. If she made the right impression, she might be able to wrangle an invitation into his secret club, or at least a temporary guest membership.

But what impression should she make? Melanie spent the day mulling over the possibilities as she worked.

After closing the shop that evening, she browsed through the merchandise considering what to wear tomorrow. At twenty-five, she considered herself to be too old and dignified to go without panties or wear anything tight enough to show her nipples. There were plenty of nubile beauties at Beardsley College who were doing just that. Melanie had to set herself apart from the co-eds, make herself look elegant and mysterious and almost, but not quite, out of reach. She settled on an outfit that would match Jason's breeches: a bottle-green velvet riding jacket with padded shoulders over a voluminous blouse trimmed with Venetian lace, paired with a narrow knee-length black skirt, with leather lace-up boots that sported spiked heels. She put her hair up in a topknot, and as a final detail she added a pair of reading glasses with schoolteacher frames.

Melanie smiled at her reflection in the mirror. She looked like a Victorian governess with a leather fetish. If only she had a riding crop or a flogger in her hand, she would be any submissive's wet dream. Melanie combed through the Alcove looking for a toy to add the finishing touch to her costume. A crop would be nice, but she wanted something a little less obvious. The wooden fraternity paddle? No, that looked like some kind of hazing joke.

'Ah, that's it. Thank you, Tom Brown,' Melanie murmured, reaching for a long, cruelly thin rattan cane. Just as she was wrapping her hand around the polished bamboo, the telephone rang.

'Hello?' Melanie fingered the ribbed rod as she spoke, picturing the stripes that it would leave across a pair of fresh young butt cheeks. Hot-crossed buns, indeed!

'Melanie, it's Harrison. Your favourite pupil.'

From the froggy tone of Harrison's voice, Melanie guessed that her 'favourite pupil' either had a cold and was doped up on medication, or had knocked back a few drinks. She heard the faint rattle of ice cubes in the background, and realised that it was the latter.

'Harrison. How's your training coming along? Have you been practising your exercises?'

'Every day. You know how I worship you.'

'Will you be ready to wear your plug at the meeting?'

A long pause followed. 'Meeting?'

'The planning commission meeting. Where I'm going to present my proposal for the shop.'

'Um, yes. That one.'

'You haven't forgotten, have you? Harrison, that meeting means everything to me!'

'I understand. The planning commission always holds its year-end meeting just before Christmas.'

Harrison's voice had taken on a vague tone that made Melanie queasy with fear. He had had too much to drink, she reminded herself. He had called her during his evening cocktail hour, while his wife was attending some quilting circle or twelve-step meeting, and he had probably hoped to jack off on the phone while he talked to Melanie about his anal training. The planning commission would be the last thing on his mind. But Melanie wasn't in the mood for one-way phone sex with a plastered investment banker.

'Listen, Harrison, I'd love to talk, but it's been a long day. I've got to go home and get to bed.'

'What do you wear to bed? Do you sleep naked?'

'How dare you ask me that, you naughty man!' Melanie stepped into her 'anal mistress' role. She could hear Harrison shudder in delight. 'What I wear to bed is none of your business. As your punishment for being so forward, you will wear your butt plug all day tomorrow. I want you to think about your rude behaviour while you sit at your desk at the bank and review your clients' portfolios. Good night.'

'Don't hang up,' Harrison pleaded. 'I have to see you.'

Melanie felt a lurch of dread. God, she hoped that was the booze talking. Drunken infatuation was OK, but the last thing she wanted was for Harrison to fall for her.

'I'm very busy these days.'

'This is important. I need to talk to you about your proposal.'

'Why don't we talk now?' Melanie didn't like the sly note in Harrison's voice.

'Because I want to introduce you to someone.'

'Who?'

'Nathaniel Wentworth. We're scheduled to have brunch Saturday morning. I want you to join us. We'll talk about your plans, and how they fit in with the museum.'

Melanie didn't know what to say. Her one consolation was that Harrison didn't want to meet her alone for some intimate rendezvous. Meeting him for anal training had been risky enough.

'Well? Can you meet us at the Golden Loon?'

'I guess I can spare an hour.'

'Ten-thirty on Saturday morning, then.'

Melanie was relieved to hang up the phone. The exchange had left her shaken and confused. The Golden Loon was a secluded hotel down the coast, a place where uppercrust businessmen met their working-class lovers for discreet rolls in the sack. Their dining room served a champagne brunch on the weekends that was infamous for leading to Saturday afternoon trysts. Was that what Harrison had in mind?

She hadn't had a chance to tell Harrison that she had already met the new curator. Harrison would expect her to gush over his Harvard buddy, while Melanie would be trying to stifle her dislike of Nathan Wentworth. She would have to pound a lot of the Golden Loon's complimentary champagne to get through that brunch.

'I hope you appreciate what I'm doing for you,'

Melanie said, addressing the vintage gowns that stood like ghosts in the half-darkened room. Then she picked up her cane and headed home to take a long, blistering-hot shower.

Melanie left for Beardsley College on Friday afternoon, grateful to get a break from Morne Bay and its petty small-town politics. The drive to the town of Somerhill was monotonous at this time of year; all the glorious foliage had been replaced by a landscape as drab as a basket of dirty laundry. The town itself, with its pretty steeples and cobblestone alleys, was as picturesque as ever, but Melanie didn't expect much from Jason's living quarters. She assumed he would live in the typical college rathole, a dilapidated wreck of a house with a weed-choked lawn and a Jolly Roger flag hanging out of one of the second-storey windows. She was pleasantly surprised when she parked her car in front of a tidy brick colonial with white shutters. Under a dusting of snow, the lawn was impeccably mowed, and a pair of well-pruned blue spruces stood guard on either side of the front door.

Melanie gave the brass lion's head knocker a few sharp taps. The door opened so quickly that Melanie toppled over the threshold, falling into a broad male chest. The owner of that chest held a tall glass of Guinness in one hand, a cigar in the other.

'I guess you were expecting me.'

'I was expecting someone,' the young man drawled, giving Melanie a devouring look, 'but no one like you.'

She looked up at one of the sexiest young men she had ever had the pleasure to fall against. He had a tall, well-made form; gloriously thick, reddish-brown hair; and sleepy green eyes. But his best feature by far was his mouth: juicy and sullen and made for debauchery. The fat lower lip had a slight cleft, as if someone had sewn a single stitch across the flesh in an attempt to restrain it.

Though Jason's cheeks were smooth and rosy, there were early signs of dissipation in his jaded pout and his puffy eyelids. Here was a boy who had already sampled quite a few of life's more exotic pleasures – and was rapidly getting bored by them. But as he took in Melanie's schoolmarm attire, her dominatrix boots, and her cruel cane, his face lit up with anticipation.

'This is going to be a hell of a night,' he said.

'Oh really.' Melanie took a clipped, haughty tone. She immediately fell into the role she intuitively knew would excite this young deviant. She gave the lad an icy look over the top of her glasses. There was no sense in letting him take the upper hand. 'But before this night goes anywhere,' she continued, 'you'll have to invite me in. An introduction wouldn't hurt, either.'

'Sorry,' he mumbled. 'I'm Jason.'

'I'm Miss Paxton. When we get to know each other better, I might let you call me Melanie.'

'Would you like to come in, Miss Paxton?'

'That's a reasonable assumption. It's colder than a witch's tit out here.'

Jason stepped aside and Melanie, her nose in the air, swept into the house. The first thought that popped into her mind, as she looked around the living room, was that the boys who lived here were either unnaturally obsessive about cleaning, or they pooled their money to pay for a housekeeper. There wasn't a trace of clutter or dust in the shabbily elegant room. The burgundy leather sofa and armchairs were scuffed and scarred, but clearly expensive, as if they had once furnished an upscale men's club. A fire crackled underneath a carved mantelpiece, and crystal decanters twinkled on a table next to the fireplace. With Vivaldi playing in the background and a selection of academic journals and fancy architectural magazines arranged on the coffee table, the stage was set for a seduction scenario.

'Are you home alone tonight?' Melanie asked. She loved the room's masculine atmosphere, but she would have preferred to see half a dozen male bodies draped like young lions across the furniture.

'No way,' Jason said with a mysterious smile.

'So where is everyone else?'

'They're around. You'll meet them soon enough.'

'Here are the pants,' Melanie said, handing him the parcel. 'I hope you like them.'

Jason's eyes took on a wicked gleam. He tapped out his cigarette in a crystal ashtray, then took the package. 'I'm sure I will. How much do I owe you?'

'Nothing. Consider them a gift.'

'Really, I have to pay you something.'

'No you don't. Your sister is a terrific employee, so think of it as a family benefit.'

He beamed. 'Would you like to have a drink while I go try these on?' he asked.

'I'd love a Bailey's, if you have it.'

'Sure. We keep a lot of chick liquor in the house.'

'Chick liquor?'

'You know, peach-wine coolers, butterscotch schnapps. The stuff girls like to drink. But we also have single malts, the finest Jamaican rum, and that super-expensive Russian vodka that doesn't give you a hangover.'

'What if I were in the mood for some cheap rotgut?' she asked. 'Would that classify as "chick liquor"?'

Jason looked confused. 'I could get you some of that . . . I think.'

'No, no. Bailey's will do just fine.'

Melanie hid a smile. She could imagine Jason and his buddies visiting a liquor store en masse in a quest for the perfect alcohol to fuel their sexual pursuits. Jason probably didn't need much extra fuel to have his way with women. One glance from those bedroom eyes triggered a vision of him lying on top of Melanie, showing her exactly what he'd been learning in school. As he handed Melanie a glass of the rich creamy liqueur, his fingers deliberately brushed her hand.

'Back in a minute,' he said. 'Stay out of trouble while I'm gone.'

Then he bounded up the staircase, leaving Melanie to her own devices.

An arrangement of group photos, framed in polished brass, hung over the fireplace. Sipping her drink, Melanie walked over to investigate. The photos featured a clan of college boys in various situations: lifting tankards of beer at an outdoor bar, wearing football uniforms at a sunny park, dressed in formal tuxedos on the marble steps of a hoity-toity Georgian mansion. In every shot the fellows were physically close, arms draped around each others' shoulders, hips and thighs pressed close together. Each member of the gang was better-looking than the last, from the blond with the cruel sneer and floppy hair to the tanned bodybuilder with the military crewcut. Together they formed a smorgasbord of cute boys, and they all shared Jason's sultry, jaded expression.

What a bunch of spoilt brats, Melanie said to herself. The pictures filled her head with homoerotic scenes as she imagined the young men nude, sweaty, engaged in wrestling matches in a grassy meadow à la D.H. Lawrence. Better yet, she pictured all of them – more than twenty-five altogether – overpowering her and taking her like a band of marauders. By the time Jason reappeared, the potent blend of alcohol and her imagination had made her more than a little horny.

Melanie opened her mouth to ask Jason about the photos, but when she saw him, her voice failed her. He stood at the foot of the stairs, one hand on the banister. With one of his feet resting on the floor and the other on the third step, his lean, athletic legs were displayed to prime advantage, and his crotch was spread to show off his wares. On top of the fawn breeches, which fit him like a second skin, Jason wore a chocolate-brown smoking jacket and a white blouse with a ruffled collar. The frilly collar, combined with his dark, ripe lips and wavy chestnut hair, gave him an effeminate beauty that contrasted powerfully with his muscular thighs, bulging crotch and leather riding boots.

'Goddess have mercy,' Melanie breathed.

'You like them?' Jason dropped his arrogant pose, and his face glowed with a boyish glee that made Melanie want to pinch his cheek and fuck him at the same time.

'Those breeches were made for you. You look absolutely perfect.'

'Come on.' Jason hurried down the steps, took Melanie's hand, and all but dragged her across the room. 'Let's show the guys.'

As Melanie rushed to keep up with Jason's long-legged stride, she caught glimpses of a formal dining room, an industrial-sized kitchen, and a game room with a bar, a billiards table and pinball machine. Jason and his friends were much better equipped than the average college fraternity. What exactly were they up to in this secret club of theirs?

Jason opened a swinging door in the game room and led Melanie down a staircase. As they pounded down the stairs to the basement, Melanie heard the sounds of male laughter, and her pulse sped up.

Time to meet the boys.

Jason stopped in front of a door painted with the words PRIVATE – NO UNAUTHORISED ENTRY. Melanie was surprised that the guys hadn't added ALL GIRLS KEEP OUT to the warning. Before he opened the door, Jason held Melanie's shoulders and fixed her with a worried look.

'Now listen. You have to swear not to tell anyone about what you see tonight.'

'I swear.'

'I mean it – you can't tell anyone. Especially not my sister.'

At that point, Melanie would have sworn away her first born just to see what lay beyond that door.

'I promise not to tell anyone,' Melanie repeated, 'if you promise not to commit any unauthorised entry.'

Jason laughed. 'You and I are two of a kind, Melanie.'

Melanie straightened her spine and tapped her cane on the concrete floor. 'We may be two of a kind, but you will remember to call me Miss Paxton.'

Jason bent over in a penitential bow, then opened the door with a flourish. 'Miss Paxton,' he said, 'welcome to the club.'

Behind the door lay a large, carpeted recreation room where some well-to-do family had probably once allowed their children to throw lavish, unsupervised parties. The house's current residents had redecorated the room to look like a meeting hall, with rows of folding chairs separated by a narrow aisle. Each chair, except for one at the very front, was occupied by one of the men from the group photos upstairs. They were laughing and elbowing each other like schoolboys at an assembly, but when they saw Melanie, they rose to their feet in unison, their faces slack with awe.

Melanie could get used to this kind of attention. Though not one of the boys was dressed as elegantly as Jason, they all wore dinner jackets, ties, and polished shoes. Their hair was freshly shampooed and streaked with comb marks, their young cheeks were clean-shaven, and every one of them looked good enough to steal away with for a holiday of nonstop screwing.

'Gentlemen, let me introduce our guest of honour.' Jason put his arm around Melanie's shoulders. 'This is Miss Paxton, from Morne Bay. I've invited her to sit in with us tonight, and if we're lucky, she might agree to participate.'

Damn right I'm going to participate, Melanie thought as Jason guided her down the aisle. You'd have to lock me up to stop me.

The men sat facing a raised platform, where a table and a high lectern stood. Melanie's mouth went dry when she saw what lay on the table: a long, thin switch, very much like the cane that Melanie held, and a rolled-up bandanna that would work very nicely as a gag.

'Please have a seat, Miss Paxton.'

Jason motioned to the empty chair, which sat facing the rest of the room. Melanie sat primly, her ankles crossed, and rested her cane on her lap. She noticed that a few of the boys, especially the insolent blond with the floppy bangs, licked their lips when she touched the rattan rod. She wished that she could spend two solid weeks in this house trying out the tool on each and every one of their bottoms. No travel agency on earth could arrange a vacation more suited to Melanie's tastes.

'I'm going to go sit down with my brothers,' Jason said, leaning down to whisper into Melanie's ear. His breath was warm, with a rich, molasses scent from the Guinness he'd been drinking earlier. 'Thank you for coming tonight. You're the best thing that's happened to us since strawberry-flavoured lubricant.'

Before Melanie could ask him what he meant, the door burst open again. Jason rushed to take a seat, almost falling over in his haste. When Melanie saw who was filling the door, she couldn't blame Jason for panicking. She recognised the man who stood there, but he looked nothing like the carefree student from the group photos. He was the bodybuilder with the massive biceps and pecs, which were now concealed by the lines of an impeccably cut military jacket. Under the jacket he wore a studded leather belt looped through pressed trousers, and a pair of polished black leather boots that squeaked menacingly as he stalked down the aisle. His face was half hidden under an officer's cap; only his hard, square jaw and lips were visible. Melanie caught a peek at his eyes under the brim of the cap, and their fierce glitter made her quiver.

For the second time that evening the boys rose, but this time they assumed an erect military posture. The Officer's gaze travelled across the small assembly, coming to rest on Jason.

'What's that you're wearing tonight, Heller?' the Officer asked Jason, in a voice so charged with deadly control that it gave Melanie chills. 'Halloween was last month. We wear jackets, ties and pressed trousers at our meetings, no exceptions.'

'I'll wear whatever I want, when I want.' Jason's green eyes flashed. He met the Officer's stare, but Melanie could see the fear underneath his defiance. She could also see a rapid thickening in the crotch of his breeches. In those tight pants, a man didn't have a prayer of hiding his responses.

All eyes followed the Officer as he walked to the front of the room, ignoring Jason's retort. With his hands folded behind his back, he inspected the items laid out on the table. Almost as an afterthought, he picked up the cane.

'It's too bad that you chose to commit a dress-code violation,' the Officer said, 'on a night that you were to be punished for the lame-ass job you've been doing on my boots. What's the matter, Heller? You can't polish leather, and you can't follow simple rules.'

Melanie looked at the Officer's boots. The black leather had been rubbed so diligently that the toes gleamed like mirrors, but apparently that wasn't good enough for this anal-retentive frat boy. Or maybe Jason, like Tom Brown, was condemned to playing the role of scapegoat. No matter what he did, Tom was always punished, teased, or thrashed; he was trapped in the net of rules and regulations and underground codes that dictated conduct at Rugby School. Tom's helplessness, Melanie realised, was what made his daily dilemmas so exciting.

Jason squared his shoulders. 'I can follow rules as well as anyone, Officer Burns,' he said, 'but tonight I chose not to.'

'Tonight you chose not to,' Burns repeated thoughtfully. He raised the bamboo and brought it down, slicing the air with a lethal whistle, then he pointed the cane at Melanie. 'Don't you think it shows a lack of respect to violate dress code in the presence of a lady?'

Jason opened his mouth to respond, but Melanie interrupted him. 'I gave Jason those breeches, and I asked him to wear them tonight.'

Now everyone was staring at Melanie again, including Officer Burns, who spun on his heel to face her. He glanced at the cane on her lap and smiled. His lips were thin, cold, reptilian.

'Very good, Miss. Then I'll give you the honour of delivering the first ten blows. I'll administer the next ten myself.' He turned back to Jason. 'Heller, approach the table.'

Jason obeyed, but he kept his chin at a proud angle, and there was a jaunty sway to his gait as he walked to the front of the room. The meaty lump in his breeches had grown so big that it strained the seams. Melanie rose, cane in hand, and met him at the table. She wished that she could give his crotch a reassuring squeeze, but if the Officer saw her, the number of blows would rise to maybe sixty – and he would probably make Melanie give him a blow job in the bathroom.

'Good luck, Jason. You'll need it,' Melanie said, stepping into her role as Miss Paxton, the heartless and beautiful schoolmistress. 'Assume the position.'

Melanie didn't know exactly what 'the position' was, but her improvisation served her well – Jason bent over the solid oak table, his palms pressed against the surface.

He curved his back inward so that his shapely buns stood out, then turned to Melanie.

'Don't forget the rag,' he whispered. 'I need to bite down on it when you thrash me.'

Melanie took a handful of Jason's curls, pulled his head back, and plugged him up with the bandanna as if she were stuffing an apple into a pig's mouth. He responded with a groan, too deep for anyone but Melanie to hear, and she knew that if she were to squeeze his cock now, he might explode.

With the whole room suspended in a hush, Melanie caressed her bamboo beauty as if she were contemplating her first blow. The truth was, she was stalling her audience. In her inexperienced hands the cane was little more than a prop; aside from a few articles she had read on the Internet, and distant memories of Tom Brown's torments, she didn't know much about this time-honoured method of punishment. One thing she did know was that Jason's bum-forward position left him vulnerable to serious pain, even injury. His skin was stretched thin over his thighs and buttocks, and if she struck his tailbone, she could break it.

Meanwhile, Jason's muscles were piano-wire taut, his comrades were drooling with anticipation, and Burns was tapping the toe of his boot.

'What are we waiting for, Miss Paxton? Christmas?'

A few guffaws erupted in the gallery. Melanie stood up as straight as she could, looked over the rims of her glasses, and fixed the wannabe officer with a glare that could have peeled paint off the walls. She had to be firm with this junior dom, or else she'd be his bitch by the end of the night.

'What you are waiting for is someone who can give your boys the kind of treatment they really crave,' Melanie said. 'If you want to thrash each other like psychotic schoolmasters, that's your business, but I prefer a more sensual touch. Do you have a problem with that, Burns?'

Burns tried to stare Melanie down, but his lust and curiosity won out over his ego. He was as hot as anyone else to see what she was going to do. 'Whatever works for you, Miss Paxton,' he grumbled.

'I'm so glad we agree.'

Her instincts, Melanie decided, would be her best guide in this performance; since she didn't know what she was supposed to do, she would do what she wanted. With Jason's young firm buttocks and thighs awaiting her attention, it didn't take her long to make up her mind. She skimmed her hand along the curves of his legs as if she were inspecting a fine stallion she was thinking of purchasing. His muscles stiffened, and he hunched his shoulders, as if that gentle caress were harder to take than the bite of the cane. No doubt the anticipation was killing him. That's what these young bucks didn't understand – they wanted to jump right into the thick of the action, when half the fun was in the delay.

'Not a bad specimen,' Melanie mused. 'Let's see a bit more.'

She whisked the tip of her cane back and forth between Jason's thighs, and he increased the width of his straddle. Melanie slid her hand between his legs and grabbed his entire package. The warm, heavy mass of his balls filled her palm, and his cock felt like packed steel between her fingers. In an involuntary motion, he ground his pelvis against her hand. Melanie let go of his cock and slapped his ass.

'What do you think you're doing, young man? You're to hold still when you're being inspected. Your "officer" here hasn't trained you very well.'

Melanie frowned at Burns, who gawked at her in

confusion. Now that Melanie had stolen the stage from him, he looked as awkward as any other ham-handed college boy.

'I never, ever start a punishment without an inspection,' Melanie explained to Burns. 'See how I manipulate his cock and balls, making sure he's worthy of my attention? I'm not going to get all hot and sweaty over a boy who's less than superb. Jason has a fine set of hardware, and I can tell from his state of arousal that he's ready to take the cane. Next, I run my thumb between his buttocks, all the way up to his spine. It's important to know exactly where the tailbone is, so you don't strike it by accident.'

Melanie sounded like the hostess of a cooking show describing the proper way to make an omelette, but the boys were lapping it up, especially Jason, who was panting through the gag. Melanie had been too enthusiastic with her inspection; now she would have to distract her victim so that she could torment him a little more. She took a few steps back, so that she was positioned at an angle to Jason's bum. The boys in the gallery held their breath. Jason moaned through the wad of cloth that filled his mouth. The cruel Miss Paxton raised her cane as if she were going to deliver a brutal blow, but she brought it down gently, with only the slightest swish, and gave Jason's bottom an experimental tap. The bamboo bounced off his flesh with only the lightest impact, but he was so overstimulated that he shuddered from head to toe.

'What a nice resilient rump,' Melanie said. 'Too bad it belongs to such a spoilt, undisciplined boy.'

Melanie peppered Jason's rear end with short blows. Though she wasn't using much force, the cane was thin enough to deliver a bite. Concentrating on the tender undersides of his buttocks, she struck him until he was whimpering like a baby. His head was lowered between his shoulders, and a drop of sweat splashed from his hairline onto the table. His thigh muscles were tense with the effort of restraining himself – a few more strokes of the cane, and he would probably burst.

'All right, I've warmed him up for you, Burns. Go ahead and finish the job.'

Burns stripped off his jacket and laid it neatly over a chair, then stepped into place.

'Now let me show *you* a thing or two, Miss Paxton.' He turned to the men in the audience. 'Gentlemen, you will count as usual. Ten blows for Heller.'

Burns raised his cane and brought it down through the air at an angle that struck Jason at the meatiest part of his ass.

'One!' roared the boys.

Jason's jaw muscles churned as he bit down on the gag. The cane came down again and again, with the audience bellowing out the count. Melanie had under-estimated Burns; for all his brutish machismo, he had an artist's precision when it came to caning. His strokes were swift and precise, hitting their mark with just enough velocity to cause pain without injury. Each time the cane landed, Jason's hamstrings quivered, his hips shot forward, and he gave an agonised grunt. Melanie thought she would die of desire.

But Jason died first, shuddering to a climax as the cane struck ten. He arched his back and cried out, the bandanna sliding out of his open mouth. Melanie noted with great satisfaction that the crotch of his vintage riding breeches was soaked through. He had shot his young load in his pants. Somewhere, the gentleman who had owned those breeches had to be spinning in his grave.

After the ritual, the gang adjourned upstairs for refreshments in the parlour. While Jason was getting his punishment, someone had set up a card table with a single pitcher of punch and a tray of unappetising store-bought cookies. It was pathetic fare for such a hearty crowd, which was probably why most of the boys were sneaking off together to parts unknown. Melanie wished she could follow them, but Burns had her in his grip – literally. He grasped her arm at the first opportunity and didn't let her go.

'We make a good team,' he said, kneading her flesh with steely fingers. 'I never thought a chick – I mean a woman – could do the kinds of things you did tonight.'

'You didn't think a woman could hold a man's balls?'

'No. I mean, yes. I mean, I didn't think a woman could take control of a roomful of men.'

Melanie took a sip of punch. She held the cup in front of her face, shielding herself from Burns's beady stare. He was studying her as if she were a rare insect, and he couldn't decide whether she were a fascinating and exotic creature, or a repulsive oddity.

'You haven't met many dominant women, have you?' she asked.

'No. None of us has. We've never seen anything like you.'

'That's obvious.'

Melanie wished Burns would leave her alone so that she could mingle. Now that he had staked his claim on her, she wasn't getting so much as a glance from the other guys, who were standing around in enticingly tight groups. A circle jerk might erupt at any minute, and Melanie would miss out if she didn't break free from Burns's cast-iron fingers.

'Where's the nearest bathroom?' she asked. 'After all that domination, I need to freshen up.'

'Next to the kitchen. I'll show you.'

Burns tightened his hold on her arm – tomorrow she was going to look like she'd been manhandled by a stevedore – and pulled her across the room towards the kitchen. Melanie had an idea where she was going to end up: down on her knees on the bathroom tile, looking Burns's cock dead in the eye. This aspiring marine was determined to overpower her, one way or another. Short of kicking and screaming, Melanie didn't see any way out of it. If she made a scene, she wouldn't be invited back to the club, and in spite of Burns's overbearing attitude, she was still dying to be the only girl in this den of boys-only pleasures.

The door loomed. Before Burns could open it and lead Melanie to her fate, another male body blocked the way.

'Jason!' Melanie cried. 'Where did you go?'

'Upstairs to change,' he said with a wink.

'Get out of our way, Heller. I was here first.'

Burns tried to shove Jason aside, but Jason didn't budge. For such a pretty boy, he was surprisingly strong. Melanie caught a distinct whiff of competitive chemistry between the lads. The adversity between these two was steeped in sexual tension. With Jason standing there, breathing heavily in his frilly shirt, Burns was starting to look a lot more interesting.

'Listen, boys. There's no reason we can't all use the bathroom, is there?'

Burns looked suspicious. Jason's eyes lit up.

'At the same time?' they asked at once.

'That's the only way you're gonna get it.'

Melanie reached past Jason and pushed open the door.

'Wait a second,' she said, 'this isn't a bathroom. It's a –'

Before she could finish her startled sentence, Melanie was engulfed by a wave of cheering boys. Here was the party she had expected to find, complete with a table loaded with deli meats, cheeses, and chips, a beer keg, and a bar lined with glittering bottles. The moment the door opened, rock music began to blare from a state-of-the-art stereo system. A sweet, hazy cloud of marijuana smoke hovered above the crowd, and on a low leather couch in the corner, a couple of boys were embracing with a passion that went way beyond fraternal love. This was the den of iniquity that Melanie had dreamed of when she first spoke to Jason on the phone.

'Welcome to the club,' Jason said into Melanie's ear, his voice rising to a shout to be heard over the music.

'Three cheers for our first female member!' Burns roared.

Female member? she wondered, dazed and delighted. Wasn't that a contradiction in terms? Then she found herself rising on a pair of male shoulders as the crowd burst into three uproarious cheers. The boys passed her around the room, each one demanding his chance to carry her, until she felt like she was surfing on a sea of men. By the time they put her down, Melanie was dizzy with testosterone fumes. A cup of foamy keg beer was thrust into her hand, and she drank half of it in one gulp. She was vaguely aware of a large male paw yanking the pins out of her hair and mauling her topknot until her hair came tumbling down. Someone else was pulling off her velveteen jacket and spiriting it away.

'Hey, be careful with that.' Melanie's protest was drowned out by the earsplitting music. The game room turned into a mosh pit as rock gave way to punk. Two stomping boys butted heads, colliding with Melanie and sloshing her beer all over the front of her Venetian lace cravat.

'All right, that's it,' Melanie shouted. 'You aren't boys, you're the spawn of Satan!'

The spawn paid no attention. One of the monsters grabbed Melanie and began tongue-kissing her with all the finesse of a Saint Bernard. Melanie squirmed out of his clutches and shoved her way through the crowd. Jason, her saviour of the evening, met her at the door.

'I'm sorry about those jerks in there,' he said, when they were safely out of the chaos. He daubed at Melanie's antique blouse with his shirt-tail. 'Let me wash this for you.'

'Don't you dare!'

'OK, OK.' Jason backed off. 'But let me at least take you upstairs, where it's quiet. The guys get out of control sometimes.'

'I guess I'm too old for this.'

'Too old? No way.'

Jason had been subtly edging Melanie towards the wall; now he had her caged, with one of his arms braced above her head. She could feel the throbbing percussion of the music vibrating through her body.

'Do you know how hard you made me come tonight?' Jason asked. 'I've never come like that. Never. I thought for sure I was having a heart attack.'

'I had no idea what I was doing,' Melanie admitted.

'Whatever you did, it was incredible.'

He was leaning in so close now that he was all but kissing Melanie as he spoke. His lips were so lusciously overripe that she wanted to gobble them like candied apricots, and the lust in his emerald eyes was driving her wild. Keeping one hand on the wall above Melanie's head, he used the other to ease up her long, tight skirt. Melanie helped him, twisting her hips, until the skirt was bunched around her waist and Jason had full access to the velvety expanse of skin between her lower belly and her upper thighs. He strummed at the suspenders on her garter belt as he kissed her. Jason was a wonderful kisser. His mouth was as soft as a girl's, but he used his tongue with the firm aggression of a man. He took his time, keeping his hands away from Melanie's hot spots, teasing when he could have been attacking.

All of a sudden, as Jason's lips melted into Melanie's, an image burst into her mind, uninvited and unwelcome. Instead of Jason's soft, coaxing mouth, she felt a hard, insistent one bearing down on hers, and a pair of big, callused hands pinning her wrists over her head. That hard mouth and those callused hands belonged to Nathan Wentworth.

Nathan Wentworth – whom she was meeting tomorrow morning. That must be why he had shoved his way into her head. In only a few hours, she was supposed to get together with the curator and Harrison Blake, and if she wanted to secure that permit, she would have to save her lips for some serious ass-kissing.

'Oh, hell,' Melanie said, breaking the kiss with Jason, 'I can't believe I'm doing this, but I'm going to have to stop.'

'Why?' Jason said, with an incredulous whimper.

'I have an important meeting tomorrow morning, and it's a long drive back to Morne Bay. I'm going to be sleeping at the wheel if I don't get some sleep.'

'Stay here tonight. It'll be safer than driving home in the dark, with all those drunken idiots on the road.'

'I thought all the drunken idiots around here were in the next room,' Melanie said dryly. But Jason was right. She hated driving late at night on the dark two-lane highway that snaked through the woods.

'Oh, come on. You can sleep in my bed. I'll sleep with Burns.'

Melanie wanted to ask if 'sleeping with Burns' involved all that it implied, but she was too tired. As she trailed upstairs, following Jason to his room, Melanie wondered where all the energy of her youth had gone. It must have disappeared once she hit the quarter-century mark a few months ago.

Jason's room, littered with beer cans and papered with posters of buxom swimsuit models, looked more like Melanie's image of a frat boy's digs. His 'bed' was a futon mattress on the scuffed hardwood floor, and the sheets that covered it were suspiciously musty, but Melanie was too exhausted to care. After Jason left her alone in the room, she undressed, put on one of Jason's oversized college sweatshirts, and flopped down in the nest of smelly blankets. She couldn't be more grateful if she were sinking into the finest satin comforters sprinkled with lavender oil. Before Jason could finish giving her his chaste goodnight kiss, Melanie was fast asleep.

Maybe it was the night's activities, or the boy-smells of Jason's bed, but Melanie had some of the most vivid erotic dreams of her life that night. She dreamed that the boys in Jason's club were taking turns eating her pussy as she lay sprawled on the futon. As soon as one of them brought her to orgasm, another one muscled his way in to take his place. The boys were gentle with her, handling her body with the utmost care as they tried to pleasure her without waking her. The climaxes succeeded each other in deep, slow waves, so many of them that she never really stopped coming. The sensual details of the dream were so real – the silky texture of the boys' hair between her thighs, their lunging tongues, the strong grip of their fingers – that when she woke in the morning she could swear that the incident had really happened.

'Welcome to the club,' each one whispered when he was done. *'Welcome to the club.'*

The orgasms had definitely been real – under the pile of blankets, she was soaking wet. Melanie scissored her thighs, enjoying the slippery feeling of her flesh. She must have been rubbing herself in her sleep; she felt swollen and sensitive, slightly bruised.

'Good morning, sleeping beauty.' Jason poked his head around the door.

'What time is it?'

Jason pushed the door open with his elbow. He was carrying two extra-large Styrofoam cups. The steam that spiralled from those cups smelled of coffee and hazelnuts. As far as Melanie was concerned, he might as well have been holding two chalices of ambrosia.

'Quarter past eight.'

'Damn! I'm supposed to open the shop at nine, and I have a breakfast meeting after that.' Melanie struggled to sit up. Her limbs felt sore, as if she'd been exercising all night instead of sleeping.

'Don't worry. I called Beth; she's going to open for you.'

'Beth?'

'My sister. Remember?'

'That's right.' Melanie was so hung over from her nocturnal orgasms that she had forgotten that her employee Pagan had been given the name Elizabeth at birth.

'Beth really likes you.' Jason lowered himself carefully to the floor. He winced when his buttocks made contact with the ground. 'But not as much as I do.'

'I like you, too, Jason.'

Jason leaned over and kissed Melanie gingerly on the lips. Under the coffee he'd been drinking, Melanie tasted something else, something musky and briny and … familiar.

'Hey! You *were* eating me out last night!'

Jason's sultry lips formed a sheepish smile. 'I couldn't help it. I came in to check on you, just to make sure that none of the other guys had come in to ravish you. You were lying here with your legs spread, and you looked so gorgeous in the moonlight that I couldn't stop myself. I made you come about eight times, and you never even woke up.'

Melanie narrowed her eyes. She felt like slapping Jason's beaming face, but he had done such a good job that she couldn't bring herself to do it. 'Did any of your friends join in?'

Jason had the grace to look genuinely shocked. 'No

way! You think I'd let any of those apes have a chance at you?'

'Maybe I would have liked it,' she said, recalling her dream.

'Well, *I* wouldn't have liked it. I wanted you for myself.'

Now it was Melanie's turn to smile. She sipped at the pitch-black hazelnut coffee and watched Jason's mouth twist into a surly frown.

'Not into gang sex? What do you call your ritual last night?'

'That's different.'

'How so?'

'The guys in the club are like my brothers. We punish each other because we love it, and it gets us off, but sometimes I want to be alone with someone. A woman who's unique, like you. I don't want to share that kind of experience with a bunch of other guys.'

'But you didn't even share it with *me*, Jason. You should have woken me up and asked my permission.'

'I know I should have.' Jason hung his head. 'But I didn't think you'd let me.'

'Not let you? After everything we did at the meeting?'

Jason chewed his plump lower lip as he struggled to find an explanation. 'I thought you'd pegged me as a sexual submissive – a bottom. I didn't think you respected me enough to let me make love to you like a real man.'

'First of all, I have a lot of respect for bottoms, so you're wrong there. Second, if you want to be treated like a real man, make sure your lovers are conscious.'

'I'm sorry, Melanie. I really am. You probably think I'm a jerk, a spoilt rich kid who takes whatever he wants without asking.'

Melanie didn't want to tell him that he was right. 'You and your friends do seem more privileged than most college students,' she admitted.

'Well, I'm not spoilt or rich. No one in the club is wealthy, except for Burns. His family has a lot of money, and they gave us some of the furniture and stuff that we have in the house, but the rest of us are strictly middle class.'

'How can you afford a place like this?'

'The old-fashioned way – we work for it. We're entrepreneurs. We all got together in the summer of our freshman year, when we were working construction on an apartment complex in Lewiston. We hated the foreman on our crew, so we decided to get our licenses and work for ourselves. We can't work full time because of school, but we make enough money to give us more than the average student has.'

'I owe you an apology, then. I have to admit, I did jump to conclusions about you.' Melanie set down her coffee. Jason had sparked an idea. 'Listen. Have you ever done any additions? Or restored any old houses?'

'Restoration is our speciality. How do you think we got such a good deal on the rent for this place? It was the first project we did together. You should have seen what a dump it was when we first started.'

'I'll keep that in mind. I may need your help one of these days.'

Jason looked at Melanie through his long eyelashes. 'Anything I can help you with before that? I promise to ask permission this time.'

'You don't have to ask, now that I'm awake.'

Melanie stretched her arms over her head and yawned. She pulled off Jason's baggy sweatshirt, then kicked her legs free of the blankets and spread her thighs so that he could have his way with her again. Jason kissed his way up and down the length of her torso, his swollen lips clinging to the skin as he went. He spent a lot of time suckling at her nipples, which responded to the attention by turning burgundy red. Younger men always wanted to devour Melanie's nipples; maybe it was because they had more recent memories of breastfeeding. Jason was an expert at it, using the inner part of his mouth, and sucking in a rhythm that made her feel primal. She was starting to feel like a bona fide earth mother when Jason's door opened.

Burns's bulky form commandeered the room. He wore nothing but a pair of red-and-white striped boxer shorts, whose fly was distended by some impressive morning wood. His military brush cut had been flattened on one side by his pillow, and his eyes blinked sleepily as he took in the sight of Melanie and Jason. He looked like a six-year-old who's been woken up from a nap – a six-year-old who pumped a lot of iron.

'What's going on, Jason? I woke up, and you were gone.'

His mouth, so severe last night, was now drooping into a pout. He looked back and forth between Jason and Melanie, as if he couldn't decide which one had left him out of the party. He appeared a lot more vulnerable and appealing in his boxers than he did when he was dressed up like General MacArthur.

'Am I interrupting something, boys?' Melanie asked. 'I wouldn't want to keep anyone from getting his morning sodomy. From what I've heard, it's more stimulating than a double espresso.'

Despite what Jason said about preferring one-on-one with a woman, he shouted over to Burns, 'Get your ass over here, Burns. Don't stand there sulking – join us.'

Burns padded across the floor on his bare feet. His thighs, with their bulging quadriceps, displayed the results of thousands of squats, but he had an endearing, bow-legged gait that prevented him from strutting like a bodybuilder.

'Lie down next to Jason,' Melanie said. 'You can each have a nipple. There's a reason why I have two of them.'

Burns followed her instructions, and the boys went at Melanie's breasts like a couple of pups. They wrestled over her body, rolling her back and forth like a toy each wanted for himself. Their bodies, still warm from sleep, enfolded her in a blanket of muscles. Melanie felt a tugging motion below her waist, and she glanced down to see that Jason had pulled his friend's cock out of his shorts. Burns returned the favour, yanking at Jason's erect organ. Soon they were going at each other so hard that Melanie was afraid they'd jerk each other's dicks out by the root.

'Slow down. We've got plenty of time,' she warned. 'Listen, Burns, why don't you give your friend a little fellatio? It's the least you could do for him, after last night.'

'Yeah,' Jason taunted, pointing to the faint marks that striped his ass. 'Why don't you suck my dick, Eugene?'

Eugene? If that was Burns' first name, it was no wonder he had such an authority complex. When his lower lip trembled in response to Jason's teasing, Melanie forgave him completely for being such an overbearing pest at the party.

'Go ahead, Burns,' Melanie coaxed, running her fingers through the stubble of his hair. 'Let's see what you can do.'

Like a pasha waiting to be serviced, Jason lay back on a heap of pillows and dirty laundry. His erection listed along his lower belly, pulsing lightly against the furred skin. Jason's handsome face, puffed with self-satisfaction, slackened into lust as Burns lay down between his thighs and took his cock into his mouth. Burns was as adept at sucking as he was at caning, making consummate use of his lips and tongue on his friend's member. Outside of a few snippets from porno movies, Melanie had never seen a man go down on another. She was astounded at the intensity Burns applied, using his hand to tug roughly at the base of Jason's shaft while he licked and sucked the glans. Jason's head fell back against the pillows, his long lashes fluttering against his cheeks as he moaned in ecstasy. As he approached orgasm, his fingers kneaded his lover's shoulders, and his thighs quivered. His climax was a stunning sight – when he arched his back and stared at the ceiling, his mouth opened in an imploring cry, Jason looked like one of Michelangelo's angels. Burns didn't give an inch when Jason came; he swallowed every drop of his friend's come, then lapped the last drops that oozed out of the slit.

'Very well done, Burns. I'm impressed.' Melanie stroked the tightly knit muscles of Burns's back. 'I never thought a man could outdo me in that department, but you've put me to shame.'

'Of course. We've spent a lot of time perfecting our decadent arts,' he announced with pride. Burns tried to mask his smile of pleasure with a smirk, but Melanie could tell he was flattered. As he shifted into a sitting position, his hard-on shoved its way through the fly of his boxers.

'My, my. What are we going to do about this?'

Melanie touched his penis, and the straining shaft jumped into her hand. Burns breathed raggedly. A moan seeped from his lips. Melanie moistened her fingertip in the milky pre-come that coated the tip of his cockhead. It quivered like a divining rod, and Burns's abdominal muscles rippled in response. He leaned back, bracing himself on his palms, prepared to receive the same treatment that he'd given Jason, but Melanie was in the mood for something different. Burns had partially redeemed himself this morning, but he still needed to be put in his place.

'You've probably fucked lots of girls, haven't you, Burns?'

'Are you kidding? I can't even count 'em all.'

'And now you're lying there with that smirk on your face, thinking that I'm going to be another notch in your belt. Isn't that right?'

Melanie reached down between Burns's thighs, grabbed a handful of his scrotal sac, and twisted. Jason looked on, grinning, as his tormentor whimpered for mercy.

'Think again, Burns. This morning we're going to turn the tables. Jason, darling, could you get my purse? And fetch me some lubricant while you're at it.'

Jason scrambled off the futon and retrieved Melanie's purse and a tube of KY Jelly from his cluttered desk.

'Could you let go of my balls now?' Burns asked in an imploring falsetto.

'I don't think so. And you should call me Mistress when I've got your family jewels in my hand.' Melanie gave his nuts an affectionate pull. 'Jason's enjoying this so much. I hate to disappoint him, especially since he's done such a wonderful job polishing your boots. Jason, please open the inner pocket of my purse. I keep one of my favourite toys in there.'

Jason's eyes widened as he pulled out a small purple vibrator and handed it to Melanie.

'This is my emergency backup,' Melanie explained, showing the wand to Burns. 'You never know when you might need some quick stimulation when you're away from home. Like now, for instance.'

Melanie rolled up two of Jason's pillows and arranged them on the futon. She instructed Burns to lie down on top of them, so that they bolstered his hips. With his bum raised at a convenient angle, she had access to his anus. He kept the tightly puckered hole very clean, most likely with the help of some of his slaves in the house. A little exploration with a lubricated finger informed her that Burns wasn't used to being penetrated. At first he resisted her, clenching his buttocks with all his might, but as he grew accustomed to being touched, he gave in to her invasion.

'When's the last time you had anything stuck up here?' Melanie asked, wiggling her digit inside the tight passage.

'Maybe when I was five or six,' Burns admitted, 'and that was only a rectal thermometer.'

'How does this feel?'

'Kind of weird, Mistress.'

'Good weird, or bad weird?' Melanie eased her finger in and out, fucking him gently. Then she pushed her finger even deeper, feeling around for the surface of his prostate. She tickled the gland with her fingertip.

Burns answered her question with a groan.

'Eugene isn't used to playing bottom,' Jason said. He was kneeling on the futon next to Melanie, enjoying the scene enormously.

'I think he likes it,' Melanie said. 'I think he's ready for more. Aren't you, Burns?'

'I guess so, Mistress,' Burns said, with a wary glance over his shoulder. He cringed when he saw Melanie pick up the vibrator.

'Don't worry – I'll go very, very slowly.'

Melanie pulled her finger out of Burns's bum. She switched on the vibrator and set it to its lowest level.

'Spread his cheeks for me, Jason. I need some room to work here.'

Jason obeyed, not bothering to hide his glee when Burns shrieked at the first touch of the buzzing vibe. Melanie circled his anus with the little instrument until he gradually relaxed enough for her to insert its head into his bunghole. Burns moaned and began to grind his pelvis into the pillows.

'Don't get too comfortable there, Burns. Jason, I think it's time to give him a taste of his own medicine. You have a ruler, don't you?'

'I sure as hell do!' Jason leaped up and rummaged through his desk until he found the wooden instrument. He handed it to Melanie, but she shook her head.

'No, no. You're going to deliver the punishment this time around. I'm just going to make sure he enjoys the experience. Shall we make him count?'

Jason joyfully agreed. He slammed the crest of Burns's sculpted ass with the ruler.

'Count, Burns!'

'One,' Burns squealed. His hips bucked.

'He doesn't seem to have much of a pain threshold,' Melanie remarked. 'Don't use so much force. We're just trying to teach him a lesson, not mark him for life.'

'I can take it,' Burns said through gritted teeth.

Jason took him at his word and delivered a flurry of energetic whacks. Melanie kept control of the vibrator, increasing the speed of the buzz and pushing it deeper as Burns's tightening muscles tried to force it out. The arrogant soldier boy had transformed into an eager submissive, urging Jason to spank him harder and begging Melanie not to stop. As Jason reached the twentieth swat, Burns humped himself to a mighty orgasm against the pillows. His muscles hardened into knots, his face turned crimson, and the blood vessels in his neck stood out in a pulsating network.

'Congratulations, Burns. You've passed your own initiation this morning,' Melanie said. 'Next time you play the Super-Top, you'll have this incident to remind you of what it's like to be on the bottom. Won't you?'

Burns, who lay in a puddle of his own sweat, moaned his assent. Jason and Melanie smiled at each other and exchanged a silent high-five.

5 **Practising Restraint**

While Melanie was having erotic dreams about the boys in the club, Nathan was having erotic dreams about Melanie. Strange, considering that he was sleeping next to Dana McGillis, who had spent the night out at Nathan's farmhouse after an evening of fun and games in his woodshop.

The fun and games hadn't turned out the way Nathan had expected, however. The professor's schoolgirl wardrobe reflected her fashion tastes more than her sexual leanings. Dana McGillis wasn't a submissive; she wasn't even a switch. She was a dominant through and through, and she had proven that to Nathan last night when she showed up at his house dressed in a leather catsuit, gauntlet gloves, and thigh-high boots. Playing bottom wasn't Nathan's style at all, but Dana had looked so incredible – like an Eric Stanton rendering of Catwoman – that Nathan had been willing to try something new. All of his fantasies about spanking the big-bottomed redhead had gone out the window. When he gave her a tour of his workshop, she took the lead, bent him over his own spanking bench, and worked his ass with a paddle he had made himself.

Being topped by a woman was definitely different, and definitely not to his taste. He had let Dana spank him, and had knelt on the floor to lap her auburn-furred slit while she guided him by his hair, but he had drawn the line at kissing her boots. He wasn't able to come until he got her into his own bed, where he could at least pretend to be in control.

Nathan knew that he should be more flexible. He knew that he should be more politically correct. But when it came to sex, Nathan Wentworth was about as submissive as Attila the Hun, and that wasn't going to change any time soon. In his dream about Melanie, she had been wearing nothing but a long red velvet ribbon around her neck, which he had held like a leash while he sat with her crouching between his legs, sucking his cock. The suction of her lips wrapped around the head, and the teasing of her pointed tongue on the strand of skin behind his glans, were so realistic that he almost had his first wet dream in over fifteen years.

Before any pre-dawn emissions could occur, he woke up to find his erection filling Dana's mouth. She was buried under the sheets, sucking him hungrily, and his body was responding with a lot more enthusiasm than it had the previous night. His balls were already tightening in Dana's fingers, which she used to massage his sac while she performed her artful fellatio.

When she realised that Nathan was awake, Dana lifted her head and threw off the sheets. Without the heavy eyeliner and clotted-blood lipstick she'd been wearing the night before, she looked young and innocent. Her near-sighted eyes squinted at Nathan as she gave him a sleepy smile.

'I was worried about you last night,' she said. 'I didn't think I was going to be able to make you come. Was I doing something wrong?'

'Not at all.'

Nathan didn't have the heart to tell Dana that nothing she had done last night, no matter how spectacular, could have brought him to orgasm. Her rumpled hair, freckled face and myopic green eyes made her look too vulnerable.

'What was the problem, then? Can you give me any advice on my technique? I'm pretty new at this, you know.'

'Nothing's wrong with your technique. Your technique is great.'

Speaking of which, Nathan wished she would go back to her superb sucking. Early morning analysis of the previous night's sex wasn't his thing. He'd much rather replace past experiences with new ones.

'When you invited me over and told me that you were into D/s, I just assumed I'd be the D, not the s,' Dana went on. 'I was so happy that I'd found a man as attractive as you who wanted to be dominated. It never occurred to me that you'd want me to be the sub.'

Nathan laughed. 'Then the miscommunication went both ways. It never occurred to me that you'd want *me* to be the sub. Couldn't you tell I was dominant?'

'No. Sometimes the classic "manly men" are the heaviest bottoms of all.'

'Well, I'm not a bottom to any degree. Now that you mention bottoms, I've been wanting to get a closer look at yours. Would you mind sitting on my cock and facing the wall?'

'Sounds interesting.'

Dana climbed out of the bedclothes. Her nude body looked good enough to eat with a spoon: small, springy breasts with peppermint-pink nipples rode high above a firm belly. By some kind of magic, she produced a condom from out of her nakedness and sheathed Nathan's cock.

'Here we go,' she said with a challenging grin, as if he were a bronco and she were about to ride him to victory in a one-woman rodeo.

Dana had chunky, freckled thighs and the tightest, roundest pair of glutes that had ever sat astride him. When she turned around and mounted him, her bum rising into the air like a pale moon, he was afraid he would blow before she could slide all the way down his shaft. Watching her ample rump wriggle around as she secured herself on the seat was more than he could stand.

He took hold of her broad hips and drove himself in up to the hilt. She leaned forwards, supporting herself on one hand while strumming her clit with the other.

Nathan took full advantage of her position, pistoning in and out of her hole. He knew that Dana wouldn't respond well if he slapped her ass, but he couldn't resist spreading her cheeks and finding her anus, then penetrating the spoked bud with his thumb while he gripped a handful of flesh with his fingers. Dana gave as good as she got, posting up and down in time to his thrusts. He had to admit, he loved watching his own rod surge in and out of a snug pair of cunt lips. His dick was thick, long and well shaped, with only the slightest tracing of veins. It was a fine tool, and he'd never had a lover who didn't go crazy when she was riding it. When he felt a sudden surge of wetness flood his cock, he knew that Dana was coming.

Her inner muscles clenched. She stopped for a moment, holding still at the crest of her ride. The assistant professor of history grunted like a farmgirl when she hit her climax. Nathan was only seconds behind, catching the last clutches of Dana's orgasm just as he peaked.

'That was fantastic,' Nathan gasped, catching his breath. He thought that Dana might want to discuss this session, too, but she collapsed face down on the mattress and instantly fell asleep. Nathan took advantage of her slumbering state, stroking her ass and marvelling at its firm white width.

Still, the Melanie dream haunted him. He had been dreaming about her on and off ever since the day he met her at the shop, but she had never been so hot, so eager, or so submissive as she'd been this morning. The ribbon she wore around her neck had been wrapped several times around his hand, and his grip on her leash had been so secure that he knew she'd never be able to slip away from him. The best part was that in the dream, she didn't want to.

He had better remember that dream, Nathan thought, because after this morning's meeting, Melanie would be so furious that he'd never get close enough to speak to her again, much less put a leash around her neck. Even so, he stopped at a dime store on his way into town that morning, a shop that was already ablaze with Christmas lights and decorations, and bought a giant spool of crimson ribbon.

It never hurt to be prepared.

An accident on the highway made Melanie late for her breakfast meeting. A moose was at fault; the animal had stepped out of the woods at the wrong moment, ambled into the road and barely escaped being turned into moose-burger by a semi-truck. The truck had veered sideways into a ditch, and was now blocking both lanes of the highway.

Why did she stay in this isolated backwater? Melanie brooded, drumming her fingers on the steering wheel. She should be in a city, taking taxis everywhere, instead of sitting around in a car waiting for the half-assed sheriff's department to clean up the aftermath of a moose's miserable timing. If Lori hadn't left her to run Chimera, Melanie would be in Boston or New York this very minute. Then she wouldn't have to worry about playing footsie with small-time bankers to get them to listen to her business ideas. She would be taken seriously, as a woman and an entrepreneur, and she would never have to suffer through breakfast meetings at sleazy hotels named after crazy water birds.

Melanie barely had time to stop at home to change into her sexy-severe charcoal business suit with a peplum jacket and slit skirt. It was after eleven when she finally walked into the dining room at the Golden Loon. Brunch was in full swing, with furtive-looking businessmen gobbling eggs and bacon while their secretaries got drunk on Mimosas and Bloody Marys, lubing themselves up for the afternoon's debauchery. The room reeked of illicit lust. Through the haze of raging hormones, she spotted Nathan Wentworth sitting alone at a table beside the window. In comparison to the aging businessmen and their ditzy paramours, Nathan didn't look half bad. He was gazing intently at the water as if he wished he were out there, on the bay.

Nathan's table should have been set for three, but Melanie saw only two place settings. 'Where's Harrison?' she asked, too annoyed with the whole morning to offer a greeting. 'He's the one who arranged this whole thing.'

When Nathan saw Melanie, the curator's look of bored desperation disappeared. He stood up and pulled out a chair for her. She accepted his courtesy with a cool nod, not about to let him off the hook for that condescending 'bad girl' remark.

'It looks like Harrison stood us up,' Nathan said, without a trace of concern.

'You don't seem very upset,' Melanie observed.

'I'm not. To tell you the truth, I'm relieved. I really just wanted to see you. For a while I thought you weren't going to show, either.'

'I got stuck driving back from Somerhill. There was an accident on the highway. You're lucky I'm here at all,' she sniffed.

'I consider myself very lucky. I wouldn't have sat in this godawful restaurant for so long if I wasn't hoping you'd come.'

The curator studied her with his serious eyes. Melanie didn't know what to do. How on earth was she going to chat with this sombre man for a suitable length of time? They hadn't even gotten past their introductions, and she was already as nervous as a cat in a packing crate. Fortunately, a waiter appeared with the bottle of complementary champagne – free because it was cheap – and Melanie pounced on him.

'Could you just leave the bottle?' she asked.

The waiter obliged. Melanie tried to pour champagne for Nathan, but he refused. A Puritan through and through, he had turned down the free-flowing booze in favour of black coffee – decaf, no doubt. He wasn't wearing the sheepskin jacket (it hung over the back of his chair), but he wore a white Oxford shirt with a frayed collar and an faded blue crewneck sweater that looked like it had seen too many washings. Good old Yankee thrift. Melanie had to admit that the navy sweater deepened the blue of his eyes, and contrasted perfectly with his wavy, light-blond hair. But he was still too big for her, too intense. He kept staring at her as if he wanted to punish her, eat her, or both.

'I've been thinking about your shop ever since the morning I stopped by,' Nathan said. 'Something about the place kept tugging at my mind. As I was going over the floor plans for the new museum last night, I realised what it was.'

'Yes?'

'Your shop is a lot like the museum that I always wanted to build, only better.'

Melanie was stunned. The champagne glass, which she had lifted halfway to her mouth, stopped in midair. 'I don't understand. Are you talking about the old clothes that I sell?'

'Not really, although the clothes are part of it. I wanted to create a museum where people could observe the history of sexual behaviour. You've created a place where people can literally explore their *own* sexual behavior. Your shop is like a museum, in that it offers a display of human sensuality, past and present.'

'But my customers don't come to look at things. They come to buy. They don't want to just observe – they want to possess. To experience.'

'Exactly. Chimera is a living entity. And that's something I've always wanted to achieve.'

'Why don't you forget being a curator, then, and open a shop?'

Nathan laughed. Laughter softened his features, making him much less fearsome. 'Believe it or not, I've considered that. But there's no easy way to sell the things I make. Not in the way I'd want to sell them.'

Melanie went back to her champagne, and was surprised to find that her glass was still full. She'd been so intrigued by Nathan's statements that she hadn't even touched her drink. She took a sip. On an empty stomach, the fizz would go straight to her head. She had better be careful, or she might end up in one of the Golden Loon's bargain rooms with a museum curator.

She was starting to think that this wasn't such a bad idea.

'What exactly do you make?' Melanie crossed one leg over the other and twirled a strand of her hair. She was flirting – actually flirting – with a man who looked like he could pose for a statue of one of the country's founding fathers. A man who, according to Hannah, had some very interesting hobbies.

'It's not easy to describe, especially in public. I'd have to show you.'

'Oh, come on. Can't you give me a hint?'

Nathan looked around the room. Melanie followed his gaze, taking in the couples who were huddled together over the remains of their meals, their hands tunnelling under the tablecloths to play in each others' laps. Within the next half hour, the dining room would be deserted, and a large number of the upstairs rooms would be occupied. Watching those lovebirds, Melanie suddenly wished that she was sitting closer to Nathan. She wouldn't mind doing a little investigation of her own, to see if his penis really matched the rest of his physique. The cheap champagne was making her feel loose and easy.

'I don't want to talk about it here,' Nathan said. 'Why don't you come out to the farmhouse with me? I'll show you my woodshed, and you can see for yourself.'

'Did you say "woodshed"?' Melanie asked.

Nathan grinned. 'Must have been a Freudian slip. I meant to say "wood shop".'

'Hmmm. Well, let's see your wood, then,' she joked.

Melanie held out her hand. Nathan got to his feet and lifted her from her chair. When she was eye-level to his belt, she sneaked a look at his crotch. If he were fully hard, he was as big as Melanie had hoped. If he were half-hard, he was going to be much, much bigger.

'By the way,' Melanie asked, as she climbed into the passenger seat of Nathan's pick-up truck, brushing a layer of sawdust off the seat, 'what was this meeting supposed to be about?'

Instead of answering, Nathan began to cough. Melanie could tell he was faking it.

'Well?' she insisted. 'What did Harrison want to discuss? Was it my expansion proposal?'

'All I know for sure is that he wanted us to meet.'

'Harrison's been acting strange. When he called me to set this up, he said that he really needed to see me. Do you think something's wrong? Maybe we should call him.'

'I don't think that's necessary. I'm sure he just got held up somewhere. Family crisis, or something like that.'

Melanie didn't like the way Nathan was evading her questions, but she was happy that her Saturday wasn't being spoilt by a business meeting. The contents of Nathan's workshop were much more intriguing than anything Harrison would have had to say. Hannah had said that he didn't have any pillories out in his barn, but maybe he had a few toys that were even better.

'Nice and quiet out here in the country,' Melanie commented, when they stopped at Nathan's farmhouse. Snow had begun to fall, augmenting the silence with its muted whisper. 'You could make all the noise you wanted, and no one would hear you.'

'Or *you* could make all the noise you wanted,' Nathan said, giving Melanie a meaningful glance. 'I'm not usually the one who makes noise around here.'

Melanie was trying to process what she thought he was implying, feeling dizzier by the second, thinking that she was about to embark on an afternoon of illicit adult games. She continued as best she could with her innocent-sounding conversation.

'Do you have a lot of company?' she asked.

'I have guests now and then. But not the ones I really want.'

Nathan then led Melanie across the yard to a large wooden shed that slanted up against the barn. He had a spacious homestead, with the large farmhouse, the barn and shed, and the pasture rolling down to the bay. It was the perfect setting for a life of rural perversion. People who lived in the city would be shocked if they knew what went on in the country. With all that space and privacy, you could follow your impulses wherever they led you.

Melanie didn't expect much from the shed. From the outside, it looked like a firetrap, but its interior was neat and cozy, a masculine retreat. The room was lined with shelves and filled with saws, work benches, power drills … and the most incredible array of wooden spanking implements that Melanie had ever seen. The paddles hung along the walls in neat rows, arranged according to their size and function. There were palm-sized pocket paddles, long fraternity paddles, paddles with holes, and paddles covered with fur. All of them showed meticulous craftsmanship and impeccable taste in wood, from the local maple, oak and pine to the imported exotics, like bloodwood and koa.

That wasn't all. At the back of Nathan's work space stood a display of spanking furniture, so elegantly designed and lovingly stained and polished that they could stand in the finest houses in Morne Bay. Surrounded by all of these elegant, cruelly inventive objects, Melanie saw Nathan Wentworth as if she were meeting him – really meeting him – for the first time. He wasn't a typical intellectual, or a rustic farmer, but a brilliantly perverted craftsman, an artist of the erotic. Here was a man who could be a strong protector, but also an exquisite tormentor. He had an Ivy League education, the physique of a lumberjack, and the genius of a true sadist. Melanie had never seen such a combination of qualities. No wonder Hannah had a thing for him.

'What do you think?' Nathan asked.

'It's incredible. Just incredible,' Melanie cried out in delight as she recognised a reproduction of a Victorian spanking horse.

'I saw something just like this in an old erotic post-card!' she exclaimed. She turned to Nathan. 'Can I try it out?'

'Go ahead.'

Melanie ran over to the spanking horse. The pommel was covered in black velvet, and the dainty legs were just the right height for Melanie's body. When she was perched on the pommel, her bum in the air, she looked over at Nathan and squirmed provocatively.

'This feels like it was made for me.'

'Maybe it was.'

'I love it! I want to buy it.' Melanie stood up, too excited to stay still. Her brain was racing at a thousand miles per minute. 'I want to buy all of this. Everything. I want to sell the things you make at my shop. This stuff is unbelievable: it's gorgeous, it's authentic, and it's local. We'll make a fortune! When I expand, we're going to have tons of extra space. The Alcove is going to have a room all its own, and we'll put the furniture there –'

'Melanie, stop.' Nathan's voice was too quiet. 'I have to tell you something.'

'Tell me what?'

Nathan walked over to Melanie, took her by the arms, and looked down at her. His face was more serious than ever, and there was something else in his eyes that made her go cold all over.

'There isn't going to be an expansion. Not the way you've been planning it, anyway. The town council has decided not to consider your proposal at their end-of-the-year meeting. That's why Harrison wanted to meet with you today.'

'What? I don't believe you.'

She dug her heel into his foot and punched his solar plexus, trying to get free. He grunted in pain, but didn't let her go.

'Melanie, listen. Hold still and listen. Give me two minutes to explain. Harrison was supposed to tell you all this, but apparently he lost his nerve. That's why he didn't show up at the hotel today.'

Melanie went limp. A tidal wave of tears was building behind her eyes. Nathan cupped her jaw in his hand so that she couldn't look away from him, then he began to speak slowly and deliberately.

'The town council has decided that an add-on to the house would diminish its value as a historic landmark, and hurt other businesses on Harbor Street. As it is, Chimera is growing faster than the available parking in the neighbourhood. The way Harrison describes it,

Chimera used to be a small, exclusive shop that relied primarily on foot traffic. No one ever expected it to become so popular. With the museum going up next door, the street is going to turn into a madhouse.'

'Chimera has been there for years. Move your fucking museum somewhere else.'

Nathan shook his head. 'It's too late for that. Besides, the council approved the site as a museum a long time ago. They just never had the funding to go ahead with the project. I helped them secure the grant.'

'Why don't we cut through all this bullshit? This isn't about parking, and it's not about historic landmarks. This is about sex. If Chimera were any other kind of business, the town would be drooling to get a piece of the pie. Free enterprise – that's what all you Puritans are so crazy about, isn't it?'

'What I'm crazy about,' Nathan said, 'is you.'

He pulled Melanie close and wrapped his arms around her. With her face buried in the sheepskin jacket, she let go of her tears. She wanted to push Nathan away, to run away and hitchhike back to town, then pack a bag and flee for Manhattan, where she would become an over-night success and show the yokels on the town council what morons they were. But Nathan wouldn't release her if she fought him. She would have to wait for his mushy mood to pass, then make a break for it.

'You don't have to give up on your dream. All you have to do is adjust the parameters,' Nathan said.

'How?'

'Instead of adding on to the house, you can expand from the inside. Knock out a wall or two, spread out into the upstairs rooms. The interior of that house is big enough to hold a lot more erotic merchandise – including mine.'

'That house will never be as big as it needs to be, not

unless I add a wing. Besides, if the town council is dead set on stopping me from expanding, they'll do it one way or another.'

'Why don't you consider moving? Choose an area of town that's zoned for larger businesses. Your customers will follow you wherever you go.'

'It doesn't matter where I go. This isn't about zoning, it's about restricting people's sexuality.'

'No. It's not. This is about a small town trying to control growth and preserve its heritage.'

'I want to believe you, Nathan. But I think you're wrong. The Alcove was a success in the beginning because it took people by surprise. The ones who didn't approve were too shocked to take action. Now that it's sinking in, becoming part of the culture, the dragon is finally waking up, and it's going to start breathing fire down my neck.'

'Don't worry about dragons. You have your own personal Saint George here.'

'Are you serious? You'd fight for me?' she asked faintly.

Melanie lifted her face from Nathan's jacket. For such a stern man, he could certainly wax sentimental.

'Absolutely. I'm not without influence, you know. The council has to keep me happy, too. Besides, look at all this.' Nathan motioned to the display of paddling instruments, the spanking horses and benches. 'We're on the same side.'

'What if the council finds out about you? Aren't you worried about what could happen if you associate with the town's most notorious bad girl?'

'Absolutely not. Listen, Melanie, you and I share a lot of the same goals. We've just pursued them in different ways. You've gone straight for what you want, while I've taken a more indirect approach. I'm older than you, and the world is a lot more open than it was when I got out of graduate school. I want to start taking advantage of that, before I'm too feeble-minded to appreciate it.'

'So you want to be my partner, in a sense.'

'In more than one sense, actually. Why do you think I built that spanking horse for you?'

Melanie sniffled and wiped away her stray tears. 'You mean you *did* build that for me?'

Nathan nodded. 'You're my new muse. Try it out again. See how it feels.'

Melanie broke away and went back to the wooden horse. Its design did suit her tastes perfectly: graceful and feminine, crafted out of rich brown oak, with the sophisticated touch of black in its velvet-covered seat. Among all the other toys in Nathan's wood shop, she had gravitated towards this one, and it had felt natural to lie across it, bent double and waiting for a spanking.

She still hadn't gotten that spanking. Melanie threw off her coat, rucked up her skirt, baring her body from the waist down, and resumed her position on the horse. Between its front legs was a spooled rung that she could cling to with her hands. She pumped her hips up and down, in case Nathan hadn't gotten the message that she was ready to test his craftsmanship.

But Nathan's face had hardened with displeasure. 'Who told you to pull up your skirt?'

'No one,' Melanie said provocatively.

In three strides, he crossed the room and yanked her skirt down. Through the charcoal wool he grabbed one of her cheeks in his broad hand and jiggled the flesh. He repeated this with the other cheek, scooping it from below. Then he stepped back. Melanie waited for his hand to fall. Anticipating a real wallop, she held her breath, screwed her eyes shut, and clenched her muscles. Hannah had loved being spanked by Nathan Wentworth, but Hannah was made of hardier stuff.

The swat never came. After a moment, Melanie glanced over her shoulder. Nathan stood there watching her as if her body were a delicate piece of statuary that he'd received as a gift, and he didn't know what to do with.

'What's the matter?' she asked.

'This isn't the right time. You look perfect there, just the way I fantasised, but it's not the right time to discipline you. Not with everything you've been through this morning.'

Melanie got to her feet and adjusted her skirt and jacket. Relief and disappointment washed through her. She was still overwhelmed by Nathan's sheer size, and as a woman who didn't enjoy serious pain, she had been afraid of the force he could deliver. On the other hand, when he had yanked her skirt down, she had felt a jolt of excitement that had practically thrown her off the spanking horse. Her legs were still trembling.

'I'm old-fashioned that way,' Nathan explained. 'I'm obsessed with spanking, but when it comes to the delivery, I can't follow through unless there's a real need for correction – not when the woman really matters to me.'

'You mean you've never spanked anyone casually?'

'I've done scenes with women I didn't know, but I've never found that satisfying. I'm not a performer. I want a relationship with a strong woman who resists me, who doesn't give in easily, but who wants to be dominated in the end. The last thing I want is a woman who's totally compliant.'

'I'm never totally compliant. I'm never even partially compliant. Ask anyone in town. Why do you think they're trying to stop me from expanding?'

'I know. That's why I'm so attracted to you. You're contentious, temperamental, and spoiled. Best of all, you share some of my deepest perversions. In fact, I think you may have some kinks you're not even aware of yet.'

'And I suppose you're going to help me discover them?'

'That depends. Do you trust me enough to give up your pride for a few hours and do what I tell you?'

Melanie considered this. Nathan still overwhelmed her, but he came with good references, and the more she got to know him, the more she wanted to see what kinds of dirty desires were brewing under that stoical exterior. She didn't want to let him have her cheaply, however. Men like Nathan liked to achieve their goals the hard way, which was fine when those goals included sex.

'What's in it for me? If I let you have your way with me for the afternoon, do I get anything out of it besides a good time?'

'What else do you expect?' Nathan laughed.

'I always enjoy a good bargain. I've got a proposition for you.'

'Are you asking for money, you little tart?' he joked.

'Never!' Melanie exclaimed, feigning indignation. 'I make enough of that for myself. I was thinking more of an exchange of services. I'll do whatever you want for the afternoon, if you agree to give me a day in return.'

'Do I get to ask a few questions about this day? Such as when will it be, where do you expect me to go, and what the hell will I be doing?'

Melanie gave him the crafty smile of a carnival fortune-teller. 'Even if I could see that far into the future, I wouldn't tell you. That's part of the bargain. Take it or leave it.'

'You want to give me an afternoon in exchange for an entire day. You're unbelievable!'

'A little of me goes a long way. I'm a sexual concentrate.'

'Fine. I'll accept your deal, but only because I can't imagine anything better than spending a day with you. I'm no fool.'

'We'll see about that.'

'You're mine for the afternoon, then.'

They shook hands solemnly, like two opposing political leaders at a summit meeting.

'One afternoon,' she agreed. 'I'll be your love slave for one afternoon – but tomorrow, it's back to being my ordinary self. Pushy, bitchy, and ready to kick the town council's ass.'

'I wouldn't have it any other way.'

Nathan reached into his jacket pocket. He produced a large roll of red ribbon and showed it to Melanie.

'What do you want me to do with that? Some holiday decorating?'

'I'm the one who's going to be doing the decorating.'

'And I'm going to be an ornament?'

'You catch on fast,' Nathan said, with a smile that made Melanie's sex start to pound like a toy drum.

Nathan looped a length of the ribbon around Melanie's neck and tied it in a bow that was snug enough to restrain her without cutting off her circulation. Holding the spool in one hand, he led Melanie into the yard. Melanie stepped along behind him, walking briskly to keep pace with Nathan's long legs. She was glad that the farm was so isolated; if anyone from town had seen her trotting along at the end of a ribbon like a terrier at the end of a leash – in her most sophisticated business suit, no less – she would have died of embarrassment.

Nathan led Melanie along matter-of-factly, as if he did this kind of thing every day. For all she knew, maybe he did. He might have a whole army of submissives who visited him out here in the boondocks, catering to his every erotic whim. Melanie was happy to fulfil the terms of their agreement, but she wasn't about to let him keep her out here past the cocktail hour.

When they reached the house, Nathan guided her

around to the back and opened the door that led into his mud room. The linoleum tiles were seamed with dried soil, and the corners were piled with old boots and rags. There was a straw mat to wipe dirty shoes on, and a row of hooks on the wall for extra coats.

'What's this? You don't take your slavegirls through the front entry?' Melanie asked.

Nathan frowned. His face was as grim as the visage of a pilgrim standing on the rocky coastline. If there had been a pillory anywhere in sight, Melanie would be locked inside it by now.

'You're not my slavegirl, you're my guest. Most of my guests come in through the mud room, especially when they've been out in the barn. If this entrance isn't good enough for you, I'd be glad to drive you back to civilisation.'

'I was only joking,' Melanie said in a small voice. Nathan had a way of making her feel chastised for the smallest infractions. Men usually fell over themselves trying to please her. The only man who had ever successfully put Melanie in her place was her father, and the effort had practically killed him.

'All right, then. Follow me. No talking until we get upstairs.'

Melanie followed Nathan through the kitchen. Judging by his profession, Melanie had expected to see all kinds of antique treasures displayed in his home, but the parlour of the farmhouse was plain and shabbily furnished, with the typical masculine clutter of newspapers, discarded clothes, and empty bottles. The flagstone fireplace looked cold and barren, as if it hadn't seen any use since Nathan moved in.

'I spend most of my time in the barn or the kitchen,' Nathan explained, reading Melanie's thoughts. 'I haven't lived here long enough to decorate the place the way I wanted to, and I've been so busy with the new museum that I haven't had much inspiration left over for my house.'

The floors were covered with braided runners. The old rugs had been worn down by so many feet over the years that their colours, probably once vibrant reds and blues, had faded into a uniform brown. Melanie knew that the rugs were genuine antiques, hand-braided by farm women who had passed away long ago. The rugs reminded her of Hannah, whose grandmother had lived in this house, and the thought of Hannah made Melanie uneasy. What would Hannah think if she knew that Melanie was here now, alone with Nathan? Would she be jealous, or would she be happy that Melanie got to experience sex with Nathan, too?

Melanie sighed. She understood how meat-and-potatoes monogamy worked, and she was more than familiar with the haphazard customs of promiscuity, but the rules of polyamory were a mystery to her. Hopefully Hannah wouldn't find out about this encounter before Melanie had a chance to explain.

Melanie's high heels clip-clopped across the hardwood floors and up the narrow stairs. She watched Nathan's denim-covered butt as he climbed the steps, and her mouth started to water. She loved the way his hamstrings flexed as he lifted one leg, then the other. The inseams of his jeans were so frayed that she could imagine them tearing without much effort at all. She saw Nathan lying on his back while she sat astride him, ripping those jeans off his thighs, kneading the marble-hard muscles underneath his skin, working her way up to the wrinkled mass of his scrotum, which would be covered with a fuzz slightly darker than his toffee-blond hair . . .

Hold on there, Mel, she corrected herself. Nothing like that was going to happen today. She had made a deal to play Nathan's submissive for the afternoon, and she was going to live up to it.

'Welcome to my private chambers,' Nathan said, opening his bedroom door with a mock flourish. 'This is where you'll spend the next four hours.'

Melanie took in the master bedroom, with its freshly painted slate-blue walls and eggshell-white crown mouldings. Here, at least, Nathan had invested some time in decorating. An enormous bed, covered with a wedding-band quilt whose blend of blue and grey fabrics matched the masculine hue of the walls, dominated the room. A weathered pine schoolteacher's desk stood under the window, looking out over the bare trees of the apple orchard, and a simple wooden table held a chipped ceramic basin and pitcher. A bearskin rug covered the floor in front of the small fireplace. Melanie hoped the afternoon's torments would include writhing naked on that rug.

'Can I talk now?' Melanie asked. 'Because I'd like to know if I can –'

'Quiet,' Nathan growled. 'It looks like I'm going to have to gag you so that I can concentrate.'

'Concentrate on what?'

Nathan opened a drawer in an oak chest and pulled out a black tie splashed with red hibiscus flowers. It looked like the sort of thing that a friend would bring back from Honolulu as a joke. Melanie was about to ask if he could possibly gag her with something more tasteful, but when she saw the look on his face she submitted without protest.

'Now I'm going to undress you,' he said. 'Don't worry,' he added, when he saw the panicked look in Melanie's eyes, 'I'm not going to wrinkle, tear, or damage your clothes in any way. You're my gift for today, and I'm going to unwrap you myself.'

Once her mouth was bound with the garish tie,

Nathan led her over to a full-length mirror with an intricately carved wooden frame. While she watched her reflection, he undressed her, removing her jacket, blouse and skirt. She made no move to help him at all, except for lifting an arm or a leg here or there. He was like a giant playing with a doll, manipulating her limbs with great care, then hanging each of her garments in his closet. Melanie was impressed to note that he used cedar hangers.

Maybe he's my kind of man after all, she thought.

He stripped her down to her matching black lace bra and garter belt, then ordered her to stand still while he pulled the pins out of her hair and unrolled the chignon. He ran his fingers through her dark tresses, then brushed them out with hypnotic strokes. Melanie closed her eyes, letting herself melt into the warm, soothing feeling of being groomed. When her body went lax, Nathan stopped brushing. He searched through his chest of drawers, pausing to look at one object, then another. Melanie would have loved to get a look at his stash of toys, but she knew better than to try to speak. He settled on two items: a black satin sleep mask, and a long chain of sleigh bells.

'All right,' he said. 'Time to practise some restraint.'

Setting the bells and mask aside, Nathan went to work with the red ribbon. With gentle artistry he wrapped Melanie in a red velvet web, crisscrossing her breasts and binding her arms to her sides. He pulled the ribbon between her legs, so that it snaked through her cuntlips, then brought it back through the cleft of her ass and tied it in a bow between her shoulder blades. Melanie's eyes widened in delight when she saw the end result. The red velvet snare contrasted with Melanie's ivory skin and the black accents of her garters and stockings. The ribbon exerted enough pressure on her breasts to make them jut out from her chest, appearing twice their normal size. She looked weird and wonderful and very, very kinky. But before she could spend much time admiring Nathan's handiwork, he pulled the sleeping mask over her head, and everything went dark.

First she heard the sleigh bells jingling merrily, then she flinched as she felt their chilly weight fall along her collarbone. Nathan was draping the bells around her neck.

'Belling the cat,' he explained. 'Just a small precaution. I have to go downstairs and get a few things, and I don't want you to move until I get back.'

How was she supposed to move? Melanie wondered. She was bound so tightly in the ribbon that she might as well have been wrapped in duct tape. And if Nathan had anything more interesting downstairs than he had up here, he had to be the most well-stocked pervert on the East coast.

Melanie heard Nathan's firm tread on the floorboards, walking in the general direction of the window. From the clanking sounds that followed, Melanie guessed that he was picking up the ceramic basin and pitcher and carrying them out of the room.

'I'm leaving the door open,' he said as he left. 'If you move a centimetre, I'll hear the bells. Believe me, Melanie, you don't want me to hear those bells.'

Gagged, bound, and blindfolded, Melanie waited. Somewhere in the room, a clock ticked away the seconds. Melanie hadn't noticed a clock when she came in, but she was well aware of it now. She was also aware that there was a chilly draught seeping in through the window, causing gooseflesh to gather on her breasts, inner arms, and thighs. Nathan was doing a lot of banging around downstairs, but Melanie knew that if she so much as shivered she would jingle like a reindeer, so she tried to distract herself from the cold by focusing on other sensations. Nathan's bedroom smelled of old wood, shoe polish, and the faintest hint of Red Door perfume.

Melanie's lips formed a smile around the bulk of the gag. Funny how your other senses went into overdrive when you were deprived of sight. If Nathan hadn't blindfolded her, Melanie might never have known that another woman had slept in his room the night before.

The thought of another woman being here so recently excited her. What had Nathan done with last night's guest – or to her? How did her 'red door' compare to Melanie's? By the time Nathan returned, Melanie was warm all over, in spite of the low temperature in the room. Still, she was relieved to hear Nathan stacking firewood in the fireplace and lighting a match. For what seemed like half an hour, he moved about the room, making preparations. Time crawled when you were under sensory deprivation. Melanie's feet were starting to go numb from standing in one position for so long in her high-heeled shoes. But the tingling in her feet wasn't as bad as the ominous rumblings of her stomach, which she hadn't filled with anything today except for coffee and champagne. If Nathan were considerate enough to use cedar hangers for her clothes and light a fire to keep her warm, maybe he'd be kind enough to feed her.

Just as her knees were starting to buckle, Nathan crossed the room and lifted Melanie off her feet. He carried her over to the bed (she couldn't help thinking of King Kong worshipfully lifting Jessica Lange) and deposited her on the firm mattress. The sleigh bells jingled furiously.

'You're doing very well, my little pussycat,' he said, removing the bells. 'We'll make a submissive of you, yet.'

There must be a local campaign to turn Melanie into a sub, because everyone in town seemed to want to take a crack at her. Playing bottom was fun once in a while, but she wasn't about to surrender her self-control without one last protest. When Nathan untied the gag, Melanie burst out with a torrent of complaints.

'Listen, Nathan, I'm already fed up with this. There is no chance that I will ever be a submissive, especially under these conditions! I'm starving, I'm cold, and my ankles are paralysed. It's a wonder I can talk, because my mouth is so parched from being stuffed up with your tie, which by the way is the most hideous –'

Nathan filled that mouth with something so heavenly that she shut up at once. She tasted rich, cool vanilla, overlaid with a sinful, semisweet burst of dark, gooey chocolate. The hot-cold ambrosia slid down her throat, making her whole body quiver with pleasure. Nathan was feeding her a hot fudge sundae. If this was his idea of torture, she might reconsider becoming his slave.

He stopped after three heaping spoonfuls, just enough to leave her longing for more. She whimpered.

'We've got a long way to go, Melanie. Don't worry, I won't let you suffer ... much.'

He lifted a glass to Melanie's lips, and she took a sip of ice water, refreshing after the sugary treat. Then he arranged her body on the bed, propping up her legs by inserting a pair of fat feather pillows under her knees. He spread her thighs wide apart, and gently ran his fingers along the ribbon that furrowed the folds of her pussy.

'I'd tell you how beautiful you look,' he said, 'but you're vain enough as it is.'

Melanie's heartbeat accelerated. Things were starting to get interesting. Leaving her in that prone position, Nathan began to arrange various objects on the table beside the bed. When he was finished, Melanie heard the crisp hiss of a match being struck. Moments later, she smelled warm, vanilla-scented wax.

'Why are you lighting a candle? It's broad daylight, and I can't exactly appreciate the atmosphere with this blindfold on.'

'I left the gag off because I'm going to make use of

your mouth, but I could easily put it on again. You don't want that, do you?'

'Anything but that,' Melanie shuddered, thinking of the Hawaiian tie.

'This is the part where you're going to have to trust me. Do you think you can?'

Melanie nodded.

'Good. I don't want you to ask any questions. I don't want you to even *think* of any questions. Try to quiet that turbocharged brain of yours, and experience the sensations I'm going to give you.'

Melanie wiggled her limbs a little, then settled into the mattress. This kind of perversion was more to her liking. Hannah could have all the old-fashioned, chastising spankings she wanted – Melanie preferred to lie still and be tempted with mysterious pleasures.

'Yow!' she shrieked, as something small and cold settled into the hollow of her throat.

'Lie still. Just lie still.'

Slowly Nathan drew the cube across her chest, painting the hills and valleys of her breasts with the melting ice. Wherever the ice travelled, cold beadlets formed on her skin, and she imagined herself covered in a net of tiny diamonds. She lost track of time as Nathan traced the lines and crevices of her body, until every nerve was alight. He must have used a whole bowlful of ice on Melanie's skin; the little cubes seemed to dissolve as soon as they touched her overheated body. He even buried a small chip inside the folds of her labia, where the cold burned like a flame until it subsided into a tingling chill. The only parts he left untouched were her nipples, so that by the time he had covered every other inch of her, those ultra-sensitive nubs were crying for attention. She heard someone moaning, but she didn't recognise her own voice. In the darkness behind the blindfold, all sensations were magnified, yet remote.

Nathan's breathing was deep, slow, and rhythmic, as if he were practising a sexual form of meditation. When he was done with the ice, he let Melanie lie there for a while, listening to the sound of his inhalations and the throb of her own pulse. Just as she was adjusting to the last of the lingering cold water, she was struck by an entirely different sensation: the drizzle of warm wax across her breasts. Nathan wasn't cruel enough to keep the wax hot; he had let the candle cool off enough to provide a contrast with the ice without shocking her. He poured the buttery liquid in a stream between her breasts and down the groove of her belly, letting it form a puddle in her navel.

'I wonder if I could ever punish you,' he said, so softly that she wondered if he knew that he was speaking out loud. 'Your flaws are what make you perfect. How could I correct a woman like you?'

Melanie liked the sound of that. She'd rather be worshipped than punished any day. A smile crossed her lips.

'What's that smug look on your face, Melanie? I suppose you think that you're in control because I took a moment to praise your beauty. Well, think again. Let me put this candle down and sort you out, young lady.'

He then took hold of her breasts and squeezed. She gasped. Suddenly Nathan was straddling her with his thick, powerful thighs. The frame of the antique bed squeaked in alarm. Before she could register the change in him, he was leaning over her, nipping and suckling at her breasts with such relish that she lost her breath. Her nipples, on full alert from being neglected for so long, sent alternating spears of pain and pleasure through her flesh. Her body tried to arch instinctively, but she was pinned under Nathan's weight. Using one of his knees to brace himself on the mattress, he foisted the other between her thighs and massaged her open sex with his kneecap. The denim chafed against the moist, hyperaroused flesh of her inner lips, and before she knew it, Melanie was hit by an orgasm that rolled over her with the speed and strength of a tsunami. It felt so rude and wanton to have used part of his body like that solely for her gratification.

'I didn't give you permission to come,' Nathan said, stroking Melanie's hair as she sank down through the last of the waves, 'but I won't punish you for that – this time. You're a greedy little thing, aren't you? You can't delay your gratification at all.'

'Judging by the way you're breathing,' Melanie retorted, 'I'd say that you won't be delaying your gratification much longer, either.'

'You're damn right, I won't. I'm going to come all over you, and you're going to watch.'

Nathan yanked down the zipper of his jeans, then he pulled off Melanie's satin mask. The afternoon daylight assaulted her eyes. She couldn't see anything but Nathan's large form hovering over her, his legs encasing her waist, his shirt-tails hanging loose as he freed his cock – which was even more magnificent than Melanie had hoped. Thank the goddess she had spent so much time experimenting with dildos and vibrators of various proportions; otherwise, she might not have been able to accommodate such a monster. He really was hung like a Clydesdale horse. The shaft, a fresh salmon pink, arched up to a heart-shaped head that was richly suffused with blood. Its veins were visible, but not too prominent, etched clearly enough to map the contours of the penis. The giant tool bobbed up and down between her breasts, its single eye seeking some land to plough.

'What are you going to do with that thing?' Melanie asked, torn between admiration of Nathan's sex organ and concern for her own.

'You ask too many questions,' said Nathan in a guttural tone. 'Be patient. You'll get everything you deserve, and more.'

Nathan's cock came to rest in the groove between Melanie's tits. He then scooped up the ribbon-wrapped mounds and pushed them together, forming an deeper canal. He settled his weight so that he was balanced above Melanie's body without resting on her. Once he was in position, he began to thrust, carefully at first, then with more abandon as his glans oozed its natural lubrication along Melanie's skin.

Being used this way was new to Melanie. Aside from trying not to crush her, Nathan didn't seem concerned about Melanie's pleasure, or even her comfort; he was simply availing himself of her body, grunting like an animal as he rutted between her breasts. She might as well have been a twenty-dollar hooker working out of a cheap motel room. To her amazement, she found this wildly exciting. Though she couldn't move, couldn't even squirm, in her restrained position, Melanie spurred Nathan on with banshee moans. Just before he came, his muscles tensed, and his thighs gripped her like a steel vice. He gave a massive shudder, groaned, and helping himself along with a few strokes of his hand he spurted a ribbon of seed across Melanie's chest. She watched awestruck at the sight of his jetting orgasm. It was a wonderful thing to behold.

After he had dismounted her and recovered his wits, Nathan wiped Melanie clean with a warm, damp towel. Then he cut her loose from her web of red ribbon, as if he were unwrapping a package. Each swish of the scissors' blades released another one of her bonds, until she was free again. Nathan lay beside her on the bed while he massaged her arms and torso. He hadn't bound her tightly enough to restrict her circulation too much, but it was a glorious relief to feel the blood flowing freely through her veins.

'How are you feeling?' he asked.

'Fantastic, but starving. Can I have some more of that

sundae?' Melanie asked, noticing the bowl of ice cream that sat chilling in the basin of ice. The dessert had all but melted, but the chocolate goo was still delectable as Nathan spooned it into her mouth. When she was finished, he daubed the sticky traces off her lips, then helped her settle into the pillows and covered her with a quilt. Melanie yawned in contentment. Being submissive wasn't bad at all, especially when it ended like this.

'You really gave me a work-out today,' she said. 'I feel like I ran a marathon.'

'Did you enjoy it?'

'I loved it, but my ego couldn't live on a steady diet of submission.'

Nathan smiled. 'That's why it's so much fun to make you submit.'

'Fun, but exhausting.'

'Why don't you take a nap?' he suggested. 'I've got a few chores to do outside. I'll wake you up when I'm done.'

Melanie was happy to doze off in a nest of feather pillows and heirloom quilts. As she napped, she had one of those bizarre, jaggedly vivid dreams that often characterised her daytime sleep. She was preparing to confront Harrison Blake in a most bizarre costume: a black merry widow under a sweeping opera cape, and a pair of glittering black boots that cloaked her legs all the way up to her thighs. On her head was a tall witch's hat, with a sharp tip that flopped out over the brim. Instead of riding a broomstick, Melanie sailed through the bank's double doors on an enormous flying Hitachi wand, which buzzed angrily between her legs as she circled the crowd.

The customers waiting in line gaped like turkeys staring up into the rain as Melanie landed her aircraft on the marble floor. She stalked over to Harrison's mahogany desk, but Harrison barely noted her arrival. He didn't seem the least bit surprised to see a dominatrix witch fly into his bank aboard a giant sex toy. He merely gave her his sphincter-tight banker's smile and said, 'Your loan application has been denied, Miss Paxton. We don't lend money to witches in Morne Bay.'

Melanie was relieved to wake up to the sounds of Nathan stoking the fire. She crawled out of bed and joined him on the bearskin rug.

'I just had the weirdest nightmare,' she said, sitting down and wrapping her arms around her knees. 'Harrison turned down my loan for the shop. And he called me a witch. Can you imagine that?'

'Well, you do have extraordinary powers.'

'But do people around here see me that way?'

'As a witch? Or as a woman with power?'

'Either one.'

Nathan pushed at the logs with a poker, coaxing the flames into life. 'Both, I'd say. People have always been intimidated by a woman with a powerful sexuality, especially when it's combined with intelligence. In a sense, you've worked a spell on the town. You've stirred desires that were safely suppressed for many years. You're going to encounter some resistance.'

Melanie straightened her spine. 'I know that. But I'm going to fight. I'm not going to run away, and I'm not going to take it lying down.'

Nathan grinned. 'Oh, really? We'll see what you *will* take lying down, then.'

He unbuttoned his shirt, then stood up to pull off his boots and jeans. The afternoon daylight had lapsed into dusk, and the only illumination in the room came from the flickering fire. Looking at Nathan's naked body, Melanie felt like she'd gone back in time. His muscles were hard and well defined, not from hours clocked at a gym, but from the labour he did around the farm and in his workshop. Hundreds of years ago, he would have been the kind of man who would have built a colony from its foundations. He might also have been the kind of man who would have punished a woman like Melanie for immoral behaviour, but in his twenty-first-century incarnation, Nathan Wentworth was as much of a pervert as she was. Any punishment between the two of them was going to be entirely consensual.

The sex they had on the bearskin rug, however, was sweet and steamy and vanilla. After an afternoon of being tied up, tormented, and treated like a slavegirl, Melanie was grateful for a traditional fuck in the missionary position. Nathan slipped on a condom then lay on top of her, balancing himself on his hands, and eased his way inch by inch into her well-lubed passage.

'You ... are ... so ... big,' she gasped in time to his first thrusts. He filled her channel to bursting, nudging her cervix with each stroke. For such a large man, he had very supple hips, which he used to penetrate her in a serpentine rhythm. Nathan wasn't one of those men who simply ploughed ahead in a horizontal line; he moved at different angles, varying the tempo to match Melanie's mounting tension. When her inner muscles started to tighten, he reached down and pulled up one of her legs, bending the knee over his shoulder. He held his thumb over the hood of her clit, rubbing the little button against the ridge of his cock, so that it was stimulated from all sides. As soon as she got close to coming, he slowed down and lifted his thumb, repeating this torture each time he felt her clamp down on his cock.

'Please let me come,' she begged, twisting and flailing like a woman with a fever.

'Not yet. Not till I'm ready.'

'Now!'

'No.'

Maybe it was his age, maybe it was years of practice, but Nathan had more control than any lover she'd ever had. By the time he let Melanie explode, she was out of her mind, and the orgasm felt like an endless, rippling extension of her madness. She wasn't even aware that Nathan had come, until he slid out of her body and collapsed on the rug, panting like a castaway who's just crawled up onto the beach. She wanted to roll over and tell him how great she felt, but she couldn't move, and she couldn't remember how to speak.

This was going to be an incredible winter.

6 **Melanie Moves In**

The day Melanie moved into Ted and Hannah's carriage house felt like Christmas morning, the high school prom, and a day of execution all rolled into one.

For days the couple had been cleaning, mending, and painting, trying to get the little house into decent shape for their new tenant-cum-lover. Melanie wanted to decorate the place herself, but she needed a fresh slate to work with, and the carriage house had been neglected for years. Hannah had taken time off work to make sure that everything was ready for Melanie's arrival. It wasn't until she saw the moving van reach the crest of the hill that Hannah realised why she had been toiling to the point of exhaustion every day, then plunging into a dead sleep every night.

'Here she comes,' Ted said. His voice had an ominous note, as if the van were transporting Ghengis Khan and his army instead of Melanie Paxton and her wardrobe.

What have I gotten myself into? Hannah wondered.

After hours of discussion, sharing fantasies, and making plans with Ted to bring another woman into their lives, Hannah had thought she was prepared for this. She had thought that she was self-assured and confident, ready to embark on the erotic adventure of a lifetime. Now that the big day had arrived, Hannah felt about as self-confident as a pubescent girl at her first formal dance.

The van pulled into the gravel driveway, then bumped down the short rutted road to the carriage house. The overloaded vehicle shuddered to a halt, and Melanie hopped out, dressed in jeans, an oversized Beardsley sweatshirt, and sneakers. Of course she wore loads of make-up, and her hair was tied back with a Givenchy scarf, but she wasn't nearly as intimidating as Hannah had expected. Without hesitation, Melanie ran across the yard and threw her arms around Hannah.

'I'm so glad to be here,' she whispered into Hannah's ear. 'We're going to be the happiest threesome on earth.'

Melanie hugged Ted, too. He looked as awkward as Hannah felt, and when he glanced at his wife over Melanie's head, Hannah knew that he shared her misgivings. Were they doing the right thing, flaunting the standards of a settled, sedate community? Were they putting too much of a strain on their new marriage? After Melanie rushed away to direct the moving crew, Ted walked over to Hannah and took her hand.

'It's going to work out,' he reassured her. He lifted her hand to his mouth and kissed her fingers, one by one. 'You know how much I love you, don't you?'

Hannah nodded. A lump in her throat kept her from speaking. At times like this, she couldn't believe how lucky she was. Sometimes she thought that her marriage was a dream, that she would wake up one day and find that she was really alone, and that Ted was with someone glamorous and sultry and sexually confident ... like Melanie.

Hannah had assumed that the three of them would have a mini-orgy to celebrate Melanie's first night in the house, but after a day of moving armloads of her clothes, books, knick-knacks, and exercise equipment – including a small trampoline on which she claimed to bounce nude every morning – no one had the energy to do anything except wolf down a Chinese takeout and collapse from exhaustion. Melanie wanted to sleep alone in her new place, but she promised that she would spend the following night in Ted and Hannah's bed.

Though she was bone-tired, Hannah couldn't sleep that night. As the clock's hands crept towards twelve, she lay on her back, watching the bare branches of a sycamore tree claw her bedroom window. The branches looked like clutching fingers, reaching in to grab the things that Hannah valued most. Hannah rolled away from the window and yanked the blankets over her head, but not even the thick goosedown comforter could muffle the insistent tapping.

Just as her eyes were closing, she felt a hand clutch her shoulder. Thinking it was the witch-hand of the tree, she almost jumped out of her skin. She threw off the blankets and sat up to find Melanie cowering beside the bed.

'I didn't mean to scare you,' Melanie whispered. 'I think the carriage house is haunted. Can I sleep with you?'

In her long white flannel nightgown, quilted robe and furry slippers, Melanie looked like a frightened child at a sleep-over party. Her dark eyes were huge in her pale, pinched face, and her lips quivered from the cold.

'Of course you can.' Hannah lifted the blankets.

With a contented sigh, Melanie took off her robe and slippers, then climbed into bed. She tunnelled under the covers with Hannah, and together they cuddled against Ted's slumbering body for warmth.

'I can't believe we haven't woken him up,' Melanie remarked.

Hannah stifled a laugh. 'Nothing wakes him up. Wait till you hear our alarm clock – it sounds like an air-raid siren.'

Melanie squirmed against Hannah's curvy bulk. 'We'd be warmer if we were naked.'

'I can't sleep naked, even on a summer night.'

'Who said anything about sleeping?'

Melanie already had her hand under the waistband

of Hannah's underwear. She stroked her mound rhythmically, soothingly, as if the furry patch were her pet kitten. As Melanie caressed Hannah's pussy, she also nuzzled her neck, and Hannah felt her doubts receding. She let Melanie help her out of her long johns, then she watched as Melanie sat up to pull her nightgown over her head. Her breasts were two shadows tipped with darker points. Hannah longed to touch them, but she was afraid. So much of her schoolgirl self remained part of her adult identity; next to Melanie she felt big and awkward and shy, uncomfortable with her attraction to a prettier, more popular girl. It was one thing to make love with another woman while her husband orchestrated their play, but with Ted sound asleep, Hannah didn't know what to do with her desires.

'It's OK, Hannah,' Melanie whispered. Her fingers had found Hannah's lower lips and were toying with the folds. She arched her back, and her breasts brushed Hannah's cheek. 'I want you to touch me. Go ahead.'

Hannah stroked the underside of Melanie's right breast. In the moonlight, she could see the areola of the nipple pucker into a goose-pimpled ring. She kissed the nipple, then the ridges of flesh around it, surprised at how warm Melanie's skin felt. When she pressed her mouth against the groove of Melanie's cleavage, she felt her heart beating as fast as a bird's. Melanie took a handful of Hannah's hair and guided her mouth back to her nipple.

'Don't be timid. You can bite or suck as hard as you want.'

Hannah sucked the rock-hard points, and Melanie rewarded her by massaging Hannah's clit with the base of her thumb. She slid her forefinger into Hannah's vagina and hooked it up into the soft crevice of her passage. Hannah yelped at the intensity of the pleasure this caused. She had never believed that the G-spot existed, but Melanie had found some kind of button up there that was driving her crazy. She pulled Melanie down onto the bed beside her and parted her legs.

To Hannah's delight, Melanie had creamed herself all the way down her inner thighs, and when Hannah found the knot at the core of her cuntfolds, Melanie responded with an animal noise. In her wildest dreams, Hannah never would have believed that she could arouse another woman that way. Melanie's excitement magnified her own, and before long the two women were entangled like a pair of fighting Siamese cats, yowling and tussling, nipping and clawing.

Suddenly Hannah realised that she was engulfed in more than one pair of arms. A hard male thigh was shoving her legs apart, and Melanie's fingers were being replaced by an erect cock. She felt Ted's mouth against her neck, his warm breath in her ear. As Melanie French-kissed her and kneaded her breasts, Ted fucked her forcefully from behind, until Hannah thought she would be torn apart by the cyclone of sensations. Ted came before she did, and his thrusts set off her own climax. She was dimly aware, as the spasms shook her, that Melanie was coming, too.

After they recovered, the three of them lay quietly together. No one wanted to break the spell of their three-way orgasm, or to abandon the heat they had generated on that frigid night. Hannah felt Ted breathing rhythmically against her back, and she knew he had fallen asleep again. She smiled to herself in the darkness, wondering if he would remember any of this in the morning. Within a few seconds, Melanie was snoring. Hannah, who had always felt lucky to be desired by one person, lay awake for another hour, basking in the joy of being wanted by two.

* * *

On Sunday morning Melanie woke up at seven o'clock and slipped out of the tangle of Ted and Hannah's arms. She hurried back to the carriage house, where she pulled on jeans, a sweater and parka, not bothering to put on make-up or brush her hair. Bridget Locke's article was appearing in the *Foghorn* today. Breaking the speed limit and an assortment of minor traffic laws, Melanie raced into town. She careened to a stop in front of Judy's Bakery, which always had the first copies of the Sunday paper. Melanie planned to surprise Ted and Hannah with a bag of Judy's famous pumpkin-walnut muffins, a pot of fresh coffee, and three copies of the article that was going to make Melanie a star of erotic retail.

A small crowd had already gathered at Judy's, having coffee and doughnuts or waiting in line for fresh muffins. When Melanie stepped through the door, the comfortable racket died down. For a few awkward seconds, everyone stared at her. At least half a dozen newspapers were open to the Living Arts page, featuring Melanie in all her glory.

Looks like I'm already famous, Melanie thought. She smoothed her hair, hoping that a serious case of bedhead wasn't going to hurt her reputation as a sex goddess, and stepped through the door. The conversations resumed.

'Hey, look who it is,' said a male voice. 'Our local celebrity.'

Melanie turned around to see Dean DeSilva, looking as devilishly attractive as ever, standing at the counter. He grinned and tapped her arm with a rolled-up copy of the *Foghorn*. Beside him stood a woman Melanie didn't recognise, a petite ex-cheerleader type with a teased pouf of blonde hair. She was staring at Melanie with a mixture of fascination and hostility.

'This is Traci,' Dean said, pushing the blonde forward as if she were a prize he'd won at a carnival ring-toss.

'She's from my home town. Came up to take in some of our local colour.'

'Some of it's a bit too colourful for me,' Traci said with a shiver. 'I didn't expect to find a shop like Chimera in a quaint little town like this.'

Melanie would have liked to have clawed her blue eyes out, if she could reach them through the thicket of fake eyelashes. Instead, she gave Traci a smile so sweet that she almost gagged on it.

'Chimera does quite well in Morne Bay. In fact, I'm planning to expand in the spring.'

'Doesn't look good for you getting that permit,' Dean said. His black eyes twinkled as he rubbed his goatee. 'But you probably haven't read the article yet.'

'Don't give away the ending, honey,' Traci giggled.

'Catch you later, babe,' Dean said, winking at Melanie behind Traci's back as the two of them walked out the door arm in arm.

In spite of her bulky coat and the oven-warmed air inside the bakery, Melanie felt an arctic chill. She looked around at the other customers, who had all stopped their reading and sipping and chewing to eavesdrop on her exchange with Dean, and saw that she wasn't famous at all.

She was infamous.

Melanie snatched up a copy of the *Foghorn*, threw a dollar bill down on the counter, and made a dash for her car. She jumped into the front seat and locked the door, then she opened up the paper to the Living Arts section.

FROM SPICE TO SLEAZE – MORNE BAY GETS A TASTE OF TIMES SQUARE blared the headline of Bridget Locke's article. Under the headline was a photo of Melanie – hands on hips, boobs thrust out, pouting like Jayne Mansfield. She looked like a cheesy small-town tramp, desperate for attention. That was exactly how Bridget portrayed her in the article, which wasn't a human-interest story at all, unless you were interested in seeing a human torn to ribbons. With each word that she read, Melanie's blood rose by a degree, and by the time she reached the final paragraphs she was way past the boiling point.

'There are three things I never turn down,' says Melanie Paxton, the new manager of Morne Bay's trendiest clothing boutique. 'Hot sex, hot clothing, and free publicity.'

To the chagrin of Morne Bay, Miss Paxton has proven that she lives by these words. Once a paradise for collectors of sensual vintage clothing, Chimera has taken a wild turn under its new management, offering merchandise more suited to Times Square than to this quiet community. The latest addition to Morne Bay's harborside retail scene adds a lot more spice than this town can handle, according to the town council. The council recently decided not to consider Miss Paxton's bid for a permit to expand her business.

'Morne Bay has an honorable cultural heritage, and we want to preserve its dignity,' said council member Harrison Blake. 'While we don't deny that Chimera adds a unique flavor to Harbor Street's shopping district, we have to maintain a certain image for our seasonal visitors. They're the lifeblood of our economy.'

Apparently Melanie Paxton and her shop are too rich for Morne Bay's 'lifeblood'. If sex toys and leather are the direction that Harbor Street is taking, it might be time for residents and tourists alike to seek a safer harbor.

Harrison Blake was a dead man. Melanie couldn't wait to confront him with the article. A hundred revenge fantasies inundated her brain. She would roll up the Living Arts section into a tight little tube and thwack Harrison over the nose with it while she told him what a cowardly little worm he was. She would make him get down on all fours and relieve himself on Bridget Locke's article, until it was literally a piece of yellow journalism. Then she would mail the paper to Bridget. That two-faced sewer rat had been armed with an agenda the moment she stepped into Melanie's shop, and Melanie had been her willing victim.

'It's my own fault,' Melanie said to herself. 'I should have seen it coming.'

She slammed the steering wheel with her fist. Her first impulse was to shred the entire newspaper and fling the confetti into the street, but after forcing herself to take a few deep breaths, she changed her mind. She folded the pages of Bridget's piece and set them carefully on the seat beside her. Newspaper made fine kindling, and Melanie had a few fires to start.

It was a clear, crystalline morning, and as she drove out to Nathan Wentworth's house, Melanie felt herself cooling down to a simmer. Ice shimmered on the branches of the trees, and a thin carpet of new snow on the open meadows gave the sunlight a prismatic twinkle. It was too peaceful in the country to think about the foul stew brewing in town. No wonder Nathan preferred to live out here, where he wouldn't have to get embroiled in all the messes that came up on a daily basis.

Speaking of messes, Melanie was happy to find Nathan out in his yard, shovelling up a fresh heap of horse apples and dumping them onto a copy of the *Foghorn's* Living Arts section.

'Samson wandered too close to the house this morning,' Nathan explained, when he saw Melanie walking up the drive. 'I thought I might as well put this paper to good use.'

'You know, I think I'm in love with you,' Melanie said. She stepped back and wrinkled her nose when Nathan tried to hug her. 'But I'd like you a lot better if you'd get rid of that shit.'

'Are you referring to the paper, or what's on top of it?' Nathan laughed.

'Both. Why don't you throw it away, and I'll give you a reward.'

'What did you have in mind?'

Melanie batted her eyelashes and stuck out her breasts. 'A blow job, at the very least. That's what you'd expect from an overspiced tart like me, isn't it?'

'I'd expect something a lot fancier than a regular blow job. Bridget Locke implied that you've spent a lot of time in Times Square, learning the tricks of the trade.'

Melanie sighed. 'I should be so lucky. I haven't been to New York in ages. I can't remember the last time I took a week off to go crazy in the city.'

'You should take a vacation, then. Treat yourself to a shopping spree.'

'I'd love to, but I can't afford the time. Especially now, with everything that's going on. Things are going to get ugly, Nathan. I hear the beating of native drums.'

Nathan tweaked Melanie's chin. 'But you're going to stand up to those natives. That's the kind of woman you are.'

Melanie followed Nathan as he walked across the yard and deposited the Sunday *Foghorn* with its smelly load into a large trash bin. He invited her into the kitchen for coffee, and she accepted gratefully.

'Are you still willing to help me, Nathan?' she asked, sitting down at the kitchen table to enjoy a much-needed dose of caffeine. Nathan sat down beside her.

'Of course. I'm at your service, whenever you want. I owe you a day, remember?'

'I may need more than that. I'm going to take a big risk, and I want you to promise that you'll back me up.'

'Tell me what you want.'

Melanie inhaled. 'I want you to help me expand the shop from the inside, the way you suggested. I want you to walk through every room of the house and tell me the best way to modify the building so that I can double my inventory. Then I want you to oversee the project with me, from start to finish, and I want you to defend me when the council raises a stink about it. And I want you to help me find the financing to do all this, because Harrison Blake obviously isn't going to lend me a cent. If you got the funding for Morne Bay to have their stodgy old museum, getting money to sell sex toys should be a piece of cake.'

Nathan was silent as he took a swig of coffee. Melanie sat back and watched him, fidgeting with the hem of her sweater. Had she demanded too much? Maybe she should have laid out her plan step by step, instead of heaping it on him all at once. Finally he put his cup down and spoke.

'I can do all of that – and would happily do it – except for getting the money. Financing a business is an entirely different process than getting grants for a museum. In some ways, it's much easier. There's a lot less paperwork involved in a simple business loan, and you don't have to kiss any ass at stuffy fundraising dinners. But you need a solid business proposal, a clean financial history, and you need collateral.'

'What about the house itself? Couldn't that serve as collateral?'

'It could. But you aren't the owner, are you?'

'No,' Melanie admitted, thinking of Lori, who was probably having almond oil rubbed all over her tanned, naked body on the balcony of some Mediterranean hotel. 'I'm a partner in the business, but the contract doesn't give me any rights over Lori's property.'

'Do you think she'd approve of the expansion?'

'Lori trusts me. She had doubts about the Alcove at first, but when I took some initiative and got things started, she came around. The bottom line is, she knows that I know how to make money. She'd support me in this; I'm sure of it.'

'All right, then, let's assume she's willing to put up her house to secure the loan. Who are you going to get to do the work? Dean DeSilva is in the town council's pocket, and no one else around here can touch him at working with historical buildings.'

Melanie smiled. 'I happen to know a group of young carpenters who would be overjoyed to help me.'

'You sound pretty confident. Are you sure they can do the job?'

Melanie set down her coffee mug and looked Nathan square in the eye. 'I'm so confident that I'm going to post a big sign in the storefront announcing that the shop is expanding. Then I'm going to call up the *Foghorn* and buy the biggest ad I can afford, and I'm going to post it there, too. That's why I need you to promise to back me up. When the council tries to beat me down, I want you there to give me your support. Can I count on you?'

'Yes.'

Nathan took Melanie's sleek, manicured hand in his callused one. He turned her hand face up and drew circles around her palm with his forefinger. That simple stimulation had a surprisingly powerful effect on her, sending delicate shivers of excitement down the length of her arm. But tender, romantic sex didn't appeal to her this morning; she wanted something rough and dirty, a hard-driving ride that would leave her bruised and sore and utterly sated.

'I don't suppose you're in the mood to punish me this morning, are you?' she asked. She rose and braced her hands against the back of her chair, then arched her back and thrust out her hindquarters in an invitation he couldn't ignore.

'That's a tempting offer,' Nathan said, his voice thick and hoarse. 'Very tempting. Especially when you're being so pushy.'

He positioned himself behind Melanie and took hold of her body, his hands reaching under her sweatshirt to hold her waist. She ground her buttocks into his pelvis, and felt him grow hard. Deepening the arch in her spine, she raised her bum even higher, waiting to feel his hand come down on her cheeks.

Instead, Nathan pulled her upright, his hands roving over her breasts, tweaking her nipples as he kissed the smooth slope of skin that ran from her ear to her collarbone. He pinched her nipples so hard that she yelped in pain, but that pain still wasn't enough.

'Why won't you spank me? How hard can it be?'

'It's not the right time.'

Melanie twisted out of his arms. 'It's the right time for me. I don't need your kisses, or your cock – I just need your hand on my ass. Why can't you do that for me?'

'You ask for a lot,' Nathan said quietly. He reached out to stroke Melanie's flushed cheek, but she backed away. 'You want me to help you with your building project, you want me to help you secure a loan, and you want me to give you public support. I'm willing to do all that, but I won't be pushed into anything I'm not prepared for.'

'It's only a spanking, for God's sake. It's sex play. Do you always take play so damn seriously?'

'Not with most women. But you're different.'

'I don't understand. Last week you led me around like your pet poodle, gagged me with the ugliest tie I've ever seen, tied me up and blindfolded me, poured wax on my naked body, tortured me with ice cubes, and fucked me senseless. But you won't give me a plain old over-the-knee spanking?'

'Oh, I'll give you a spanking, Melanie. I'll give you the

spanking of a lifetime. Believe me, when I'm done with you, you won't be using your pretty ass as anything but a clothes hanger for three weeks. But not now. You haven't earned it.'

'What do I have to do? Commit a felony?'

Nathan's face was as dark as a thundercloud. He clenched his large fists, and once again Melanie saw the fierce taskmaster who had frightened her when they first met. Worse than his anger, though, was the disappointment in his sea-blue eyes. She had pushed too far, and let him down.

'I'm not going to let you dominate me, Melanie. I will help you achieve your business goals, and I will be your lover, but I will not let you top me. I'm not that kind of man.'

'Screw you, then!' Melanie kicked the base of Nathan's table. She was so frustrated by the way this day was turning out that she wanted to throw a full-scale tantrum, complete with flying dishes, overturned furniture, and banshee screams. The only thing that stopped her was the forbidding scowl on Nathan's face as he towered over her.

'I don't need your help,' she said, grabbing her parka and shoving her arms through the sleeves. 'I can get by on my own. I've been doing it my whole life.'

'Are you sure about that?'

Melanie's answer was the sound of Nathan's kitchen door slamming as she left his house. Scalding tears blurred her vision as she drove home, and by the time she got back to Ted and Hannah's house her face was as red and swollen as a stewed tomato. She stormed through the front door and into their library, where she found Hannah combing burrs out of her golden retriever's fur, and Ted reading a worn copy of The Importance of Being Earnest.

'This town is insane,' Melanie moaned. She flopped down in a leather armchair and threw her arm over her face. 'How did I end up in this provincial hellhole?'

'You know, Melanie, if my students were as dramatic on stage as you are in your daily life, they'd be starring on Broadway instead of languishing in high school,' Ted said, giving Melanie one of the schoolmaster glares that used to make her cream her panties when she was in the tenth grade. 'Must you blow everything out of proportion?'

'I'm not exaggerating this time. Have you read the Sunday paper?'

'We don't read the *Foghorn*,' Hannah said sheepishly. 'Ted won't allow anything but the *New York Times* in the house.'

'Good. That's another reason why moving in with you two is the best decision I ever made. If I see one more copy of Bridget Locke's article, I'm going to go on a rampage.'

'Tell us what happened,' Hannah urged.

'I thought this article was going to help me. I thought I could wave it in the town council's face and show them why they should let me expand. Instead, Bridget did a smear job on me. Every single one of those smug prudes on the council is reading that article and congratulating himself on making the right choice.'

Melanie sniffled and wiped her nose on her sleeve. Hannah put down her comb and went over to Melanie, kneeling beside her on the floor. She wrapped her arms around Melanie's thighs and looked up into her face.

'Melanie, you know that Bridget Locke is a vicious bitch.'

'I know that now, but she was so friendly in the beginning, so warm and enthusiastic. When she first called me, I was ecstatic. I made a joke on the phone about how I never turn down hot sex or free publicity, and she actually quoted me, as if I'd said that in the interview!'

'I wouldn't trust Bridget any farther than I could throw her. She uses everything, and she's famous for her poison pen.'

'I never saw it coming. She seemed truly interested in what I'm doing, when all along she was twisting my words in her sick head.'

'That's what journalists get paid to do,' Ted said, 'especially in small towns like this. Don't worry about it, Melanie. The publicity will work to your advantage.'

'I don't see how that's possible. Now that Bridget has attacked me in print, other people are going to come forward. The town council is already against me. And once the word gets around that I'm living here, they'll be against you, too.' Melanie touched Hannah's hair. 'Are you sure you want me to stay?'

'Of course we do.' Ted got up from his chair and crossed the room. He lifted Melanie's chin so that she was forced to meet his eyes. 'We walked into this relationship with our boots on.'

'That's good, because you're going to be knee-deep in some serious mud pretty soon,' Melanie said, laughing weakly.

'They can bury us in mud if they want to. I'm not going to let a lot of closed-minded people determine how I live. All my life, I've dreamed of having a relationship with two beautiful, sexy women who complemented each other. I'm living out one of my oldest fantasies here, and I'm not about to let it go.'

'But you're a teacher,' Melanie said. 'The school board isn't going to like it that you're renting out your carriage house to the village slut – even if they never find out that we're all sharing a bed.'

'The school board does not have the right to tell me whom or what I can have in my bed. This is my home, and I'm sharing it with two women who are well beyond the age of consent. If the school board doesn't like that, they can kiss my ass.'

'I see your point, now that you put it so eloquently.'

'No more theatrics, then. You've got your work cut out for you if you're going to go through with this expansion, so don't waste time on small-town melodrama.'

Melanie knew Ted was right, but she still wished she could kick and scream at the world, with its narrow standards and unfair judgments. All she wanted out of life was everything she could get. Why was Morne Bay trying to stop her?

Nathan sat down at his kitchen table and finished his coffee with deliberate, measured sips. His head – and his groin – were still pounding from his argument with Melanie, but he wasn't going to let her shatter his composure. God, how he had wanted to give her what she asked for! When she leaned over the chair, thrust out her ass, and challenged him with that saucy look, he would have loved to have thrown her over his knee, yank down her jeans and spank her until her pampered ivory skin turned fire-engine red. But Nathan had already yielded enough ground to Melanie; one more inch, and he would be *her* bottom.

She would have to wait for that spanking. Nathan had a feeling that the time would come soon. Melanie was on a collision course with the conservative element of Morne Bay, and it would only be a matter of time until they drove her to commit some serious misbehaviour. When that time came, Nathan would be waiting.

After he had finished his coffee, Nathan straightened up the kitchen, then went out to his woodshop. For the past few weeks he'd been working on a new project, a reconstruction of a seventeenth-century pillory. It was the most ambitious piece he had built in a long time;

Melanie had inspired him to take new risks. The pillory looked like one that had stood in any town or village square, in a time when public corporal punishment was the order of the day. The pillory worked with beautiful simplicity – the victim simply stood behind the framework, placed her neck and wrists in the grooves provided, and was imprisoned between two hinged partitions. Once she was on display, she was vulnerable to the mockery and torment of the villagers who gathered to point and stare. As Nathaniel Hawthorne put it, in his classic novel of sexuality and public humiliation, *The Scarlet Letter*, there could be 'no outrage more flagrant than to forbid the culprit to hide his face for shame'. The punishments that Nathan visualised were far more private, but he had reproduced the device with such attentive detail that it could have functioned perfectly as a means of torture and humiliation.

Nathan ran his hand along the surface of the wood, which he had sanded to a satin-smooth finish. No colonist had ever devoted such loving attention to the instruments of torture. Looking around his workshop at the benches, horses, and paddles he had worked so hard to create, Nathan felt his chest swell. Though he had never confessed it in public, Nathan took pride in being part of a longstanding historical tradition of formal discipline. He could never have been one to persecute, oppress, or torture unwilling victims; it was much better, he believed, to acknowledge one's sadistic impulses and pursue them with women who loved to receive pain as much as Nathan loved to inflict it.

'You know, you really should share your work with others, Nathan. It's a shame to keep these beautiful things hidden away.'

Nathan looked up. 'Dana! What a surprise.'

The professor stood in the open doorway, her curves silhouetted by the morning light. To Nathan's relief, she wasn't wearing her dominatrix catsuit or her thigh-high boots. She stepped into the shed, her eyes devouring the collection of instruments displayed in Nathan's work area. 'I'd love to buy some of these things for myself,' she said, running her finger along the elevated platform of a spanking bench. 'Are they for sale?'

'Not officially, though I'd be happy to make you a deal. I'm not ready to expose my secret identity to the public.'

'You won't be able to hide it for very long around here. Not in a town of this size. You might as well come clean – that's what I've found. Everyone in Beardsley knows about my tendencies.'

'Beardsley is a college community. It's much more liberal than Morne Bay.'

'The community isn't really the issue, is it? It's the individual who ultimately determines how he feels about his – or her – sexuality. We're not living in colonial times anymore, Nathan.'

'I see your point. Actually, I have been thinking about going public. I'd love to sell some of these things, if only to free up some space.'

'Good. Then I'll take one of those gorgeous maple fraternity paddles. I need to establish more authority with my students. I've got something for you, too, by the way. It's a peace offering.'

Under one arm, Dana held a thin leather-bound portfolio, which she handed to Nathan. The leather was cracked and warped, as if the volume had been sitting underneath a pile of boxes and papers for decades.

'A peace offering? What for?'

'I felt bad about our last date. I wanted to start again, get back on a solid footing with you. We're much better colleagues than lovers, I think.'

'I'd have to agree with you, though there were parts of that date that I wouldn't have missed for the world. What have we got here?' Nathan opened the portfolio. The brittle papers inside released the scents of dust and mildew, an odour that was sheer perfume to an historian like Nathan. The pages were covered with lines of spidery writing, in ink that had faded to sepia. At first he wasn't sure what he was looking at, but as his eyes grew accustomed to the lines of flowery script, he recognised their purpose.

'These look like shopping lists!' he laughed. 'Silk, porcelain china, French perfume. But where was the writer shopping?'

'All over the world,' Dana said with a satisfied smile. 'These papers belonged to Amélie Morne. They're the lists that she made for her husband when he went out on his purchasing expeditions in Europe and Asia. But you've only seen one page so far. The best is yet to come.'

Nathan leafed through the pages. His jaw dropped when he saw what the shipping magnate's wife had written on one of the following pages. Her wish list wasn't limited to fabrics and flatware; the former bawdy-house dancer had asked her husband to buy ben wa balls, an ivory dildo, and a special balm from the Orient that served both as an opiate and an aphrodisiac.

'My God, this is incredible! I always knew that Darius Morne's wife was said to have purchased erotic items from abroad, but no one has ever proven it. No one around here ever wanted to prove it. Are there any documents to back this up, to show that Amélie actually received these things?'

'I don't know,' Dana admitted. 'There may be some official shipping lists in the Morne family archive at Beardsley.'

'I've been through that archive a dozen times, but I've never seen anything like this. Where did you find it?'

'The portfolio was wedged behind a couple of boxes. It had been there so long that the leather was practically plastered to the wall. I would have missed it myself if I hadn't caught my fingernail on the binding. I don't think it's ever been catalogued. That's why I didn't feel too bad about stealing it.'

Nathan frowned. 'Shame on you, Dana. You're faculty – you should know that those documents aren't supposed to leave the library.'

'I know I should. Especially since I have no intention of returning it. I want you to keep these lists, Nathan. They could add a whole new dimension to the museum.'

'Yes, they could. But you should still be punished for taking such a treasure from the Beardsley archives.'

Dana hung her head and scuffed the sole of her leather shoe along the ground. The gesture was girlish, charming. Along with her tasselled loafers, Dana wore white knee socks, a forest-green corduroy skirt, and a crisp white blouse with a tartan blazer. She had shifted back to her schoolgirl look, and it was having its usual effect on Nathan. Now that the shock of her gift was subsiding, he was being bombarded with images of spanking her.

'Well?' Nathan pressed. 'What do you think your punishment should be?'

Dana's eyes were fixed on the pillory. She lifted her finger to her mouth, and sucked the tip. Nathan's heart pounded as he remembered what it was like to have his cock wrapped up in those lips. 'I've always had a fantasy about being displayed inside one of those,' she said shyly. 'Let me see what it's like.'

'I'd love to accommodate you, but I'm afraid it's not that easy,' Nathan said.

Dana's face sank in disappointment. 'Why?'

'Well, once I had you inside, I don't think I could restrain myself from acting out a few fantasies of my own.'

A blush darkened Dana's freckled cheeks. 'That would be all right.'

'Are you serious? But after last time, I thought you were a dominant through and through.'

Dana lifted her chin. 'Maybe you just didn't push the right buttons.'

'Apparently not. Follow me.'

Nathan placed the portfolio on a workbench and led Dana to the pillory. He lifted the top partition, then instructed her to bend over slightly and assume her place inside the device. He lowered the partition, and her wrists and head were encased in wood.

'As you know,' he said, stepping back to admire his handiwork, and the woman trapped inside it, 'the pillory used to be a nearly universal method of punishment in England. The Puritans brought it over to the States, where they used it with great enthusiasm. It was used primarily for minor crimes, but as you can see, being locked inside one of these things has some major psychological effects.'

'You can say that again.'

'Is it what you expected?'

'Um . . . no. Not exactly.'

Dana was already squirming in the device, flapping her hands and wiggling her hips. Nathan was enjoying the look of self-conscious distress in her green eyes; the pillory had a way of imposing guilt on the innocent. But what he really loved was the view from behind. Dana's stooped position forced her to stick out her bottom, whose curves were accentuated by her snug skirt. Nathan squeezed one of the cheeks, feeling the heft of her flesh under the layer of corduroy. Last time they had played the game Dana's way. Today they would play by Nathan's rules.

'If you were a young woman living in the colonies, you wouldn't have enjoyed the kind of sexual freedom that you do now,' Nathan said. 'If your secret desires had come to light, you would have met the same fate as

Hester Prynne, scorned and shunned by the people of your community. It's very likely that you would have had to serve time in one of these pillories, standing on display in the centre of town while your neighbours gathered to stare at you. The villagers would have contributed to your humiliation by calling you names and pegging you with rotten food and stones.'

'I'm grateful that I didn't live back then,' Dana said, with a tremor in her voice. 'People shouldn't be punished for their sexual fantasies.'

'You're right,' Nathan said softly, reaching under Dana's skirt, then delving into the warm, humid nook between her thighs. 'And if I were one of the village's officials, I would have opposed your sentence. I would have offered to punish you myself, in private.'

'What would you have done?'

Nathan pushed his finger into Dana's juicy cleft. When she moaned and widened the spread of her legs, he inserted a second finger.

'I would have taken you out to the town square at midnight, on a night when the moon was full and high. I would have ordered you to undress, then I would have locked you in the pillory, reminding you that whatever punishments I inflicted would be much more merciful than anything the villagers would deliver.'

'I appreciate your mercy, sir,' Dana whispered.

Nathan, who had been stroking Dana's cunt, suddenly stopped. He couldn't believe what he had heard, but he decided to follow her lead.

'You know that you deserve everything I'm about to do to you, don't you?' he asked in a harsh, dictatorial tone.

'Yes. I do.'

'Being the wayward slut that you are, you'll probably enjoy yourself. Keep in mind that you're here to suffer for your sins, not to receive pleasure.'

'Yes, sir.'

Nathan emphasised his point with a swift smack to Dana's behind. Her buttocks quivered. He unzipped her skirt, then eased it down along her thighs and let it fall in a pool around her loafers. She wore white cotton panties printed with tiny blue forget-me-nots. Nathan found the sight of her girlish underwear, stretched thin by the broad dimensions of Dana's ass-cheeks, far more exciting than the most revealing lingerie. Through the cotton he traced the shadowed groove of her crack with his thumb.

'You are being punished for being too generous with your favours, Miss McGillis. Instead of praying to God to release you from your desires, you have cast away your virtue in order to follow your darkest impulses. You have led many innocent men astray, and have set a dismal example to the maidens of the village. You have not heeded the warnings of your mother, your sisters, and the other good women who have tried to save you from your downfall. Instead, you pursued pleasure recklessly, and your pursuits have lead you here to this sorry state.'

Dana chuckled. 'Very convincing, Nathan. You sound just like Cotton Mather.'

'Silence!'

Nathan rewarded Dana's impertinence with a dozen increasingly hard swats. By the time he reached eleven, the smacks were ringing through the room, Dana's cheeks were bright red through the thin cotton, and she was yowling like a wounded cat.

'I usually give women more preparation, but you needed immediate correction. Now, I don't want to hear any more smart remarks, Dana. Do you understand?'

'Yes,' Dana sniffled.

'Good. If you were a woman of the colonies, you could have been subjected to much worse pain than that. People who stood in the pillory were often whipped or beaten. Consider yourself lucky that you're getting away with a spanking.'

Nathan pulled down the cotton panties, leaving them tangled around Dana's thighs, then stood back to enjoy the view of her buttocks. The milky skin was stained bright pink, streaked with a deeper crimson where his fingers had landed. Between the twin moons peeked Dana's labia, protruding like an impudent mouth. Walking stiffly, his cock too swollen for any kind of comfort, Nathan went over to the wall where his spanking implements hung and took down a tawse. The tawse, a strip of leather split into two strips at the end, was perfect for reaching those crevices and cracks that were too narrow for a standard paddle. The tawse was one of the few toys in the barn that Nathan hadn't made himself, but it was one of his favourite implements, and he kept it with the other tools for guests like Dana.

Nathan pushed Dana's legs further apart, then smacked her pouting pussy with the leather thong. A web of silken moisture clung to the pockets of flesh at the very top of her thighs, and Nathan knew that if he continued to spank her, the fiery tongue of the tawse would make her come in no time. But he wanted to give Dana more of a treat, a little positive reinforcement for her venture into submission.

'You've withstood your punishment well, Miss McGillis,' he said, as he knelt behind her, stroking her ass. 'I daresay it will be a long time before you forget the penalties you've suffered today.'

'No, sir. It'll be a cold day in hell before I forget this experience.'

'I'd be remiss in my duties as a village magistrate if I didn't give you one more reminder of the price of easy virtue. Let me show you the kind of treatment that a woman like you really deserves.'

On his knees, Nathan spread Dana's cheeks. The thin white crescents of skin inside her cleft contrasted with the flesh that Nathan had reddened with his palm. Nathan moistened the groove with his tongue, savouring her ripe taste. When he reached the bud of her anus, he replaced his tongue with his finger, which was already moistened with her natural lubricant. His finger slipped easily inside, as Dana pushed backwards in response to the penetration. Her eager groan made him wish he'd tried more anal play when he had her in his bed. He pushed four fingers into her cunt, so that her lower body was planted securely on his hand. As he rotated his wrist, giving her an internal massage, he could feel the knot of her clit against his knuckle. On the other side of the pillory, Dana was crying out her approval. Her muscles clamped down on his fingers as she got close to coming, but he wouldn't let her push him out. When he felt the rippling forewarning of her orgasm, Nathan used his free hand to spank Dana with the tawse. He crisscrossed her bottom with quick, stinging strokes, knowing that the pain would amplify her climax. She came with such intensity that the wooden structure shuddered.

While she recuperated, Nathan rubbed Dana's striped cheeks. Too bad she was a natural dominant; Nathan could happily spend hours spanking that bum of hers. He had rarely met a woman who was so appealing to him on both a physical and an intellectual level. He was dying to fuck the hell out of her, but he didn't want to mount her like a mad dog after she'd submitted to his punishment so agreeably. Instead, he pulled up her panties for her and readjusted her skirt, then got to his feet and unlatched the hinge of the pillory.

'You did a magnificent job,' Dana said, wincing as she massaged her neck. Her cheeks were as red as if she'd just finished a 10K run, and strands of her auburn hair were glued to her forehead. 'When you open your erotic museum, I'll volunteer to perform as the Puritan maid in distress. That pillory is brilliant.'

'I doubt my museum will ever be a reality, but I appreciate the compliment.'

As Dana noticed the denim-covered ridge that rose along Nathan's groin, a sly smile spread across her face. 'I bet you'd appreciate something else even more.'

Dana made a grab for Nathan's fly, and before he knew it, her nimble fingers had freed his aching prick. This time Nathan didn't mind giving up control. He submitted happily to Dana's attentions as she sank to the floor and proceeded to work over the crown of his cock with her lips. Her mouth made lewd, liquid sounds as she sucked, and when she gripped his shaft and stroked him while tonguing at the strand of skin that ran from his head to his shaft, he came into her mouth. The orgasm was long and hard, the spasms brutal in their intensity. He finally looked down to see her wiping her hand across her mouth like a naughty pantry maid who's just swallowed a mouthful of forbidden booze. Her eyes glowed behind the steamed-up lenses of her glasses.

'Lovely,' she said. 'You almost make me want to change my stripes.'

'Only almost?' Nathan asked wistfully, knowing what her answer would be.

7 Pony Training

Except for the *Foghorn* disaster, Melanie's first week in her new home passed smoothly. Melanie gave Ted and Hannah a lot of space, allowing them to carry on with their life as a couple while she set herself up in the carriage house. When she wasn't at work, she spent most of her time redecorating her place, which turned out to be haunted by nothing more than a family of mice. In the evenings she had dinner at the main house with Ted and Hannah and, if she were invited, she joined them in bed. After their first night together, Melanie usually slipped away after they'd made love, braving the cold outside to go back to her own bed. She insisted that she preferred sleeping alone, but Hannah knew that this was a bald-faced lie. A woman like Melanie wouldn't face arctic temperatures after a night of hot sex unless she were trying very hard to respect Hannah's marriage, and Hannah loved her for it.

Hannah couldn't help worrying that such harmony wouldn't last. She still had numbing pangs of jealousy whenever she saw Ted look at Melanie with anything deeper than animal lust in his eyes. It was impossible not to admire Melanie – on top of being gorgeous, she was creative, tenacious, and intelligent. But could Ted admire Melanie without loving her? And if he did fall in love with her, where would that leave Hannah?

As the days passed, and the novelty of Melanie's presence wore off, Hannah's attacks of insecurity subsided. During the work day she found that she couldn't wait to get home; living with Melanie was like having a sister, a girlfriend, and a lover wrapped into one. Her vibrant sensuality charged the air, so that Hannah was in a constant state of arousal, experiencing the world with renewed awareness.

Unfortunately, all the excitement at home was making Hannah useless at work. She spent her days mixing up charts, misplacing the surgical tools, prepping the wrong pets for the wrong procedures. The dogs and cats seemed to forgive her for her mistakes, but her boss wasn't so understanding. All through the week that Melanie moved in, he watched Hannah bungling her way through her tasks with growing impatience. When she almost gave a constipated Pekinese an overdose of laxatives, Dr Heath ordered her into his office and closed the door behind him.

'What's going on, Hannah? You're the best technician I've ever had, but your work has gone to hell,' the veterinarian said, in his usual direct manner.

Speechless with shame, Hannah stared at the surface of the doctor's desk. She had known that her work was suffering, but the disappointment in her boss's voice struck her like a blow to the stomach. But the worst part was that in her state of heightened erotic awareness, Hannah was turned on. She had always thought that Robert Heath was a handsome man. He was the classic strong-but-sensitive type, a man who could turn the most rambunctious stallion into a calm, mountable beast, yet who would stay up all night feeding an abandoned newborn kitten with an eyedropper. Unlike a lot of veterinarians, he was comfortable working with small and large creatures alike, and his knowledge of the animal kingdom seemed unlimited. Hannah was in awe of him, but as she watched his competent hands heal and mend his patients, she had never allowed her feelings to go beyond professional respect.

Now as he confronted her, wearing his white lab coat, with his sturdy arms crossed over his chest, Hannah was feeling a lot more than respect for her employer. Her shame and excitement heightened each other, resulting in a minor flood in the crotch of her jeans.

'I could let you go with a reprimand, Hannah, but I suspect that wouldn't solve the problem. You're going through some major changes in your life, aren't you?'

'Yes,' Hannah gulped. Had the whole town guessed what was going on at the drama teacher's house?

'Don't worry, I won't ask you for details. Suffice it to say that I've seen a difference in you lately. You're acting much more like a self-confident adult, less like a timid girl. You're standing up for yourself, dressing in more flattering clothes. If it weren't for all these mistakes you've been making at the clinic, I'd be damn proud of you, Hannah. You're turning into the woman you were meant to be.'

Hannah's eyes stung. She hoped he would dish out his punishment soon, because if he lavished any more praise on her, she might start crying.

'In my opinion, you're going through some growing pains. That's the only explanation I can think of for these mistakes you've been making. But these errors of yours are getting serious, Hannah. I can't have you endangering the animals' health.'

'No, sir,' Hannah whispered. 'What can I do to make up for it?'

Dr Heath stroked his chin with his forefinger. He had a strong, clearly etched jawline that reminded Hannah of an actor from one of those old Western movies – the kind where men were known to turn women over their knee and spank them. Back on the wild frontier, the rules of political correctness didn't apply.

'Well, I want to steer you in the right direction without

breaking your spirit, and I think I've found the solution. Tomorrow, instead of coming to the clinic, I want you to meet me at my house at five o'clock.'

'In the morning?' Hannah asked. Early morning was the time she and Ted usually enjoyed a cozy round of sex, just the two of them, while Melanie was getting her beauty sleep in the carriage house.

'That's right – five a.m. I want to get started well before the sun comes up. As soon as we're done here, I want you to reschedule my morning appointments. I've asked a student from the veterinary college to come in and cover any emergencies.'

'You've gone to a lot of trouble just for me.'

'It's very important that I set you on the right course.' Dr Heath looked at her over his glasses. 'As much as I'd hate to let you go, I'll have to do that if you keep making mistakes that put our patients at risk.'

'I understand,' Hannah said.

She was shaking when she left the doctor's office. How could she let herself lapse that way, doing so poorly at a job she loved? He would probably make her muck out his stable and feed his nasty chickens, but she would endure anything to keep her job.

Except for her doubts about the next morning, Hannah had no trouble focusing on her work that day. Dr Heath's warning had left her so sober that she didn't even crack a smile at the antics of Mabel Butterworth's West Highland terrier, who usually made her laugh like a maniac. That evening she stayed late to file all of the day's paperwork and give the exam room a second cleaning. Dr Heath didn't comment on her extra effort, but she saw a glimmer of approval in his eyes as he wished her good night and reminded her not to be late for their meeting. By the time she got home, she felt that she'd gotten a step closer to redeeming herself, but she knew that she still deserved to be punished.

'I think Dr Heath is going to do something terrible to me tomorrow,' she announced to Melanie and Ted, who were in the midst of preparing dinner. Melanie was tossing balsamic vinegar into a bowlful of greens, and Ted was stirring a pot of oregano-laced marinara sauce. The low strains of a Bach cello suite drifted from the stereo in the library. The calm domesticity of the scene soothed Hannah's spirit. She felt a twinge of possessiveness when she noticed that Melanie was wearing the apron that Ted had given Hannah the week after they got married, but she chalked that up to the insecurity that she'd been feeling ever since Dr Heath reprimanded her.

'Something terrible? Tell us more,' Melanie said. She gave Hannah a hug and a kiss and handed her a glass of merlot.

'I'd better not drink anything tonight,' Hannah said, although she would have loved nothing more than to down a whole bottle of wine after a day like today. 'I have to meet him out at his farm tomorrow at five.'

'At five in the morning? That alone is cruel and unusual punishment. Especially for me.' The lenses of Ted's glasses were fogged by steam from the pot, but Hannah could see the concern in his blue eyes. His reference to their early morning lovemaking reassured her that she was still the love of his life, even if he let another woman wear her apron.

'I deserve it. I've been slacking off at work,' Hannah admitted, sitting down at the rustic pine table. 'At first it was only a matter of misfiling charts, but yesterday I almost made a serious medication error. I deserve whatever he does to me. If anything had happened to that dog, I'd never have forgiven myself.'

'Poor baby.' Melanie perched on the bench beside Hannah and smoothed her hair away from her forehead. 'It's not your fault. You've had to make some big adjustments here at home. Dr Heath should be more understanding.'

'Oh, I'm sure he'd be completely sympathetic if he knew you were sharing your husband with another woman,' Ted said wryly. 'Maybe I should call him up and explain.'

'Then he'd want to steal your secrets,' Melanie said. 'Look, Hannah, you don't have to tell your boss anything. Just let him know that you've had some serious changes going on in your life.'

'He already knows that, and he does understand. But he wants to make sure I don't let my job slide as a result. He's right, you know.'

'Then you'll just have to take your medicine like a big girl. Hopefully it'll be a good, stiff dose,' Melanie said with a wink.

Ted frowned. 'Whatever he does, it had better not involve any sexual favours.'

Hannah felt a surge of defiance. 'Why shouldn't I give my favours to a good-looking man? We do have an open marriage.'

'And Robert Heath *is* quite attractive,' Melanie said. 'He's got those marvellous dark eyes and that glossy black hair, and he looks like he's always thinking about something noble. Reminds me of Gregory Peck in *To Kill a Mockingbird*.'

'I've always loved him in that movie,' Hannah sighed.

'And there's something about a man who's good with animals ... makes you wonder what he's like with humans. Why do you think he isn't married? He's probably got some totally deviant sexual fantasy that he can't share with anyone, and he's been waiting for years for the right woman to come along so he can live it out.'

'Well, he's not living it out with Hannah,' Ted broke in.

'Why not?' demanded the women in unison.

'I'm not going to have my wife subjected to any sexual harassment from her boss.'

'It's only harassment if she doesn't want to do it,' Melanie argued.

'Listen, you two.' Hannah stood up and slapped her palms down on the table. 'This is all beside the point. I'm not meeting Dr Heath for sex tomorrow morning. I'm meeting him because I screwed up at work, and he's going to set me back on track.'

'Hmmm.' Melanie smiled knowingly, swung her legs off the bench and went back to her salad.

'I want to hear a full report tomorrow.'

'You will,' Hannah assured her husband.

Ted gave a noncommittal grunt and poured himself another glass of wine. Hannah sat down again and began to chew at the remains of her fingernails, which she had bitten to the quick during the course of the day. Dr Heath was an exacting, demanding man, a professional who held himself and his staff to the most rigorous standards. Whatever he had in store for Hannah was bound to be one of the most difficult tests she had ever faced.

Hannah didn't sleep well that night, and by four in the morning she was dressed and ready to go. A swarm of bees seemed to have taken up residence in her belly, attacking the lining of her stomach; she couldn't swallow so much as a drop of coffee. By the time she pulled her pick-up truck into the gravel lot outside of Robert Heath's house, she was a nervous wreck.

The vet's house was a neat white saltbox tucked inside a semicircle of tall pines. It was true that the darkest hour was just before dawn, Hannah thought as she approached the place, her boots crunching on the frosted grass. Except for a golden square of light at the back of the house, the entire property was sunk in frigid blue darkness. She felt as if she were entering a world that had fallen under some northern wizard's spell.

The front door swung open, and light spilled onto the yard.

'Hannah! I didn't expect you so early.'

Dr Heath's calm, approving voice made the bees in Hannah's stomach settle down to a mild buzz. Maybe she could do this after all, she thought, as she stepped into Dr Heath's house. As soon as she walked through the door, the fragrance of freshly ground coffee, hickory smoked bacon and maple syrup greeted her nostrils.

'We'll start with a good breakfast. You'll need your energy,' Dr Heath said. He pulled out a chair from the kitchen table and motioned for Hannah to sit down.

'I'm afraid I'm not very hungry.'

'Hannah,' said the doctor, in a tone that allowed no resistance, 'you are going to follow every one of my instructions this morning. Now I want you to relax, sit down, and eat.'

She complied, wondering how she was going to swallow anything. But as soon as he set the steaming plate of pancakes, bacon and eggs in front of her, Hannah succumbed to her instincts and dug in. Dr Heath sat across the table from her, cutting his food with surgical precision. A muscle in his jaw worked neatly as he chewed. The intimacy of the setting and the quiet darkness of the morning made Hannah feel much more at ease; in fact, from the mounting tightness between her thighs, she realised that she was starting to look forward to the morning's activities. Surely if he were going to torture her, the doctor wouldn't start the session by stuffing her with pancakes.

Or would he?

'First, you'll wash the breakfast dishes while I go outside and get things ready,' Dr Heath said, as soon as they had finished eating. 'When you're done, I want you to come outside and meet me in the stable.'

He pulled on his black parka, the one that Hannah had

seen him wearing a hundred times on their visits to local farms, and stepped outside into the pre-dawn gloom. In his well-organised bachelor's kitchen, Hannah easily located everything she needed to wash and dry his dishes. She hurried through the chore as fast as she could, her body tingling with anticipation. When she stepped outside, the light that rimmed the doors of the large Quonset hut where the doctor kept his horses guided her across the yard. Hannah opened the heavy sliding door and stepped inside.

She had never been inside Dr Heath's stables, and the sight stopped her short. The stalls, which housed two mares and a gelding, were set up at the back of the structure. Strategically placed floodlights shone brightly, their beams crisscrossing a wide central arena. An oval running track ran the circumference of the interior. Hannah knew that her boss was an avid runner who had competed on his college track team years ago, but she had never known that he'd taken his enthusiasm this far.

Dr Heath stepped out of one of the stalls. An assortment of tack was draped across his arms. The metal hoops jingled as he approached.

'What do you think about this place?' he asked. A smile of boyish pleasure illuminated his handsome features. 'I have to admit, this is my pride and joy. I've invested a ridiculous amount of money in this project. It's a damn good thing I'm not married, because any reasonable woman would divorce me and have me committed.'

'I never knew you were so passionate about running.'

'Running is only one of my passions.'

'What are the others?'

'You'll soon find out,' he said. 'Come over to the stalls. I'm going to get you ready, then you'll see what this track was really made for.'

Hannah followed Dr Heath over to the stalls, where the horses were contentedly munching their morning grain. The horses occupied three of the stalls, but the fourth was empty. The floor was carpeted with fresh straw, and a small wooden platform stood in the middle.

'Take off your clothes,' Dr Heath instructed, 'then step up on the platform. Go on, Hannah. We don't have all day.'

The veterinarian issued his orders in a sharp, no-nonsense tone that was more exciting to Hannah than the most seductive persuasion. A space heater in the corner of the stall kept Hannah warm as she stripped off her jacket, boots, jeans and sweater. Dr Heath stopped her before she could strip off her socks.

'Keep those on. You'll need them when you wear these.'

Hannah gasped. He was holding out a pair of boots made of white butter-soft leather and laced from toe to knee with golden thread. The boots had athletic soles with metal taps, and the toes were adorned with gold pompoms. Hannah had never seen anything like those boots; they might have been crafted in a twisted fairy tale.

'Go ahead. Try them on.'

'I don't think they'll fit,' Hannah fretted. 'I have such big feet.'

'I know your shoe size, Hannah. Trust me; these will fit perfectly.'

Hannah took the boots and sat down on the platform. Dr Heath was right; they slipped onto her feet as easily as if they'd been made just for her. With intense concentration, he laced the boots for her, and when he was done, her legs looked like the limbs of a fine, strong horse. As soon as she stood up, she had the urge to prance around the stall. When she walked, the taps click-clacked on the concrete floor.

'Very good. Now, step up onto the platform and take those braids out of your hair.'

Hannah loosened her braids and combed out her hair with her fingers.

'Beautiful,' Dr Heath said. 'You have hair like hammered copper. I've always wondered what it would look like hanging down.'

'Thanks, but the ends need to be trimmed.'

'Hannah, you need to learn how to accept praise graciously. Your hair is gorgeous. And your pubic hair is only a few shades darker. Grooming you is going to be a real pleasure.'

The doctor's frank admiration gave Hannah an attack of self-consciousness. The reality of her nakedness hit her like a speeding truck, and she felt her body go hot in a head-to-toe blush. Dr Heath excused himself for a moment, then returned holding an assortment of brushes. While Hannah stood there on the platform, he brushed out her hair, using the long, slow strokes that he used on his cherished horses. Since she had to submit to the veterinarian's attentions, Hannah decided that she might as well enjoy herself. She closed her eyes and pretended that she was his pet pony, well-fed and happy, enjoying a good grooming. Before long, her scalp was tingling from the mesmerising brush strokes, and her body was humming with contentment.

Once her hair was silken-smooth and crackling with static, Dr Heath picked up an oval currying brush and turned his attention to the fur between Hannah's legs. The brush made small, light circles around her pubic mound, until her bush was a puff of copper curls. He whisked the strands into a feathery shape, then put down the brush.

'Widen your stance,' he ordered, slapping her rump. 'I need to reach between.'

Using a thin, stainless-steel comb, Dr Heath untangled the strands on Hannah's lips. When she flinched at the chill of the metal, he calmed her by rubbing the back of her thigh. That rubbing turned into a lower-body massage, his fingers kneading the tense muscles of her hamstrings and buttocks. Though his touch was sensual, even erotic, his face never lost its look of professional attention. Hannah wondered if he were as turned on as she was, or if this activity was as routine to him as the medical tasks he performed every day. When he began to press the soft inner flesh of her thighs with his thumbs, Hannah almost lost her head. Was this whole morning going to be one long tease?

'That's enough,' he said. 'Now for the next step.'

He reached into the shadows and presented Hannah with something so fabulous and strange that she cried out in surprise. The headdress consisted of a white leather mask with a pair of large eyeholes and a chin strap. Like the boots, its seams were stitched with gold thread, and a triangle of gold sequins adorned the place that would cover Hannah's forehead. Most spectacular of all was the proud white plume that rose in feathery splendour from the top of the headdress. As if that weren't enough, he had also produced a belt rigged with a flowing synthetic tail that matched the white purity of the plume.

'Welcome to my fantasy, Hannah.'

Dr Heath placed the headdress on Hannah's head and secured the strap under her chin. Then he helped Hannah step into the belt, which had a strap that ran from her waist down to her crotch, fastening in the back. He tightened the belt so that the crotch piece fit snugly against her cuntlips, then buckled it at the small of her back, just below the tail.

'Well, what do you think?'

'I never dreamed you were going to turn me into a circus pony.'

'I don't know about the circus part, but you'll certainly be my pony.'

Are you going to ride me? Hannah wondered, but she

didn't dare to ask. She wasn't sure if she liked this part of Dr Heath's game. The plume of the headdress, though it looked like a spray of foamy water, was astonishingly heavy, and she had to keep her head and backbone unnaturally straight just to prevent it from toppling over. The costume made her feel like a Las Vegas showgirl, and the belt with the tail was something straight out of a pervert's wet dream.

'How do you like your new identity?'

'Well,' she hesitated, 'do you want the truth?'

'Nothing less.'

'I feel like a big, naked fool with a silly feather on her head and a fake tail sticking out of her bum.'

'That's because you haven't submitted to the experience. I'm trying to help you regain your focus, Hannah. What I want you to focus on now is being a pony. You're not a woman, you're not my employee – you are a beautiful pony who is being trained and disciplined. Would a pony think of herself as a fool because she was dressed up to please her master?'

'No.'

'Of course not. A pony doesn't have a complex self-image to maintain. Her goal is to do her master's will and obtain a reward. A pony would be proud to wear a magnificent headdress like that.'

Dr Heath held out his hand. On his palm rested a small, perfect apple, its skin streaked with hues of pale green, pink, and red. Hannah imagined her teeth sinking into the fruit's crisp white flesh, its tart juices trickling down her lips, and her mouth began to water.

'You want this apple, don't you?'

'Yes.'

'You want it so much you can taste it. But you have to please me first. You're going to spend the morning performing, and if you succeed, you'll have a treat. Now I want you to warm up. Stretch your hamstrings, your quads, and your calves, as if you were getting ready for a jog. Meet me outside at the arena when you're finished.'

Then he left the stall. Hannah did her best to follow the veterinarian's instructions. It had been months since she had done any serious exercise, except for the chores she did at work and around the house. She bent over and attempted to touch the gold pompoms on the toes of her boots, then straightened up and raised her legs one after the other in a slow-motion prance. With the boots on, the movement felt like a natural extension of her pony identity. She could see herself high-stepping around the doctor's track, and when she left the stall, she realised that she was going to be doing just that.

Dr Heath stood in the arena, loading a cart with firewood. The wooden cart was charming, painted shiny red and stencilled with Pennsylvania Dutch designs of hearts and doves. He called Hannah to join him. She stood straight, tall and obedient while he hitched her to the cart, using two metal D-loops around her belt to harness her.

'All right, now you'll start slowly. Lift each leg to about the height of your crotch, making the shape of an upside-down 'L'. You'll march around the track, pulling the cart behind you. I don't want you to rush at first; we're just getting you warmed up. But don't slack off, or you'll get a taste of this.'

Dr Heath flicked the backs of Hannah's thighs with a long, flexible switch. The switch had a bite to it, making Hannah bolt down the track. The cart tipped over and spilled its load of wood on the floor.

'I'm disappointed in my pony.' As he knelt down to rearrange the cart, Hannah saw that his handsome face was dark with displeasure. She hung her head. The plume drooped.

'I'm sorry. Please don't punish me.'

'I understand why you're skittish, but I'm afraid you

have to be punished, anyway. Otherwise your training won't be effective.'

Hannah squeezed her eyes shut and waited for the cutting bite of the switch. Instead, Dr Heath lifted her tail and gave her bottom fifteen swats with his hand. When he was done, he reached between her legs and toyed with her labia, arranging the folds so that they fitted neatly around the crotch strap.

'Your cunt is wet. I think you may be enjoying yourself too much. Let's step it up a bit. I want you to trot around the track six times. Keep your chin up, and lift your knees as high as you can. Go.'

Hannah set off at a brisk pace. It took a few minutes to get used to pulling the cart, but as soon as she picked up some momentum, its rubber wheels ran smoothly behind her. At first it was easy to maintain her showy gait. Once she adjusted her steps to balance the weight of the long tail with the heavy headdress, she found herself strutting along without much difficulty, her bare breasts bobbing, plume and tail waving. But after her fourth or fifth lap, her thighs started to burn, her ankles began to ache, and she could feel the headdress wobbling. Her heavy breasts, slick with sweat, felt tender and sore as they swung back and forth. The crotch piece of her belt was chafing her, and though she couldn't see her tail, she knew it had to be sinking as she slowed her pace.

'Keep it up,' Dr Heath shouted, jogging along beside her. 'Don't stop. Chin and shoulders *up*! You'll do another six laps.'

'I can't,' Hannah moaned.

'Yes, you can. Focus on each step as if it were the only thing you have to do all day, and try to execute it perfectly.'

The switch swished against Hannah's thighs. She picked up her pace again, forcing herself to think about her posture, even though her mind was filled with images of cool glasses of water and fresh, clean towels. Her scalp itched and sweltered under the headdress. Were horses this miserable in their bridles and harnesses? If this was how those poor beasts felt, Hannah swore that she would never go riding again. She knew that she must have circled the track a hundred times, but whenever she turned to look at Dr Heath through the eyeholes of the white leather mask, he showed no sign of relenting. She realised that she had been incompetent at work, but why couldn't he have simply demanded that she clean up her act and give him a blow job? If only he would let her stop, she would be a model employee ... the very best ... if only he would let her stop ...

Finally, when Hannah had decided that she would rather drop dead from exhaustion than play a Lippizaner show horse for one more second, Dr Heath stopped her with a sharp whistle.

'Very good. A fine performance,' he applauded. 'I've never seen a pony adapt so quickly to a cart. You're a natural.'

Hannah groaned in relief when he unhitched her from the cart and unbuckled her belt. Then the elaborate headstall came off, and the boots, and Hannah was herself again – hot, sweaty and thoroughly corrected. Dr Heath draped a light blanket across her shoulders to cover her naked body and absorb some of the sweat that was streaming down her skin. Then he folded his arms across his chest and fixed her with a severe look that made her even hotter.

'What have you learned this morning, Hannah?'

'How to stay focused,' she panted. 'I won't be making any more mistakes at the clinic. You can count on that.'

'I'm sure your performance will improve a hundred per cent. But we have a few more things to do before we go to the clinic today.'

'Like what?' Hannah asked in dread.

The veterinarian's steely, authoritarian glare melted into a smile, and Hannah saw once again how good-looking he was. 'First, I'll give you a good rubdown. After that, it's up to you.'

Hannah helped him carry the pony paraphernalia into the stall. She felt a twinge of regret as he put away the headdress, boots and tail. Now that she was herself again, she missed her animal identity. As uncomfortable as it was, the pony get-up had made her feel sexy. Horny, too. When Dr Heath removed the blanket and began to rub her skin with a terrycloth towel, the arousal that Hannah had been suppressing all morning came flooding through her body. Just because she wasn't wearing a fancy costume didn't mean she wasn't an animal at heart. As the veterinarian wiped her down with brisk, sure motions, Hannah made soft nickering noises. When he pushed the towel between her legs, she moved her hips to meet his hands, urging him to rub harder. But the doctor's movements remained strictly professional as he abandoned her mound and began swabbing her thighs and calves.

'There,' he said, giving her a smack on the rump. 'Now you can put your clothes on and go back to the house. I've got a big old clawfoot tub in my upstairs bathroom; you can take a nice long soak and loosen up those muscles.'

'For God's sake, I don't want a bath,' Hannah cried. Here she was, standing around with her nipples erect, her pussy throbbing, and her skin humming all over from the abrasion of the nubbly cloth, and all he had in mind was a bath?

'Don't worry. I know exactly what you need.' Dr Heath lifted the damp ropes of hair off her shoulders. His breathing grew unsteady as he touched her breasts, then tugged at her nipples. 'I'm a doctor, and I know how to treat my animals.'

He took Hannah in his arms and ground his pelvis

against hers. She groaned when she felt the long hillock of flesh that rose through his jeans, but as soon as she made a grab for his belt buckle, he caught her hands and lifted them away from his crotch.

'Let me touch your cock,' she begged. 'Let me at least see it.'

'Not yet. You've done enough work for the morning. I always make sure that my pets are well rewarded for their efforts before I take any pleasure for myself.'

He spread the blanket out on the straw-covered floor of the stall and told Hannah to lie down. The floor felt as cold as a stone slab, and pieces of straw poked her through the thin blanket, but Hannah forgot all about those sensations when the veterinarian straddled her, securing her body between his lean thighs, and began to massage her breasts. As he kneaded the handfuls of flesh, Hannah closed her eyes and remembered all the times she had observed Dr Heath performing intricate procedures with those long fingers, or watched him soothing a frightened animal. Because he was her boss, she had never let herself get excited when she watched him work, but the truth was, Hannah had always wished he would use that gentle expertise on herself.

'Your tits are magnificent,' he said.

His voice was strained, but still controlled. Hannah couldn't do anything but moan in response. He moved lower, his fingertips dancing down her torso and palpating her belly. While he worked her over, he breathed deeply and steadily. This was the way the doctor breathed when he was concentrating on an examination, only now Hannah was the animal being examined. That thought made her so aroused that she spread her legs as wide as she could and lifted her ass, pumping her hips up and down in an invitation for him to touch her pussy. He did so, expertly parting her labia so that he could slide his forefinger into her hole. She felt wild and lewd, with her cunt splayed out in front of her boss like a bitch in heat. Meanwhile, Dr Heath remained as calm as ever, except for a slight acceleration of his breathing. Wouldn't he ever just let go and start rutting?

Hannah couldn't wait any longer. When the doctor hooked his finger around the curve of her pubic bone and tickled the sweet, spongy spot behind, it was too much for her to take. She squirmed out from underneath him, rolled over on her stomach, and raised her rump in such a way that he'd have to be a eunuch not to see what she wanted. Making animal noises, she arched her back and parted her legs so that the glistening fruit between them was practically in his face.

'All right, Hannah. I've been trying to hold back, but you're not giving me much choice. I'm going to have to fuck you.'

She looked back over her shoulder and watched him fumbling with his belt buckle and zipper. He was so eager that his hands were shaking as he pulled his erect cock out of his pants and sheathed it with a condom. If Hannah had had any doubts about whether he wanted her, they vanished when she saw his turgid member jutting out from his pelvis, and the beads of perspiration sparkling on his dark pubic hair.

'This is what you've been waiting for, isn't it, my hot little bitch?' he asked, sliding into her with a grunt. Her skin was so slick that his hands could hardly gain any purchase on her hips, but once he was securely inside her, he had no problem thrusting in and out of her seeping channel. The doctor and Hannah were only inches off the floor, with just enough room for him to lean forwards and grip her breasts. The stall filled with guttural moans and grunts. Hannah's knees ached from the pressure of the doctor's body, her hair flopped in her face, and her palms hurt from the straw and specks of dirt and gravel that were digging into her hands, but in spite of all that, she was delirious with pleasure. Then Dr Heath bit her neck, heightening her excitement to such a pitch that she came. It was a primal orgasm, a series of blunt spasms that took her breath away. She heard the doctor making bestial sounds, and she knew that he was coming, too.

After they recovered for a moment, he eased her onto her side and wrapped his body around her, spoonlike. He plucked away the strands of hair that were plastered to her damp cheeks and murmured comforting nonsense into her ear. She had never felt so thoroughly spent; every muscle in her body had been used to the fullest.

'You don't have to go back to work today,' the doctor said, running his hand along her heaving ribs. 'You can go upstairs and spend the day resting in my bed. I'll call the clinic and have one of the students fill in for you this afternoon.'

'No. I'll go in with you. I don't want to let you down again.'

Dr Heath chuckled. 'Believe me, Hannah, you won't let me down. You've made me so happy this morning that giving you a day off is the least I can do to show my gratitude.'

'Actually, there's something else,' Hannah said, after a moment's thought.

'What's that?'

'Don't let anyone else wear the pony costume that I wore today. I want that one to be mine.'

Dr Heath was silent for such a long time that Hannah was afraid she had pushed him too far with her request.

'You don't have to worry about that. I probably shouldn't tell you this, but that costume was custom-made for you, Hannah. No other woman will ever wear it.'

'Are you serious? You had that headdress and those boots made for me?'

Hannah was so shocked that she could hardly get the words out. She couldn't believe that such a composed, serious professional had had such a long-standing obsession, especially about *her*. She didn't know whether she ought to feel supremely flattered or afraid for her safety. Dr Heath didn't seem like a psycho, especially when he was making her come like a ton of bricks, but it was always those quiet types who fooled you.

'And the belt with the tail, and the red cart,' he continued. 'All for you. The first time I saw you, I pictured you as a pony girl. You're the perfect size and shape for pulling a cart, and with those long legs and that glorious mane of hair, I knew you'd be the living image of my fantasy.'

'But how did you know I'd ever wear those things? They must have cost a fortune,' Hannah sputtered. She sat up and clutched at the blanket, suddenly nervous about being naked. 'What do you want from me in return?'

'Relax, darling.' Dr Heath laughed and patted her thigh. 'You've already given me what I wanted – and much more. You can wear the pony costume again, if you want, or you can pretend that it never existed. I'd even destroy it for you, if that's what you want. Believe me, you have nothing to be afraid of.'

The doctor's glasses had come off during their bout of bestial sex, and his black hair fell into his smouldering brown eyes in a way that made him look as compelling as any movie star Hannah had ever seen. Hannah found it hard to believe that he was a psycho. A pervert, yes, but some of her best friends (not to mention her husband, her new lover, and herself) were perverts.

'Don't you dare destroy that costume,' she said. 'I'm not afraid of you, Robert.'

Then Hannah helped him clean up and remove all his clothes, so that she could give his body a thorough inspection. Robert Heath had a sinewy athlete's build, and for the next hour Hannah gave him a work-out worthy of what he had given her. Years of running marathons – and living by himself without a regular sex partner – had given him more stamina than any man she'd ever been with. The women of Morne Bay, who thought of the veterinarian as an aloof, reclusive bachelor, had no idea what they were missing.

Though she knew she was being greedy, Hannah decided to keep that secret to herself.

8 Bad Girl Backlash

Chimera wouldn't open for another two hours, but the few pedestrians who walked down Harbor Street on Saturday morning were treated to the sight of some extraordinary activity behind the snowy storefront window. Melanie was directing a crew that consisted of Hannah, Pagan, Luna, and a gang of the girls' Goth friends who were staunch supporters of the shop. Melanie had made sure that the Goths, who were unaccustomed to seeing the dawn, were fuelled by enough black coffee and bagels to keep a gang of teamsters going. Everything had to be ready by nine o'clock, when the doors opened on the soon-to-be-expanded Chimera.

'All right, everyone – listen to me.' Melanie waved her arms, and the chatter ceased. 'As you already know, managing Chimera isn't just a job to me. It's my life. I've tried to make this shop a secure, attractive setting where my customers could feel good about buying sexy clothes and toys. Apparently certain residents of this town, who happen to have more power than they deserve, don't agree that shopping for sexy clothes and toys should be a positive, public experience. They'd rather have all of us squirrelled away in our bedrooms, buying things off the Internet and having them delivered in anonymous packaging.'

'Internet shopping isn't such a bad thing, is it?' Pagan asked, through a mouthful of bagel.

Melanie glared at her. 'No, of course not. In fact, that's how I purchase most of the inventory. But I want to offer the locals an alternative. I want to take this shop a step further than it's ever been. That's why you're all here today. By the time we open, this place isn't going to be a boutique; it's going to be a microculture. There will be music playing on a stereo system that we're going to install – let's have something lush and seductive, like Theatre of Tragedy. Pagan, who is a budding erotic artist, is going to hang her paintings on the walls. And Luna has agreed to sell some of the clothes she designed herself. So in addition to offering the finest sensual clothing from the past and present, we'll be featuring the artists and designers of the future as well. If the members of the town council want to shop at some sanitised mega-department store, that's their choice, but for those who have a sense of adventure, a hunger for something different, we'll be here to welcome them into our world.'

The crowd burst into cheers and ragged applause. Melanie scanned the room. She hadn't been able to reach Nathan all week. Finally she had left a message on his answering machine, asking him to join the group this morning. She had hoped that he would go through the house with her to propose his suggestions on remodelling, but after her outburst last Sunday, he had probably decided that she wasn't worth the trouble.

Nathan Wentworth didn't matter, Melanie decided, assessing the crowd. Out of the twenty-odd people who were gathered here today, fewer than ten had been invited. The others had arrived via word of mouth, wanting to be part of the counterculture that Melanie was creating. If she'd thrown this shindig at midnight, when these thrift-store vampires were at their best, the shop would be packed.

'OK, let's get to work,' Melanie said. 'Anyone who's electronically inclined can hook up the stereo. Pagan will need three or four of you to help her hang her paintings. A couple of you can post the signs in the window announcing that we're expanding, and if someone's feeling especially horny this morning, you're welcome to set up a display using as many of the sex toys as you possibly can. Our mannequins love to pose with the merchandise, so let your imagination run wild.'

'What do you want me to do?' Hannah asked. 'I'm afraid I'm not very creative.'

'Keep the coffee circulating. The Goths look like they're ready to slink back to bed. I think it has something to do with the threat of work.'

'The mere fact that they showed up is a miracle. Where should I put this stuff?'

Melanie jumped at the sound of a familiar voice. Nathan Wentworth stood behind her, holding a large cardboard box.

'I didn't think you'd come,' she said, trying not to broadcast her happiness at seeing him.

'I figured it wouldn't hurt to have a grown man on the premises if you had to lift anything heavy. Some of these kids look distinctly undernourished.'

'They work very hard to achieve that stylish pallor, so don't belittle them. Besides, they were here when I opened the doors this morning. That's more than I can say for you.'

'Believe me, I was up earlier than these kids. I had to do my morning chores, then load up the truck.' Nathan tilted the box so that Melanie could see its contents. 'I brought every paddle I've made in the past three years, plus the custom furniture. I hope you have a spare room.'

'A *room*? You can have half the house, if you want it.' Melanie jumped up and down, no longer bothering to hide her happiness. Nathan's toys were exactly what she wanted to offer the community: custom-made, impeccably crafted products of the local culture. The fact that he was willing to risk his reputation by offering them for sale at her shop touched her more than she could say. She threw her arms around him – as far as she could, considering that he was holding an unwieldy box – and gave him a long, deep French kiss. She wasn't aware that her crew was watching until she let him go, and everyone hooted in admiration.

Everyone except Hannah. When Melanie called her over to see the box of toys, she saw a strange expression on her friend's face, a look of pained confusion that Hannah quickly masked with a smile. To all outward appearances, Hannah seemed pleased with the custom-made wooden paddles and leather tawses, but Melanie saw her hands shaking as she held the items.

Oh, shit. Now I've done it, she thought. She felt like crawling under a counter. She should have told Hannah that she and Nathan had something going, but she wasn't sure what that 'something' was. On the other hand, did she really owe Hannah an explanation? Just because Hannah had a crush on Nathan didn't mean she owned him. Hannah was married to an incredibly sexy man, and she worked for a gorgeous veterinarian who starred in the fantasies of every pet-owning woman in town. Hannah had had her fun with Nathan, and with Melanie, and undoubtedly with many others. For God's sake, Melanie thought, her guilt turning into anger, Hannah was the last person on earth who had a right to be jealous.

But jealousy wasn't an emotion that played fair. Jealousy was notorious for demanding more than its due. As she watched Hannah, Melanie could tell that her friend was struggling with a demon. Within the span of fifteen seconds, a dozen conflicting emotions displayed themselves on Hannah's face.

'Listen, Hannah,' Melanie said, putting her hand on her friend's arm, 'can we go upstairs and talk?'

Hannah shook her head. 'I don't think so,' she said in a choked voice.

'Hannah, you're being childish,' Nathan said. 'Let's all go upstairs and sort this out.'

'No.' Hannah flung her arm back, jerking away from Melanie's touch. 'I have to go.'

'What are you talking about?' Melanie cried. 'You're staying right here until we settle this.'

'There's nothing to settle. Everything's fine. It's just that I have to work today.' Hannah wiped her nose with her sleeve and gave a shrill, false laugh. 'Stupid me – I forgot all about it.'

Hannah hurried out of the shop, her head hanging between her shoulders, hair swinging down to hide her face.

'Was that what I think it was?' Nathan asked Melanie.

'I'm afraid so.'

The crew, which had grown quiet while everyone watched the scene unfold, returned to their tasks with renewed concentration.

'This is my fault. I misjudged her feelings,' Nathan said. 'Hannah made it clear to me that she had an open marriage. When she came over to my house that morning, I assumed that she wanted some casual play. I had no idea that it was anything more than that.'

'Neither did I,' Melanie sighed. 'And apparently neither did she. I should have told her about us days ago, so she'd have some time to digest it. Do you think I should go after her?'

'No. You need to be at the shop this morning, and Hannah needs time alone to think about the way she behaved.'

'But she was so upset –'

'Listen.' Nathan held Melanie's arm. 'Hannah's a grown woman. She chose a lifestyle that requires a great deal of self-knowledge and maturity. If Hannah is going to continue to have multiple partners, she'll have to learn how to handle those feelings of jealousy and possessiveness. You can't go running after her to console her whenever she acts like that. Let her come to you, after she's had some time to cool down. Now, let's get to work.'

The next hour of preparation passed quickly, although the crowd's festive spirit was dampened by Hannah's departure. Melanie gave Nathan a tour of the house, and he took notes on the building's structure, noting the locations of its supporting beams. At eight-thirty, a caterer stopped by to set up a buffet of pastries, crêpes, fruit, and coffee that would be served to the morning customers. Nathan unloaded the spanking furniture from his truck and arranged it outside of the Alcove. The place was starting to take shape, looking exactly the way Melanie had dreamed. Minutes before the shop was to open, a florist came by to deliver lavish bouquets of exotic flowers: birds of paradise, rare purple tulips, and orchids, all grown in some hothouse far from the cold climate of Morne Bay.

'What's all this?' Melanie cried, in a fit of delight and panic. 'I didn't order flowers. These are going to cost a fortune!'

'They did cost a fortune,' Nathan grinned.

'You mean you bought them? But you're so ... uh, thrifty,' Melanie said.

'I may be thrifty, but I'm not cheap, if that's what you meant to say. The flowers were an investment in my future. This is a big day for me – my debut as a retail seller.'

'Are you sure you want to stay around for the opening?' Melanie asked. 'I'm grateful for your support, but you don't have to face the firing squad with me.'

'Frankly,' said Nathan, 'I'm looking forward to it. This town is too small for me to hide who I am. I could do it when I worked in Boston, but not in Morne Bay. People are going to find out about my hobbies. At least this way, it won't be a nasty little secret that's uncovered by a nosy neighbour. I believe in what you're doing here, Melanie. I want to be part of it.'

'I noticed that you didn't bring the spanking horse that you built for me.'

'Of course not. I'd never sell that. It's in storage.'

'In *storage*?' Melanie shrieked. 'Will I ever get to use that thing, or is it going to gather dust for the next fifty years?'

'I'm sure it won't take fifty years for you to earn a good spanking,' Nathan laughed. 'But you're going to have to be patient. In the meantime, you've got plenty to keep you busy.'

He nodded towards the door, where a cluster of shoppers had already gathered, waiting for the door to be unlocked. Melanie's heart swelled with pride as she surveyed the shop. Chafing dishes filled with breakfast delicacies steamed on a table draped with snowy-white linen. The smells of the pastries and coffee mingled with the scent of the flowers and the sensual strains of the Gothic music. Pagan's paintings, voluptuous women arranged on canvases splashed with colour, reminded her of Gauguin's nudes. The dresses that Luna had designed, creations of lace and velvet and leather, stood proudly next to the graceful vintage gowns that had been worn by women over a hundred years ago. In the Alcove, the toys shimmered like an array of gems. The place was a temple of sensuality – predominantly feminine, but with masculine touches in the leather and wood, and the jaunty vibrators and dildos.

'I don't think I've ever been so happy,' Melanie said, watching the customers surge through the door, their faces alight with wonder as they saw the banquet of delights spread out before them.

Then her gaze turned to the window, and her mood fell like a bird shot out of the sky. She had been so entranced by her own vision that she hadn't looked beyond the storefront to see what was going on in the street. Amassed on the sidewalk was another crowd, one with an entirely different purpose. Melanie couldn't mistake that purpose: it was written in enormous, angry print on the picket signs that they held high above their heads.

NO SEX FOR SALE! DECENT SHOPS FOR DECENT PEOPLE! SAVE OUR CHILDREN! SAVE OUR TOWN!

One poor fellow, who seemed to have found his way into the wrong demonstration, was carrying a sign that said BUY AMERICAN – KEEP OUR JOBS AT HOME. In spite of her distress, Melanie couldn't help smiling at that one. Maybe she could sell the guy one of Nathan's heirloom-quality, Yankee-made spanking benches.

But for now she had to deal with the more serious protestors, who were marching back and forth in front of Chimera's door. The protestors merged with the customers who were still waiting to get in, forming a welter of confusion. The customers who had already entered the shop had been distracted by the chaos outside, and they were gathering at the window to see what would happen next. A few of the more self-conscious shoppers slunk out the door and hurried back to their cars.

'Now they've crossed the line,' Melanie said. 'They can chant about how twisted and evil I am till they're blue in the face, but when their free speech starts interfering with my free enterprise, the blood starts flowing. If they want a battle, they've got it!'

Melanie marched out the front door, followed by Nathan, Pagan and Luna, and the Gothic army. She grabbed one of the protestors, a thin, tight-lipped woman who was holding a sign that read SEX IS A SICKNESS, by the arm.

'Who's responsible for this?' Melanie demanded. Looking into the woman's pinched, belligerent face, Melanie felt a flicker of recognition. Miss 'Sex is a Sickness' was none other than Harrison Blake's wife. Melanie couldn't remember her name, but she remembered the lethal looks that the woman had given her when she passed her on the streets or in the shops.

'We're *all* responsible,' declared Harrison's wife, raising her sign and her pointed chin at the same time. 'That's what sets us apart from you. You're poisoning this community to serve your own sick interests. You don't care about the town, or our children, or anything but your own fat bank account.'

'If I wanted a fat bank account, do you think I'd be trying to scratch out a living around here?' Melanie said, with a derisive laugh. 'I could be making a fortune in the city, but I'm trying to do this town a service.'

'A service like the ones you've performed for my husband?'

The beams of hatred shooting from Mrs Blake's eyes were hot enough to fry eggs. Melanie felt herself shrinking under the woman's stare. She might have backed away if Nathan hadn't stepped in.

'Now, listen, all of you.' When Nathan's deep voice rang out through the cold morning air, the protestors stopped their chanting. 'You have a right to express your opinions, but you can't block the entrance to Miss Paxton's shop. Local regulations require that you maintain a distance of at least twenty yards from a place of business. You'll have to take your protest across the street.'

'Bullshit!'

'Take your filth twenty yards away from my kids, then. Better yet, make it twenty miles!'

'This is *our* town; we play by our rules!'

As Melanie surveyed the crowd, nausea spread through her stomach. Every single face in that hateful group belonged to someone she knew, someone she had thought was a friendly acquaintance, if not a friend. Some of them had made purchases in her shop, had bought items that they were probably hiding in the drawers of their nightstands or under their beds. People who would never confront Melanie face to face were out here now, their courage bolstered by the presence of the crowd. Was this really the twenty-first century, or had Melanie somehow fallen down a chute that took her back two or three hundred years? At least there was a ray of hope in the form of Jason and his young chums; not everyone was against exploring their decadent selves.

Nathan was trying to reason with some of the more rational demonstrators, but before he could make any progress, a fist fight broke out between Pagan and an acne-ridden teenage evangelist. The Goths, eager to release their pent-up social frustrations, began to throw things at the crowd. Melanie felt like crying as she saw that the fruit and pastries she had bought for her celebration were being used as weapons. The Battle of the Puritans and the Pervs had officially begun.

Melanie shielded her face with her arms to protect herself from the missiles that filled the skies. A cheese Danish struck one of the signs with a heavy splat; another one hit Melanie in the back of the head. The breakfast that was supposed to have been served to Melanie's first customers of the day was now flying through the air and landing all over the sidewalk. Through the shouting and tussling, Melanie was aware of Nathan pushing back the crowd, which seemed to have grown larger and angrier. She saw Luna trying to fend off a couple of demonstrators with a bamboo cane from the shop, and Pagan threatening one of the town bullies with a silicon dildo. Goths were everywhere, kicking and flailing like an army of black spiders. Melanie might have burst out laughing if she hadn't heard the sound of shattering glass. One of the Goths had smashed a champagne bottle against the side of the house, and was waving the jagged end at the protestors, offering to cut their throats if they came any closer.

'Stop!' Melanie screamed. 'This is going too far!'

She ran to the front of the shop, which was now a deserted wreck inside, slammed the door shut and locked it. Then she turned around to face the protestors, the Goths, and her employees.

'There. I've given you what you wanted – for now,' she said to the demonstrators, her whole body quaking with rage. 'No one's going to come to the shop today, and they might not come tomorrow, but you can rest assured that they *will* come in the future. Whether you like it or not, people around here want what I have to offer, and there's not a damn thing you can do to stop me from offering it. You've won the battle this morning, but you haven't won the war.'

Everyone looked shocked, uneasy, and even ashamed, as if they couldn't believe their own behavior. The wail of a siren broke the silence as the sheriff's four-wheel-drive vehicle rounded the corner. Someone had managed to rouse the sheriff out of bed early on a Saturday morning. Too bad he had arrived too late to do anything but stomp around like a disapproving uncle, eyeing the ruins of Melanie's celebration.

'Are you responsible for this mess, young lady?' the sheriff asked.

Melanie looked around, trying to see who the sheriff was talking to. Then she saw that his bloodhound gaze was directed at her.

'Am I responsible? Absolutely not! I'm the victim here. This gang of criminals is trying to drive me out of business. This "mess", as you call it, is the remains of a very expensive breakfast that I was planning to serve my customers. I want people arrested, and I want them to pay for what they've done.'

As Melanie spoke with the sheriff, the protestors and Goths hurried away. By the time she'd finished her speech, the street was all but empty. No one was left but Pagan, Luna, and Nathan, who were trying to pick up the wreckage. Pagan looked like she was about to cry, and Luna was flat-out sobbing. Nathan was trying to calm Luna while rescuing some of the merchandise that was lying about in the aftermath of the battle. The last thing Melanie had wanted was for her toys to be employed in acts of violence.

'Where were you when all this was going on?' Melanie demanded, jabbing her finger into the sheriff's chest. She had always wanted to jab one of the law enforcement officials around here; their ugly brown uniforms were a disgrace to the public aesthetic.

'Listen, Missie, you're lucky I showed up when I did. If I'd seen you and your hooligan friends making this mess, I'd have arrested you for disturbing the peace. In fact, I might do that anyway.'

'Hold on.' Nathan nudged Melanie aside and stood in front of the sheriff. 'There's no need to arrest anyone. The protest is over.'

'All right, then. But you folks had better get this street cleaned up before I change my mind.'

'Wait, I want justice!' Melanie cried. 'I want compensation. What are you going to do for me? I was just attacked and vandalised.'

The sheriff shrugged his beefy shoulders. 'You're the one who decided to open a sex shop. What do you expect?'

'Listen, Mister, I pay taxes like everyone else. I deserve police protection.'

The sheriff chuckled and shook his head. He was still chuckling as he waddled back to his vehicle, pulled the revolving light off the rooftop, and eased his bulk into the car, munching on a Danish he had slyly pilfered from the remaining plate. As soon as he was gone, Melanie turned on Nathan.

'Why didn't you back me up?' she demanded. 'You didn't contradict a single thing that sheriff said.'

'Of course I didn't. I don't argue with rural law enforcement officers. The last thing I want to do today is to spend time in a county jail for obstruction of justice. Trust me, Melanie, if you or I had said one more word, he would have had both of us in handcuffs. We're lucky he didn't stick around to harass us.'

'I can't believe you,' Melanie said. 'I can't believe any of this. How did this happen? Why did it have to happen to me?'

She could have answered her own question. Dean DeSilva had been right; this town wasn't going to tolerate a woman like Melanie. Bad girls had their place – in the back seats of cars, in cheap motel rooms, serving drinks at dive bars or greasy hamburgers at roadside diners – but if they dared to take their sexuality out into the open, they would be driven away like stray cats. In a place like Morne Bay, everyone had a slot to fill. Melanie had overflowed her slot long ago, and Morne Bay was fed up with her.

Well, Melanie was fed up, too. Her backbone sank as she looked around at the rubble that filled the street. An abandoned sign lay in the middle of the road. In livid red letters, it read TAKE YOUR TRASH OUT OF TOWN.

Fine, Melanie thought. That's exactly what I'll do. All of a sudden she felt deflated. She didn't want to fight any more. She didn't want to reopen Chimera. She wanted to pack her things, change her hair colour, and move somewhere sane.

'I'm out of here,' Melanie announced. 'I've had it. I can't take this any more.'

'Wait a minute,' Nathan said, 'we've got a lot of cleaning up to do. And I think we should stay open today.'

'You and the girls can deal with this,' Melanie said, flicking her hand at the rubble. 'Please, just get rid of all of it. Keep the shop open if you want – I really don't care.'

'All right. When are you coming back to help us? An hour? Two?'

'God, I don't know. Maybe not for the rest of my life,' Melanie said.

She stomped off to her car, got inside, and drove away.

Nathan stood on the sidewalk, watching Melanie's shiny red Volkswagen speed down Harbor Street, round the corner and disappear.

'I can't believe she's running away,' he said to Pagan, who was peeling the last of the ham-and-cheese croissants off the asphalt.

'I can't either. She's never been one to abandon ship before.'

'She can't do that. She's got to stay and stand up for herself.'

'Maybe she's finally gotten burned out. Can't say I blame her, after today. What a mess!'

A cluster of pedestrians, sensing the aftermath of a disaster, had gathered to watch the small, sad crew that remained, but these bystanders were nowhere near as hostile as the protestors who had gathered earlier. One woman even came over to help Pagan and Luna clean up.

'This is such a shame,' she said, looking wistfully at the abandoned shop. 'Chimera is like an oasis in the desert around here.'

'Well, that hasn't changed,' Nathan said. 'There's no reason we can't be open for business today, is there? You girls know how to run things.'

'I don't think that's such a good idea. The protestors might come back,' Luna said, but for the first time since the battle started, her eyes had a light of hope.

'Don't worry about that,' Nathan assured her. 'I'll stay here to make sure there's no repeat of this morning.'

'I doubt they'll come back, anyway,' added Pagan. 'By now they're all out at their kids' soccer games or warming up their Breadmakers. Besides, I'm sure they all think that we chickened out and closed down.'

'Only one of us chickened out,' Nathan said darkly, thinking about what he was going to do to Melanie when he caught up with her. So much for all her bold assertions about defending her rights; as soon as things got tough for her, she had fled like a yellow-bellied dog.

They didn't sell much merchandise that morning, but at lunchtime a wave of tourists from New York came through town and stopped to browse at Chimera. The tourists were charmed by everything they saw inside the shop, from a vintage Dior evening gown to the rainbow-glass dildos to the bold paintings on the walls. One young couple, sophisticated in their city attire, bought two of Nathan's pocket paddles, a cock ring, a pair of crotchless leather panties, and a high-necked Victorian nightgown with tiny buttons running from stem to stern. Their sleek urban detachment dissolved into adolescent giggle fits as they whispered to each other about their purchases. Nathan could only guess at what they were going to do with such an eclectic assortment of items. Watching their transformation, he understood why Melanie loved her work so much, and why she would love it even more without the bitterness that Morne Bay was dishing out to her.

Even so, Nathan found that he couldn't forgive Melanie for fleeing the scene that morning. Her two employees, overburdened by the responsibility of running the shop alone on such a discouraging day, were dead on their feet by three o'clock, and Nathan decided that they should close up early.

'But what if Melanie comes back, and we're already gone?' Pagan asked. 'She'll think we ditched her.'

Looking at Pagan and Luna, who were gazing at him like a pair of disappointed children, Nathan felt a wave of anger at Melanie that left him reeling.

'Don't worry,' Nathan said. 'You two aren't the ones who ditched anybody.' He thought for a moment. 'By the way, if Melanie were going to leave for a while, say for a vacation, where do you think she would go?'

The girls looked at each other.

'Come on, you can tell me,' Nathan coaxed. 'You two want to know where she is, too, don't you? Surely you don't want to have to run this place every day until she gets back.'

'She went shopping,' Pagan blurted. 'You can count on that. When Melanie gets stressed, she goes for retail therapy.'

'Shopping, eh? Where's her favourite place to shop?'

'Around this time of year, I'd say Boston,' Luna suggested. 'Melanie loves to walk around Fanueil Hall, and it's so pretty at Christmastime.'

'Well, let's give her a day or two to blow off some steam. Can you handle this place for that long?'

'I think so,' Pagan said, but her shoulders were already sagging at the thought.

'Don't worry. I know I can persuade her to come back,' Nathan said.

'How are you going to do that?'

'I'm going to hunt her down, abduct her, and spank her until her bottom's too sore for shopping. Then she won't have a choice but to come home with me, will she?' Nathan said jovially.

Thinking that he was joking, Pagan and Luna shook their heads and laughed.

* * *

Hannah didn't know how she was going to break the news to Ted. Sitting at her bedroom window, she looked down at the carriage house and watched Melanie's car, its trunk packed with suitcases, tearing out of the driveway. She was driving so fast that her tyres sprayed gravel.

Melanie was moving out, and it was Hannah's fault.

Ted was going to be furious.

'Why didn't you stop her?' he would ask his wife. 'Why didn't you go down and apologise, before it was too late?'

Hannah would have to admit that she didn't know. Something inside her had remained frozen while she watched Melanie throwing her suitcases into the car. Hannah couldn't go downstairs because as much as she cared for Melanie, she was still madly, hopelessly jealous. It was one thing for Melanie to fuck Ted, which only happened when Hannah was around to watch and participate. But Melanie had gone off alone to pursue Nathan. Even worse, she had made Nathan fall in love with her. When Nathan looked at Melanie, his eyes glazed over as if the grey matter in his skull had turned to porridge. He had never – would never – look at Hannah that way.

Hannah let out a long, unsteady breath, stood up and brushed off her jeans. No doubt about it, she was going to be punished tonight. It wouldn't be a fun punishment, either; Ted would assume his schoolteacher persona and lecture Hannah on her failures, and she would feel exactly the way she did years ago when she was his student, and he had taken her into his office to scold her for failing to memorise her lines for a play. Then he would chastise her severely, probably with the peeled switch that he saved for her worst misbehaviour, and he wouldn't bother to make her come afterwards.

When Ted came home that evening, Hannah was sitting in the library. She had a fire going, and a bottle of

Ted's favourite merlot sitting open on the table beside his favourite leather armchair. She wore her blue velvet dress, the one that she had worn on the first night Melanie came to dinner, and her hair hung loose over her shoulders. If Ted saw her in this light, as a mature, loving wife instead of a spoiled, jealous girl, maybe he wouldn't be too hard on her.

'Ted,' Hannah said, standing up as the door opened, 'I have to tell you something –'

The words died in her throat as she saw not one, but two men coming through the door. Ted carried a bottle of wine in one hand and a single rose in the other. Hannah recognised the flower, a cultivar called Scarlet Lady that was the same shade as Hannah's bum after she'd had a good spanking. Ted had given her one of those roses after he'd disciplined her for the first time.

'You can tell me later, darling,' Ted said, kissing Hannah on the cheek. He brushed the fragrant flower across Hannah's nose, but when she reached for the stem, he pulled the blossom away from her. To Hannah's hurt surprise, he handed the flower to his male guest instead.

'Hold this for me, would you, Ryan? I know you can make use of it later.'

The stranger stuffed the rose into his jacket as thoughtlessly as if it were a used handkerchief. The man was about Ted's age, but he reminded Hannah of every snide, superior 'upperclassman' she'd known in high school, the slick rich boys who dated only cheerleaders and junior beauty queens and never noticed Hannah. If they did take notice of her, it was only to make comments about her stringy hair or thunder thighs. Hannah could tell that this Ryan was used to getting – or taking – anything he wanted. He walked confidently around the library, helping himself to wine, using the glass that Hannah had put out for Ted.

'Wait a second. That's my husband's glass,' Hannah protested.

'You mean he only has the one?' Ryan said, lifting his eyebrows in mock surprise.

She didn't like the stranger's bold self-assurance, though she had to concede that he was one of the most attractive men she'd ever seen. His thick hair was a silvery ash blond, while his brown eyes were so dark that they bordered on black. Though it was midwinter, he had the perpetual tan of a man who travelled year round; he had probably gotten that affluent, toasty colour sun-bathing on a yacht in the South of France or strolling around the Acropolis in Greece. In his tweed jacket, black turtleneck sweater and cashmere scarf, he looked like someone who would be more at home in a Manhattan art gallery or martini bar than in a highschool teacher's library in a small, secluded town.

So what was he doing here?

'It's all right, Hannah. Ryan can have whatever he wants. That's why I brought him home tonight. He's our guest. Or maybe I should say, he's *your* guest.'

Ryan smirked. He pulled a pack of cigarettes out of his pocket and lit one. Ted, a die-hard anti-smoker, didn't blink an eye. He gave Hannah's arm an affectionate squeeze.

'I'm going to start dinner, darling,' he said. 'Ryan, you can go ahead and begin.'

Begin what? Hannah wondered. She had no idea what to say to Ted's guest, who was squinting at her through the scrim of cigarette smoke. She really didn't want to say anything to him, especially not before she'd had a chance to tell Ted that Melanie had moved out. Ted probably assumed that Melanie would appear at the front door any second, dressed in shantung-silk evening paja-mas and bearing a bottle of chilled champagne. Maybe that's why he had brought Ryan home, as a date for Melanie.

'I have to talk to my husband,' Hannah said to Ryan.

She tried to move past him to go after Ted, but Ryan was too fast for her. In one agile motion he moved from the mantel to the door, blocking her path.

'What's the hurry, pretty lady?' he said softly. 'You can talk to Ted any time.'

With the cigarette clamped between his teeth, his eyes narrowed behind the smoke, and his hands braced on either side of the doorway, Ryan looked tough, sinister. Hannah felt something flare into life in the pit of her belly.

'Take that dress off,' he said. 'Let me see what you've got underneath.'

'Are you kidding?' Hannah said, with a nervous laugh. He couldn't possibly be serious. Men like Ryan didn't look twice at big, shy, workaday women like Hannah. They went for the hothouse orchids of the female gender, the models and ballet dancers and the concert violinists who posed for *Playboy* in their spare time.

'Take that dress off,' he insisted. 'I want to see you naked.'

There wasn't any heat in those carbon-brown eyes as they travelled up and down Hannah's body, only a detached curiosity. Hannah wished that Melanie were here; she would use one or two razor-sharp insults to cut this guy down to size. Hannah could only stare dumbly at this man who had suddenly turned from a guest into master of the household. His eyes were like a snake's, beady and intensely hypnotic. As numb as a mouse in a trance, she reached back to unzip her dress. The blue fabric fell in a pool around her feet. She hadn't bothered to wear a bra or panties that night; she had hoped to seduce Ted before he had a chance to punish her.

'Nice,' he said, taking one of Hannah's nipples and

pulling at the pink flesh. 'Now, turn around. Close your eyes. Don't open them until I tell you to.'

Hannah did as she was told. She heard the sound of Ryan grinding out his cigarette, and she hoped he wasn't dirtying up some valuable antique or keepsake with his ashes. She flinched as Ryan's hands, as icy as she would have expected, roamed along her back, buttocks, and thighs. She had the feeling that he was appraising her, to see if she were suitable for some secret criminal activity. Who *was* this Ryan fellow? A stranded motorist whom Ted had picked up? A criminal with a hidden agenda? An escaped inmate from the psychiatric hospital?

'Step forward,' he said, 'keep your eyes closed, and keep walking until I tell you to stop.'

'Ted?' she whimpered. She realised that she hadn't heard a sound from the kitchen in the past few minutes. 'Where's my husband?'

'I'm right here, darling.' Ted spoke from across the room. His voice had the hoarse, guttural sound that it took on when he was strongly aroused.

'What's happening? Ted? What's going on?'

'Just a lesson for my beautiful, jealous wife,' Ted said. 'I know about the scene you made today, Hannah. When I went by the shop to pick you up this afternoon, one of Melanie's salesgirls told me everything. You should be ashamed of yourself.'

'I am,' Hannah whispered.

Ryan laughed. The sound chilled Hannah to the bone, but underneath that chill, a molten pool had opened up inside her and was spreading its heat through her body. The wicked mix of excitement and fear coursed through her veins like a whisky. Her legs were shaking so much that she could hardly stand upright.

'You have to learn to trust the people who love you, Hannah. Tonight, you are going to learn that lesson by placing your trust in me. I'm going to sit here in my favourite chair and watch Ryan, who has an exquisite gift for sadism, do whatever he wants with you. Ryan is one of New York's most prominent young stage directors. He knows how to tell women what to do, but he rarely gets the opportunity to order them around the way he wants to.'

'What is he going to do to me?'

'Don't worry, my love. He's not going to give you anything you won't enjoy . . . or don't deserve.'

'Walk over to that wall,' Ryan ordered. 'You can open your eyes, but just long enough to find your way across the room. Then I'm going to blindfold you.'

'No. Please don't do that.' Hannah hated being blind-folded. That was the one thing she couldn't stand to surrender – her power to see what was going on around her.

'Hannah,' Ted warned, 'you're not going to disobey my guest. That would be rude, and rudeness will be punished severely.'

Hannah peeked over her shoulder at Ted, who sat sprawled in the leather armchair. His fly was open, and he held his erect cock in his right hand. In his left hand, he balanced a glass of brandy. Ted looked as if he had settled in to watch the pornographic performance of a lifetime. Hannah hated the self-satisfied grin on his face. He wasn't the least bit jealous at watching another man enjoy his wife.

With Hannah nude and vulnerable, Ryan seemed excited for the first time that night. His eyes glittered, and he was breathing fast. Ryan pulled a pair of gloves out of his tweed jacket. Made of soft, supple kidskin, they were only a few shades darker than his tanned wrists. With the swift, sharp motions of a surgeon gloving up, he covered his hands. Mere centimetres separated Han-nah from the arrogant stranger. Hannah could see into the dark wells of his eyes, and the intentions she saw there drove her excitement up another few notches. He smiled.

'You want this as much as I do, don't you?'

Hannah gulped.

'Turn around,' he ordered. 'Raise your arms and flatten your palms against the wall. If you move your hands, I'll have to bind your wrists. You don't want me to have to do that. Plant your feet firmly on the floor, two feet apart. Two feet, I said. There you go. Now say goodnight, Hannah. Time for your blindfold.'

Hannah gritted her teeth as he pulled the long black cashmere scarf over her head, wrapped it twice around her eyes, then knotted it at the back of her neck. Once she had been blindfolded, Hannah thought for sure that she would be paddled, cropped, or even whipped. Ryan was the type of man who would be as cruel and harsh as he could be, within the boundaries that Ted had set for him.

Had Ted bothered to set any boundaries for him?

Instead of striking her from behind, Ryan stepped between Hannah's outstretched arms, so that he was standing between them, facing her. Hannah heard his breathing grow deep and rough as he held her breasts, considering their weight and fullness, then moved his hands down to her hips.

'You have a fine body, Hannah. You have the body that I see in my darkest fantasies, the ones I never share with anyone. Whenever I see a woman like you, as big and strong as a fertility goddess, I think about taking her away somewhere, to a remote and quiet place, and making her my slave. There's no sport in enslaving a small, delicate woman; it's easy to dominate a woman like that. I prefer more of a challenge. What do you think about that, Hannah?'

A lump in her throat kept Hannah from speaking. Though she felt nothing but distaste for Ted's guest, her body was responding to his stealthy fingers, which were now crawling down the curves of her hips, crossing her flanks, and moving into the places between her thighs, one hand touching her in front, the other in back.

'But I don't know if you'll be much of a challenge, Hannah. You're already soaking wet, and we've barely gotten started. You've got a volcano on your hands here, Ted. Big and quiet on the outside, bubbling lava on the inside. I wonder what it will take to get her to erupt?'

From his armchair, Ted laughed. Hannah didn't have to see her husband to know that he was stroking his cock as he watched Ryan handling Hannah's body. Ted had told Hannah months ago that he wanted to watch another man discipline her, but Hannah, in her naivety, had assumed that she would choose her own disciplinarian. She had imagined someone gentle but firm, like Nathan or Dr Heath, not a cold, arrogant sadist like Ryan.

Hannah felt a silky bundle of petals whisk across her lips, and she caught the scent of the rose Ted had brought home. The blossom travelled down her throat, back and forth along the dips of her collarbone, and down through the valley between her breasts. She shuddered when the blossom glanced on her nipples, one after the other. The nubs stiffened in response to the fleeting stimulation of the petals.

'You know, I've never had much use for manufactured sex toys,' Ryan mused. 'As the Marquis de Sade knew so well, nature provides us with everything we need for sexual torture.'

Something viciously sharp stung Hannah's right nipple. One of the rose's thorns was digging into the tender, ridged flesh of her areola.

'Stop it!' she shrieked. She pulled her hands off the wall and clutched her breasts with her fingers. If she could have seen Ryan's face, she would have slapped him.

'Sorry, dear,' Ryan said, in a casual tone that was far

from apologetic. 'I couldn't resist. There's something about the sight of a rose thorn sinking into a tight, erect nipple that turns my cock to steel. Feel how aroused I am now.'

He pulled Hannah's hand away from her chest and brought it down to touch the bulge at his groin. Through the denim of his jeans his cock was warm to the touch, and she felt a pulse throbbing in the hardened flesh. Gripping her wrist, Ryan pulled Hannah's hand up and down along the crest, which grew even harder under her palm.

'I know you couldn't help yourself,' Ryan said, 'but you disobeyed me. You took your hands off the wall. Now I'm going to have to bind you.'

He let go of her hands to unbuckle his belt. The strip of leather made a harsh, whooshing noise as he yanked it through the loopholes of his jeans. Disoriented, Hannah felt herself being turned around, her arms pulled behind her. She moaned and struggled, but Ryan held on tight.

'This is the part I love,' he said. 'Ted, let go of your cock and give me a hand here. Your wife needs two men to keep her under control.'

Next thing she knew, Hannah was in the grip of two pairs of hands. She thrashed her arms, but Ted and Ryan were too strong for her. Ted wrapped one of his legs around her calves so that she couldn't kick.

'Settle down, Hannah. You're going to be corrected tonight, whether you like it or not. Don't resist – you'll only make it worse.'

He held her by her upper arms while Ryan wrapped his belt around her wrists. Panting angrily, Hannah gave in and let him have his way.

'Very good,' Ryan said. 'That's much better. Ted, change places with me. I haven't finished what I started earlier.'

Hannah moaned when she felt the rose's petals caressing her again. With Ted holding her tightly, she couldn't flinch away when Ryan pressed one of the thorns into her left breast, into the outcropping of flesh just below her navel, and finally into her inner thigh. Because she couldn't escape the pain, she took deep breaths and let herself relax into it, so that with each penetration, the torment was easier to take. Standing behind her, Ted wrapped his arms around her and caressed her breasts, tweaking and tugging her nipples. The head of his erection nuzzled the small of her back. Hannah moaned.

'This isn't so bad, is it?' Ryan asked, piercing her thigh again. He must have been kneeling in front of her now, so that he could watch the tip of the thorn sink into her skin. 'Every time the thorn goes in, you feel a little burst of adrenaline, don't you? That sweet rush is your own natural opiates, coursing through your body.'

He spread Hannah's legs slightly and slid the long stem of the rose between them. Thorns dug into the tenderest part of her thighs, in the twin hollows just below her vulva. If she moved, the thorns would be driven deeper into her flesh, and their bite would be excruciating. She did her best to hold still, although the pleasure of having Ted fondle her breasts while Ryan pricked her had left her shaking like a leaf.

'Coming with that rose between her legs would be very painful, wouldn't it?' Ted asked. He sounded as if he weren't far from coming himself.

'Not if she were a very good girl and stayed absolutely motionless,' Ryan laughed. 'But what woman can do that when she's having an orgasm?'

Ted's erect penis, rubbing against Hannah's buttocks, had spread its lubricant across her skin. She could tell by the way he clutched her arms, his fingers squeezing her rhythmically, that he wanted to push her down on all fours and fuck her. Hannah wouldn't have minded that one bit, but with the rose's thorny stem so close to her lower lips, she didn't want to move a muscle. Still on his knees, Ryan grasped the backs of Hannah's thighs and buried his mouth in her pubic curls. His tongue prodded through the moist fur, seeking the kernel at the heart of her cuntflesh. As he dug for his prize, Ted milked Hannah's nipples. Hannah rocked back and forth, trying to find a release for the sensations that were swarming through her. If she undulated just a little, she could let go of some of the tension without pressing her thighs together...

Then Ryan's tongue met Hannah's clit, and her back arched, her buttocks pushing into Ted's groin. Ted, who couldn't hold back any longer, spurted against Hannah's buttocks, and his spasms pushed the flower's stem into Hannah's legs. The thorns stung her at the same moment that Ryan's tongue drove her into an orgasm, and she came with a rush of pleasure, agony, and sheer relief, grinding her mound into Ryan's mouth. She felt the rose slip out the crevice between her thighs. Ryan kissed the stinging marks that the thorns had left on her skin, and she wondered if he were really as cruel as he pretended to be.

'You did very well,' he said to Hannah. 'You took your punishment as bravely as Ted said you would.'

'Now, Hannah,' Ted added, 'to show you what a generous husband I am, and how far we've gone beyond petty jealousy, I'm going to let you make Ryan come. I'm sure you want to.'

By now, Hannah *did* want to. With Ryan's permission, Ted unbuckled the belt and released Hannah's wrists, Then she and Ryan switched positions, with Hannah sinking to her knees and Ryan standing, his crotch at a level with her mouth. Ted untied the cashmere scarf and pulled it off Hannah's head. While her eyes adjusted to the light, Ted helped Ryan unbutton his jeans and remove his hard on, which looked swollen to the point of pain. Hannah was surprised to see Ted's hand lingering on

Ryan's erection, his fingers gripping the shaft as he pulled his hand away. She was even more surprised when Ryan grabbed Ted's forearm and kept his hand there, resting on his cock.

The two men drew very close, and stayed in that position for several pulsating seconds while Hannah watched, fascinated. She had never known that Ted had homoerotic desires – perhaps he had never realised it himself. Moving slowly, so as not to disturb the scene that was unfolding, she left her kneeling position, crawled out of their way, and found a comfortable vantage point on the couch beside the fire. The two men shifted wordlessly to fill the space Hannah had left. Ted knelt down in front of Ryan and began to work his mouth around the head of the other man's member. Ryan ruffled Ted's hair, murmuring instructions and words of encouragement.

The sight of the two men together stirred new emotions in Hannah. She had never seen two men make love before – and what Ted and Ryan were doing was definitely making love. As her husband's mouth paid court to Ryan's cock, Ryan massaged the back of Ted's neck and gazed down at his lover with something close to adoration in his eyes.

This man really loves Ted, Hannah thought with surprise. The cool New York stage director was melting under the touch of a small-town drama instructor. The intimacy between them made Hannah want to come again. When Ted took his friend's cock down his throat, Hannah leaned back on the couch and began to rub her pussy. Her clit, hypersensitive after the orgasm Ryan had given her, stiffened immediately under her fingers. Ryan held on to the base of Ted's head with both hands, leaned back and closed his eyes. His hips thrust in the rhythm of Ted's sucking. As his tempo quickened, Ted eased back to accommodate him and gripped the root of his shaft. The added stimulation sent Ryan into a frenzy. He exploded into Ted's mouth, and Ted, choking only a little, swallowed his seed.

Hannah came violently, bucking up and down on the couch, but the two men didn't see her. They were too absorbed in each other, rapt in the glow they had generated.

'I've wanted to do that for years,' Ted said, when he'd come back to earth.

'I know you did,' Ryan replied. He knelt and kissed Ted on the mouth.

Ryan left soon after that. Ted invited him to stay for dinner, but the director begged off, saying that he had to drive back to the city for an early rehearsal the next day. He left as mysteriously as he had come, taking the rose with him. As he stepped out the door, he gave Hannah a kiss on the cheek and thanked her for indulging him that night.

'Who *was* that?' Hannah asked, after Ryan's black Porsche had sped off down the road.

Ted sighed. 'That was my half brother.'

'Your *what*?'

'Ryan is the only child of my father's first marriage.'

'I never even knew you had a half brother!'

'We lost touch over the years. But when I was growing up we spent some time together. The summer I was seventeen, we got very close. There was one afternoon in the pond behind the house, when we almost...' Ted's voice faded, and his eyes took on a distant, dreamy cast. 'Listen, Hannah, I'm wiped out. I'm going to get ready for bed.'

Offering no more information, Ted disappeared upstairs. Hannah couldn't believe what she had heard, but when she recalled the mutual affection in the men's eyes, the emotion between them started to make sense. She went back to the library, sat down on the couch, and tried to recapture the feelings that had washed through her as she watched the scene. The room was still warm with the energy that the two men had created. Hannah would never forget the way Ryan's steely demeanour had softened into tenderness as Ted sank down to his knees and kissed the crown of his cock.

Hannah curled up on the couch and yawned. She was beginning to drift off to sleep, but she didn't want to leave the library yet. She had too much to think about. There were so many forms of intimacy, so many variations on the conventional themes of love. Far too many for one person to experience in a lifetime. Jealousy poisoned the erotic well, making natural attractions seem ugly and threatening, killing the magic of desire. As Hannah's eyes closed, she vowed that she would replace that destructive emotion with thoughts of beauty and sensuality.

Her imagination drifted to a scene of two teenage boys, swimming naked in a green pond illuminated by summer light, meeting each other underwater, shying away from a contact that would take them years to fulfil.

9 Melanie Gets It

Running away had never felt so good. As Melanie strolled past the brightly decorated shops of Faneuil Hall, Boston's picturesque outdoor marketplace, she felt as if she had been transported back to the Christmas seasons of her childhood, when the holidays were graced with enchantment instead of burdened with stress, and all she had to think about was the loot that awaited her under the dazzling tree in her family's living room. Of course, the magic of Christmas was always tarnished by her stepmother's alcoholism, her father's brutish temper, and her Uncle Bernie's roving hands, but on the whole, December had always been Melanie's favourite month.

All of that changed when she started working in retail. The long hours, impatient customers, and the pressures of keeping popular merchandise in stock had been wearing Melanie down. Watching the shopgirls ring up her purchases, Melanie realised that this vacation was long overdue. It was such a sweet relief to be standing on the opposite side of the counter, to be the one who stretched out her hands to receive the bags full of goodies, the one who had to be pleased and pampered. Melanie recognised herself all too well in the shopgirls' weary faces, and she went out of her way to treat them kindly. After spending the day ratcheting up the balances on her credit cards, Melanie would go back to the economy hotel where she was staying, collapse into bed, and have pizza or Chinese food delivered to her room. Then she would while away the rest of the night pigging out on high-calorie treats and watching cheesy action movies on television.

Once in a while Melanie felt a stab of guilt about abandoning Chimera, but she suppressed those feelings quickly enough. Pagan and Luna would survive without her. If they were anything like Melanie had been at that age, they would be running the whole show by the time she got back. Melanie was having so much fun that the thought of being replaced by her own staff hardly bothered her at all.

The first few days of retail therapy were sheer heaven, but before long Melanie's demons caught up with her. Maybe it was the inevitable build-up of stress that drove her to commit the crime. Maybe it was the flashbacks to holidays of her adolescence, when she had been known to release her tensions at the local shops by sneaking a new lipstick or a piece of jewellery into her backpack. One moment she was browsing through a rack of lingerie, fingering a corselet made of wine-red satin; the next moment her mouth was as dry as cotton, and her heart was rollicking at a pace she hadn't experienced in years. All of a sudden Melanie was a teenager again, standing in front of a tempting piece of merchandise, her purse open and waiting at her side. Craving that thrill of transgression, she considered her next step: purchase or theft?

She lifted the undergarment off its hanger. The corset was a size too small for her, but if its laces were pulled very tight, it would fit. If necessary, she would sacrifice cocktails and chocolate for a few weeks to streamline her waist. The corset's delicate ribbing, scalloped edges, and genuine silk lining were too perfect to pass up.

Melanie looked around. She must have come in during a rare lull in the Christmas rush; she was the only customer in the boutique. The salesgirl stood at the counter, her back turned while she chatted on the telephone. Melanie heard nothing but the roar of her own pulse. Her hands shook as she unsnapped the flap of her black leather bag.

'Hand it over.'

Suddenly she was aware of a male presence towering over her. The blood that had been racing through her veins rushed straight to Melanie's sex. If there was anything more thrilling than committing a crime, it was being caught.

But being caught shoplifting was the last thing Melanie needed right now. She couldn't afford to be involved in a scandal, and she had no desire to be dragged off to a grubby urban police station by some cocky rent-a-cop. This person hadn't caught her doing anything more criminal than admiring a piece of lingerie that was a size too small for her. Melanie whirled around.

'Hand it over? I don't think so. Not unless you're going to buy it for me.'

Nathan Wentworth stood inches behind her, looking taller and more imposing than ever. She had never seen him look so handsome: clean-shaven, his blond hair combed into waves that curled over the edge of his collar. He wore a navy-blue cashmere overcoat and double-breasted suit instead of his usual sweaters and jeans. Staring at the wall of his chest, she realised that his breathing was as ragged as hers, and his eyes burned with something a lot hotter than a civic duty to prevent shoplifting. Nathan was just as turned on as she was.

'As a matter of fact, I *am* going to buy that corset for you,' he said. 'And you're going to model it for me. While you're wearing it, I'm going to punish you for planning to shoplift.'

Melanie hooted with laughter, but her legs were so limp that she swayed in her four-inch heels. 'You have no idea what I was thinking. Even if you did, there's no law against planning.'

'You're wrong.' Nathan's grin contradicted his stern tone. 'I do know what you were thinking. And if you knew what I'm planning to do to you, you'd wish there were a law against it.'

Nathan glanced over at the salesgirl, who was touching up her fingernails with metallic green polish as she giggled into the telephone. He drew Melanie against his body and, under the cover of a rack of lingerie, he yanked up her tartan wrap-around skirt and pulled down her black woollen tights. Then he cupped her ass in his hand and groped the mounds roughly, as if he were gauging the ripeness of a pair of cantaloupes.

'What are you doing?' Melanie hissed. She looked over her shoulder. The salesgirl was oblivious, but a flock of holiday shoppers was standing outside the window, staring curiously at the scene that was unfolding behind the window display of scantily clad mannequins romping in artificial snow. 'Nathan, put my skirt down! There are people watching.'

'You know what I'm doing,' Nathan said calmly. 'Don't worry about those people. They're adults; they'll survive.'

Melanie gulped. She did know what Nathan was doing. He was sizing her up for the long-delayed spanking. Standing so close to her, he felt as broad and hard as a brick wall. His fingers clamped down her flesh; she could already feel the marks forming. All of a sudden, he relaxed his grip, lifted his knee, bent Melanie halfway over it, and gave her a swat that resounded through the shop like the crack of a whip.

'Yee-ow!' Melanie cried.

The salesgirl shrieked and dropped the telephone receiver. 'Damnit! Look what you made me do,' she moaned, as a pool of green nail varnish spread across the countertop. She looked accusingly at Nathan and Melanie. Nathan had whisked Melanie into an upright position, and Melanie was hurriedly readjusting her tights and skirt – not an easy thing to do, with her ass on fire. She had been fantasising about being spanked by Nathan for weeks; now that she had had a taste of his hand, she wished she'd never encouraged him.

'I think you'd better just turn me in,' Melanie said to Nathan under her breath. 'I'd rather spend the night in jail than have any more of that.'

'But you see, it doesn't matter what you'd rather have,' Nathan said, 'because I've already decided what's going to happen to you.'

Cool and composed, he led Melanie over to the counter, where the salesgirl was smearing the varnish into the glass with a scrap of tissue paper.

'I'm going to get it when my boss comes back,' she grumbled, glaring at Nathan and Melanie. 'Did you two do any damage back there?'

Yes, this man damaged my backside with one blow, and he's only getting started, Melanie wanted to say, but with Nathan's fingers clamping her elbow, she didn't dare.

'Not a bit,' Nathan said, 'but here's something extra for your trouble.'

He handed the girl a couple of folded bills and a large handkerchief to help her wipe up the mess. The money softened her up, and she chatted with Nathan as she rang up the corselet for him. When Nathan let go of Melanie to take the fancy silver bag, Melanie considered making a break for it, but she knew that she wouldn't get very far in her high-heeled boots. Cursing the impulse that drove her to wear impractical footwear, she followed Nathan out of the shop without protest. A bouquet of mistletoe hung over the doorway, and as they were leaving, Nathan bent down to kiss her.

'You have no idea how much trouble you're in,' he whispered into her ear, grazing her throat with his fingertip.

'I think I know,' Melanie said, wishing that she didn't.

They walked arm in arm along the mall, like a normal couple out for an afternoon of shopping. Whenever they passed another couple similar to themselves, Melanie checked out the woman and wondered if she were being led to the same fate. Any one of those strangers might be awaiting a spanking when she got home, but Melanie was sure that she would be hurting more than any of them by the end of the night.

'Why don't we have a late lunch?' Nathan suggested, stopping in front of a bar and grill called O'Toole's.

'I'm not very hungry, Nathan. Really.'

'Well, I'm famished, and I need fuel for the evening ahead. We'll stop here, then head back to my hotel.'

Melanie had no choice but to follow Nathan through the tastefully weathered wooden door. The interior was dark and cozy, with a long bar at one end of the room. A gang of yuppies, unwinding from their work day, played pool at a table in the corner. O'Toole's was known for offering beers from local breweries. After the waitress led Nathan and Melanie to a secluded booth, with high seats that hid them from view, Nathan ordered a pint of amber ale for himself and hot tea for Melanie.

'Wait, I could use something a lot stronger than tea. I'll take a gin and tonic,' Melanie told the waitress. 'And go easy on the tonic.'

The waitress nodded and scribbled on her order pad.

'No, scratch that,' Nathan said. 'My companion won't be drinking alcohol.'

'So she'll have the tea, like you said, sir?'

The waitress and Nathan looked at each other for a long moment. Melanie could swear that she saw collusion in the exchange. The waitress was a curvy brunette with pale freckled skin and crystalline blue eyes that spoke of an Irish ancestry. Waiting for Nathan's response, she clasped her hands behind her back, thrust out her breasts, and batted her coal-black eyelashes. Oh, goddess help me, Melanie thought. Is this whole town filled with Nathan's subs?

'Yes. She'll have the tea. And what would you like to eat, Melanie?'

'I'll just have a dinner salad with Roquefort dressing,' Melanie said glumly. 'I don't have much of an appetite.'

'Well, I'm starving. I'll have the Porterhouse steak, medium rare,' Nathan said, in a jovial tone that made Melanie want to kick him in the shin.

As soon as the waitress left, Nathan dug into the pocket of his overcoat. He tossed a handful of small metal objects onto the table. They skittered across the varnished maple like the jacks that Melanie played with when she was a girl.

'What are those?'

'Just a few souvenirs I brought from the shop. I thought they might jog your memory. You do remember that you manage a shop, don't you?'

'I was doing a fine job of forgetting, until you came along.' She picked up one of the shiny objects and inspected it in the light of the overhanging Tiffany lamp.

'You know what that is, don't you?'

In spite of her irritation, Melanie felt a twinge in her cunt. 'Of course I do. I ordered these myself. They're body clamps.'

'Vicious little buggers,' Nathan said, twirling one of them in his fingers. 'I'll bet they have quite a bite. You know, when I was working at Chimera on the day you left, I couldn't believe how many people bought these. The customers were snapping them up like candy.'

'What can I say? There are a lot of closet masochists among my clientele.'

'There certainly are. That's why you created the Alcove,

isn't it? To fill the needs of people who had been keeping their desires a secret. You wanted to provide a safe, comfortable place for people to realise their fantasies.'

'That's right.'

'I've always admired you, Melanie. You're a woman with a vision, goals, commitments. Yet you abandoned all that without any notice, leaving two young employees with the responsibilities of management.'

'Don't be so pompous. I needed a vacation. You suggested it yourself.'

'I suggested a vacation, not a full-blown escape. You handled yourself with all the maturity of a juvenile delinquent.'

'Oh, please.' Melanie yawned. She was doing her best to look bored, but sitting across from Nathan under the lamp, she felt like a suspect at an interrogation.

'Take off your tights,' Nathan said.

'Nathan, don't be ridiculous. It's freezing outside.'

'But it's nice and warm in here. Take off your tights. Roll them up and give them to me.'

'What if someone sees me?'

'Believe me, Melanie, no one is going to see you. Now do as I say before I run out of patience.'

The booth was framed by tall wooden wings that concealed Melanie and Nathan so effectively that they might as well have been sitting in a packing crate. Add to that the fact that Nathan had chosen a seat in the corner, and Melanie was all but invisible to the patrons and staff.

With a sigh, Melanie leaned down to unlace her boots. The sigh was sheer drama; in truth, Melanie was so excited that her fingers fumbled with the laces. Finally she managed to free her feet. The waitress arrived with their drinks as Melanie was squirming out of her tights. Melanie froze, but when the brunette saw what she was doing, her eyes registered only sly amusement.

'Does she need a little help?' the waitress cooed, addressing Nathan as if Melanie were a three-year-old who couldn't negotiate her booster chair. Melanie would have liked to grab the girl by her perky black bow tie and say, 'No, as a matter of fact I don't need your help! I've been undressing myself for over twenty years,' but she controlled herself – just barely.

'I think that's an excellent idea, Wendy,' Nathan said.

So the two of them did know each other. Melanie wondered if they had ever been romantically involved, if they had played casually, or if Wendy were just one of those indiscriminate submissives who kowtowed to any dominant male who lifted his leg in her vicinity. Wendy scooted into the booth next to Melanie, and with swift, efficient movements, began rolling down the waistband of her tights. Melanie's face burned. It was mortifying to have another woman undressing her while she wiggled around like a cranky child, but at the same time, she could feel herself getting wet. Her arousal made the experience even more humiliating, especially when Wendy noticed.

'I think your sub is getting excited,' the waitress informed Nathan. 'She's all wet and shiny. Did you give her permission?'

'No, but that's all right. Unlike you, she hasn't been trained to control her arousal.' Nathan turned to Melanie. 'Wendy was trained with a chastity belt. She only gets excited when she's allowed to do so, and she can climax on command.'

'Sounds like my personal idea of hell,' Melanie muttered. 'Where did she get her training, at the Spanish Inquisition?'

'I trained her myself,' Nathan said. 'She was one of my best students.'

Wendy blushed prettily. 'Thank you, sir.'

Melanie wanted to puke.

'And since you've been trained so well, you'll know exactly how to apply these clamps to Melanie's pussy. Go ahead and put them on. I want her to wear them for a while, so don't let them pinch her too hard.'

'Should I put one on her clit?' Wendy asked.

'You put one of those things on my clit, and you're dead,' Melanie warned.

Nathan smiled. 'Just put them on her lips, Wendy. She's new at this.'

Wendy pushed Melanie's thighs apart. Melanie cringed as the waitress took a generous fold of her labia and secured it with one of the clamps. At first the bite was excruciating, but after a moment, the pain subsided into a keen, almost pleasurable ache. Melanie had never tried the clamps on herself; she had purchased them at her customers' request. She knew of at least three people in Morne Bay who wore the clamps under their clothes at work. How did they sit at the office typing on their computers and sipping coffee with these little jaws attached to their bodies?

By the time Wendy applied the rest of the clamps, Melanie's whole nether region was throbbing. Wendy rolled up Melanie's tights and handed the black woollen bundle to Nathan.

'Anything else I can do for you, sir?'

'You've done very well, Wendy. Why don't you go see if our order is ready?'

Wendy slid out of the booth and pranced away, her hips twitching.

'How long do I have to wear the clamps?' Melanie moaned.

'Until I say you can take them off. You'll love taking them off. Be patient.'

'Why don't you just take me back to your hotel so we can get this over with?'

Nathan gave her a look of mock confusion. 'Get it over

with? I'm having the time of my life. I want to make this last.'

Make it last he did. Melanie sat as stiff as a board, trying to ignore the pounding between her legs, while Nathan polished off his steak. Melanie picked at her salad, but she couldn't swallow a bite. She was too busy worrying about what Nathan had in store for her later, and counting the seconds until she could take off the clamps. Just when she was finally accepting the pain, when the pounding of the blood in her head had taken on a mesmerising rhythm, Nathan put down his steak knife and took his napkin off his lap.

'You can take them off now. Do it slowly.'

Taking the clamps off hurt more than putting them on. The release of each set of metal teeth was followed by a mini-flood of renewed pain, but when Melanie had removed all of them, the relief sent powerful shock waves through her body. Why hadn't she ever tried these things before? The sensations she was feeling had her twisting like a snake on hot asphalt.

'You want to come, don't you?' Nathan asked. He drank the last of his ale, then leaned over to peer out of the booth. It was time for happy hour, and groups of exhausted shoppers were piling through the door. 'I want you to make yourself come, Melanie.'

By now Melanie didn't care if the whole restaurant was watching. It took only a few flicks of her finger across her clit to bring herself to orgasm. The spasms of delight were coloured by the aftermath of pain, and as she hit the pinnacle, she couldn't hold back a cry. The sound melted into the noise of the crowd, but as Melanie's pleasure ebbed away, she saw Wendy watching her from behind the bar. When the pretty waitress gave Melanie the thumbs-up sign, Melanie couldn't help but return her smile.

* * *

Nathan's hotel was a magnificent old Art Deco building, with gold-veined marble floors, endlessly high ceilings, and an elevator with ornate antique doors wrought in brass. The place was paradise compared to Melanie's cheap lodgings, and as she and Nathan walked through the lobby, with its magnificent fir tree draped with tinsel and strings of glass beads, Melanie pretended that they were a vanilla couple heading upstairs for a hot weekend of holiday sex. Straight fucking – no toys, no implements of torture, no pain – just a couple of warm, naked bodies wriggling and cuddling under a goosedown comforter while snow fell outside.

Her fantasy screeched to a halt when Nathan unlocked the door of his room. Standing in the middle of the luxurious red carpet, less than a foot away from the king-size bed, was the spanking horse that Nathan had made for Melanie. That single piece of furniture, which had seemed so pretty and quaint in Nathan's wood shop, looked menacing and archaic in this glamorous hotel room.

'Come inside,' Nathan laughed, when Melanie balked at the door. 'I'm not going to hurt you ... yet. You didn't eat anything at O'Toole's. Let me order you something from room service.'

Melanie's stomach growled. 'It was kind of hard to eat when I was writhing in agony.'

While Nathan called the kitchen to order hot chocolate and a grilled cheese sandwich, Melanie explored the room. No matter where she went – over to the French doors, to the vanity table, to the bed itself – the spanking horse never seemed to leave her field of vision. When the bellboy arrived with Melanie's food, Nathan let her sit down at the table to eat. He himself remained standing in front of the French doors, his hands clasped behind his back like a prosecuting attorney hearing testimony. Melanie did her best to ignore him, fixing her attention on the crisp golden triangles of grilled bread and cheese on her plate.

'So what are you going to do when you get back to Morne Bay, Melanie?' he asked.

'You know, I don't think I'm going back. I might stay right here in Boston.' Melanie took a bite of her sandwich and munched noisily.

'Oh, you're going back. You may decide to move, but before you're going anywhere, you've got to go home and resolve things.'

'Who says I have to go back? *You?*'

'No – your conscience says it. You know that you can't hide from Morne Bay. If you leave without confronting your opposition, those narrow-minded people will haunt you for the rest of your life.'

'I could forget about that place in the blink of an eye, if you'd leave me alone.'

Nathan turned to Melanie and arched an eyebrow. 'Really? You could forget about all of your steady customers so easily?'

'I'd find other customers. There would be more perverts in an urban area, anyway. And people know more about fashion.'

'What about all the young women like Pagan and Luna who need a place that encourages their brand of creativity?'

'They should get out of Morne Bay, or they'll end up just like me,' Melanie said bitterly.

'What about the people who care about you? What about Ted and Hannah?'

'They have each other. I'm interfering in their relationship, anyway. Hannah thinks she wants to be a full-fledged swinger, but what she really wants is a wholesome 'Ozzie and Harriet' marriage with a little play on the side.'

'What about Lori Marwick? What do you think she'll say

when she comes back from Europe and finds out that the woman she made a partner has abandoned the business?'

The bread Melanie had just swallowed stuck in her throat. What *would* Lori think? When Melanie was a teenager, rebellious and miserable, Lori had given her a job at Chimera. Trusting Melanie's instincts, she had allowed the girl to take on more responsibility over the years, letting her help with the accounting and purchasing. On Melanie's twenty-fifth birthday, Lori had presented her with a partnership contract as a gift, and Melanie had promised that she wouldn't let her down. Now, only months later, she was planning to bail out.

Nathan was standing close to her, so close that Melanie could hear his rapid breathing. He must have sensed that he had finally hit a nerve. He placed his hand on the back of her neck as if he were going to stroke her hair, but instead, he took hold of the entire skein and tugged.

'Get up,' he said, in a quiet voice that made Melanie's blood freeze in her veins.

She rose. She let Nathan lead her away from the table. Without letting go of her hair, he picked up the shopping bag that held the corselet and handed it to her.

'Take off all your clothes and put this on,' he said.

'Do I have to?'

The wine-red garment, which had looked so tempting in the boutique, seemed cheap and tawdry now. It reminded her of every piece of merchandise that she had stolen in her childhood. She had never once worn or used anything that she had pinched from a shop. As soon as she got home and pulled the items out of her backpack, the objects would lose their lustre, and in the aftermath of her kleptomaniac high, Melanie would feel like nothing more than a thief.

The look on Nathan's face said that Melanie was going to wear the corselet, anyway.

She took her time undressing; if Nathan was going to play the overbearing lord and master, then Melanie would make him wait. His face was cold and impassive as he watched her peel off her mohair sweater, unwrap her tartan skirt, and unbutton her blouse. She posed with her arms over her head, let him admire the view of her breasts in her ecru push-up bra from France.

'You aren't doing yourself any favours, Melanie. The longer you make me wait, the harder your punishment is going to be.'

'You could just skip the whole thing, and fuck me on that nice, big bed,' Melanie said. She unsnapped her bra and let the fleshy mounds tumble out of the lace cups.

'Not a chance. Keep going.'

Melanie tossed her bra on a chair and picked up the corselet. Pulling its satin panels around her waist, she gazed wistfully at the snowflakes spinning past the window. Beyond the glass, the city looked like a Victorian Christmas card. That picturesque scene would make an intriguing backdrop for kinky sex. Melanie pictured herself restrained to the bedposts with fur-lined cuffs while Nathan tormented her with his mouth and hands – she might even let him use the clips, if he would forget about her punishment – and finally treated her to that big cock of his.

'The problem with you, Melanie,' Nathan said, as he helped Melanie lace up the corselet, 'is that you want to have everything on your own terms, with no compromises. You expect people to conform to your whims, wherever and whenever a mood strikes you.'

'I've always been that way. Did you think that you could suddenly turn me into the perfect little submissive?' Melanie sneered.

'I don't want you to be the perfect submissive. I've never gotten much pleasure out of dominating a complete submissive. But I don't want you to run away from your responsibilities just because people won't play the game your way.'

'Ow! You're pulling the laces too tight!'

'No, they're just right. The corset emphasises your hips and ass perfectly. You couldn't have made a better choice.'

'Believe me, if I'd known what I was doing, I wouldn't have chosen anything that emphasises my ass.'

'Well, today that's exactly what you need.'

The corselet, already too small for Melanie, was squeezing her waist like a satin fist. Her breasts were about to erupt from its scalloped contours; she had more cleavage than the star of a Wagnerian opera. Her waist, by contrast, was small enough for Nathan to span with his hands. He did just that as he picked her up and carried her, kicking and complaining, over to the spanking horse. He tossed her over the pommel as if she were a sack of potatoes, with her bum raised so high that her forehead almost touched the floor.

'I thought long and hard about how I wanted to punish you today,' Nathan said. 'I considered every tool in my collection. I thought about using a belt, a switch, a crop, a slapper. Finally I realised that nothing would give me more satisfaction than using my hand on you.'

'Don't be too hard on me,' Melanie pleaded. 'If I scream, the staff will come running.'

'No, they won't. I've paid them off. Besides, I'm going to make sure that any screaming is well muffled.'

Nathan knelt down on the floor, produced a long scarf, and stuffed a good portion of fabric into Melanie's mouth. Then he tied the ends securely behind her head. Melanie could already feel tears stinging the corners of her eyes. She had never felt so vulnerable or so ashamed, not since the age of sixteen, when she had been dragged off to the police station after a department store detective had caught her stealing a pair of nylon panty hose – on sale for two dollars. For two dollars' worth of synthetic fabric, they had actually brought in a cop to bully her, and as Melanie sat shivering in the grim interrogation room, she could feel how much the officer wished he could subject her to some private penal correction. Until this moment, that session had been the most humiliating experience of Melanie's life.

'Don't worry, my beautiful pet,' Nathan said, caressing her uplifted rump. 'I'm not going to traumatise you. I only want to teach you a lesson.'

Then Nathan did something that sent a tremor through Melanie's body – he took a step back and rolled up his sleeves. How much exercise did he think he was going to get? For once Melanie wished that she wore panties. If she did, there might have been a slim chance that Nathan would have allowed her to keep them on, and she'd have more than air to cushion her bottom.

Melanie's fingers clenched the lower rung of the horse and steeled herself for agony, but Nathan's first swats were fast and light. They landed across Melanie's cheeks and upper thighs, never striking the same spot twice, so that within a few minutes her backside was a tingling pleasure centre. Muscle by muscle, her body relaxed, surrendering to the sweet burn. Each blow pushed her lower body into the pommel of the spanking horse, creating a blunt friction. The pounding of the wooden pommel reminded her of the way a hard cock felt grinding against her mound, just before it slid into the wetness below.

Melanie was beginning to enjoy the ride, when she realised that the delectable heat in her hindquarters was growing into a wildfire. The first few minutes had only been a warm-up; now Nathan was getting serious, laying into her bum with the force of his whole arm. Nathan had to have the biggest, hardest, coarsest hands of any man alive. On her oversensitised skin, Melanie could feel every ridge and callus in his palm, and she wondered if his hand would leave permanent imprints in her flesh. If she ever made it out of this hotel room, she was going to pay Nathan back by forcing him to submit to weekly manicures.

Melanie looked up at her tormentor and whimpered imploringly through her gag.

'Whatever you're thinking, forget about it,' Nathan said. 'I'm not stopping until I'm damn good and ready.'

In his strained voice, Melanie could hear how aroused he was. He was channelling all that lust into punishing her, when he could be fucking her on the four-poster bed, like a normal, vanilla lover. As if he had seen her thoughts written in her eyes, Nathan upped the intensity of the spanking. Melanie squeezed her eyes shut and bit down hard on the scarf that filled her mouth. The cloth was already soaked with saliva; now tears added to its sogginess. As if she hadn't been mortified enough, the rhythmic percussion of the pommel gave Melanie a sudden, unexpected orgasm. She didn't know how it happened – suddenly the pain simply swelled into a tingling sensual awareness, her cunt felt full enough to burst, and the percussion of Nathan's hand pushed her over the edge. If Nathan hadn't caught hold of her, the climax would have jolted her off the horse.

'Bad girl,' he said. 'I didn't say you could come, did I?'

With one hand bracing the small of her back, he used the other to part her legs and slap her swollen pussy. She hadn't had time to recover from her first orgasm before she found herself in the grips of another. Her body was betraying her, sending her into fits of ecstasy when she should have been feeling nothing but pain and rage. Melanie's brain reeled. By the time Nathan stopped spanking her, and lifted her body off the horse, she was so limp and light-headed that she had all but forgotten where she was.

Melanie was surprised to come back to her senses a

'You aren't the one who's going to be humiliated today. I promise you that.'

Nathan knelt down so that he was facing Melanie through the window as she sat stubbornly in the driver's seat. She looked into his face, and saw sincerity in his blue eyes. In his navy-blue trenchcoat he looked so distinguished that no one could possibly diminish him, not even the back-biting council members. He was holding an antique leatherbound portfolio that sparked Melanie's curiosity.

'What's in that portfolio?' she asked.

He patted the cracked leather. 'My secret weapon. You'll find out all about it if you come to the meeting with me.'

'Oh, Nathan, I can't face those people right now.'

'Please, Melanie. Come with me. Let's show them who you really are.'

Reluctantly Melanie unlocked the door.

'All right. I'll go with you. But I reserve the right to leave if anyone attacks me.'

'If anyone even thinks about attacking you, they'll have to deal with me first,' Nathan said, and from the rock-hard set of his jaw, Melanie knew that he meant it. Nathan took Melanie by the arm. She was grateful to have his large body for support as they walked through the doors of the town hall. The hall had been constructed in the nineteenth century, and it smelled as if it hadn't been dusted since then.

This was supposed to be the day of my big triumph, Melanie thought sadly, as Nathan escorted her to the room where the council was meeting. Instead, I'm being led to the slaughter.

Council meetings were open to the public, and considering that it was the holiday season, a considerable crowd had gathered. Melanie hoped that Nathan would take her to a seat at the back of the room, but he led her straight up the aisle between the rows of chairs. Some of those chairs were occupied by Melanie's customers, others by the demonstrators who had protested against Chimera. Everyone turned to stare as Melanie made her appearance. A few people smiled; some frowned; most simply looked shocked to see Melanie, as if she didn't have as much right to be here as anyone else. In the front row, Pagan stood up, waved both arms and hollered.

'Hey, Mel! Over here!'

The council members, who sat in a row at a long table, scowled at Pagan, then glared at Melanie. Melanie stared straight at Harrison Blake, whose face suddenly turned the same sickly off-white as the wall behind him. Melanie and Nathan slipped into the chairs beside Pagan.

'You probably want to kill me, don't you?' Melanie asked. 'I'm sorry I left you and Luna by yourselves.'

'Don't worry about it,' Pagan said, with a flippant wave of her hand. 'I was kind of hoping you wouldn't come back, so I could run the shop by myself.'

Melanie hugged her. 'I knew there was a reason I hired you.'

Then Harrison Blake rapped on the table with a gavel, flipping his wrist officiously. Melanie wondered why she had ever wasted her time on such a pompous fool. The crowd quieted down, and the meeting began. For the next hour, the public was treated to a long agenda of zoning and development issues – an agenda on which Melanie was conspicuously absent. She should have been up there with the other shop owners of Morne Bay, presenting her plans for expansion. Instead, she was sitting on the sidelines, watching the 'respectable' businesspeople receive support for their projects.

Melanie knew that most of them weren't as strait-laced as they appeared. Priscilla Lawrence, the owner of a quaint bed and breakfast, was also the owner of the largest collection of vintage spanking photographs in the state. Ed Jenkins managed a hardware store, but the type of hardware he preferred was usually applied to his girlfriend's genitals. Then there were the council members themselves, who had enough secret fetishes and peccadillos among them to fill an encyclopedia of alternative sexuality. Melanie was just as good as any of these people; in fact, her business sense was stronger and her financial skills sharper than most. The only difference was that she displayed her sexuality for all to see, instead of burying it in the back of a closet.

Judging by the disgusted look on Nathan's face, he was thinking along the same lines. As the meeting wore on, Melanie wondered why he had bothered to drag her here. Was this the final phase of her punishment, to have her face rubbed in her own disappointment? If so, this was far worse punishment than the spanking Nathan had delivered yesterday. Listening to Ethel Billingsley twitter on about her plans to open a needlework shop, which would donate a portion of its proceeds to finding homes for abandoned cats, Melanie decided that Nathan was a monster of psychological cruelty.

'Didn't you torture me enough yesterday?' Melanie hissed.

'Just wait,' Nathan assured her.

'Why are we here? I'm not on the agenda, and you know it!'

'You're not, but I am.'

'Now, to conclude,' Harrison Blake announced, with a doting glance at his college buddy, 'Nathaniel Wentworth will bring us up to date on the progress of the new Morne Bay Historical Museum.'

The council members applauded when Nathan got to his feet and took his place at the podium. Pagan squeezed Melanie's hand.

'This is going to be good,' the girl whispered.

'Work on the museum is progressing as scheduled,'

Nathan said. 'Thanks to Dean DeSilva and his crew, everything is right on track, and we should be cutting the ribbon on May first, as planned.'

The council members murmured approvingly. Harrison applauded. Melanie rolled her eyes and tried not to be sick when Dean DeSilva's name was mentioned.

'But I've come here today to suggest a new angle on our project,' Nathan continued. 'When I research the history of a community, I look for the key to its vitality, the ingredient that makes it unique. These days, tourism is the primary industry in Morne Bay, but this town really got its juice from the importers who settled here in the nineteenth century. Darius Morne was a shrewd businessman, but he was also a sensualist. He had worldly tastes, and he didn't mind spending money to satisfy them. Before he infused this area with his wealth, the community was little more than a struggling fishing village. If not for Darius Morne, his wife Amélie, and their hunger for the exotic, there might be nothing here today but a few old lobster buoys lying around on the beach.'

Nathan paused to let his words sink in. The council members' faces had turned from fawning to furious. Harrison looked like he might implode. Nathan smiled to himself and opened the leatherbound portfolio.

'A few days ago, a colleague of mine from Beardsley College gave me a rare historic treasure. This portfolio holds the shopping lists that Amélie Morne composed for her husband. I'd like to read to you some of the items that she ordered from abroad. "Fifty yards of silk – pink, green, and yellow. Perfume – French. Erotic statuary – Chinese. Carved wooden *diletto* – Italian." A *diletto*, by the way, was an Italian device that allowed women to give themselves pleasure without the assistance of a penis. Amélie Morne loved to give herself pleasure, and she was always seeking out new ways to do it. It's even been rumored that she was one of the first women in the country to own the newly introduced rubber dildo, but we don't have any proof of that. Not yet, anyway.'

Nathan closed the portfolio. The room was so quiet that Melanie could hear her own heartbeat.

'Is there a point to this?' Harrison asked, his voice emerging in a squeak.

'Yes, there is, Harrison. This town was founded by sensual adventurers, people who craved beauty and novelty – and yes, sexual variety. Darius and Amélie Morne dedicated themselves to enjoying new experiences and seeking out unusual objects overseas to enrich their lives. The point of my digression is that we need to acknowledge this part of our history, not only acknowledge it, but broadcast it. There is one person in the community who embodies that spirit of novelty, the craving for sensual adventure, and that person is with us this morning. Melanie Paxton, could you come up here, please?'

From the day she was born, Melanie had never hesitated to take centre stage, but today her knees knocked as she made her way past the blur of faces to stand beside Nathan at the podium. She couldn't tell if it was terror or jubilation that made her so weak and shaky that she could hardly stand. If Nathan hadn't been there to prop her up with his bulk, she might have collapsed under the council members' withering stares.

'In honour of the entrepreneurial spirit behind this community, I'd like to propose a new addition to our local historical project, an adjunct museum and gift shop dedicated to the memory of Amélie Morne. I'm asking the council to approve the expansion of the shop currently known as Chimera, so that it can be remodelled as the Amélie Morne Museum. As the manager of the project, Melanie Paxton would continue to offer vintage clothing and erotic merchandise for display and for sale. I realise that the council has already rejected Miss Paxton's proposal to expand Chimera, and that it disapproves of the role she's taken in the community as a leader in matters of sexuality.'

'Yes, that's right. So why are you wasting our time with this?' asked Melanie's arch-nemesis, Bridget Locke. Melanie had to restrain herself to keep from shouting obscenities at the two-faced sneak who called herself a journalist.

'Ladies and gentlemen, I encourage you to pull your heads out of your asses,' Nathan went on. 'This enterprise would be unique. It could put Morne Bay on the map. It could bring in some much-needed money to a town that's striving to distinguish itself from every other seaside tourist town. So before you shut down your minds altogether, think about the financial possibilities.'

'In other words, if the shop were a museum, it could bring in additional public revenue?' Harrison asked, rubbing his jaw thoughtfully.

'That's right.'

'Wait a minute,' Melanie interrupted. 'I'd like to say something.'

With the mention of money, the implications of Nathan's proposal had started to register. She could see all too well what would happen if Chimera were turned into a museum. Her personal creative dreams would be roped into the public domain, and everything she did, every item she offered to her customers, would have to bear the town council's seal of approval. Where was the edginess in that? Where was the fun, the thrill of the alternative, if everything she did was homogenised by the mainstream?

The council was waiting for Melanie to speak. She cleared her throat.

'Thank you, Nathan, for supporting me, but I couldn't do what you're asking. It wouldn't be right. It wouldn't be fair to the friends who have stood behind me, my employees and my customers, if I were always bending to the will of the town council. I'd be happy to work with you on a display for the museum, maybe a room dedicated to Amélie Morne. She was an awesome woman, way ahead of her time. But when it comes to business, I have to be independent. That's just how it is.'

Melanie glanced at Nathan. She was afraid that he'd be crushed by her refusal, but she saw only pride as he smiled down at her. Harrison, on the other hand, seemed miserable as he watched his hopes of a new cash cow disappear. Melanie stood up as tall as she could and looked him straight in the eye.

'Harrison, you were on my side at one time, then you turned against me. I never knew why, but I assume it had to do with pressure from your wife, your friends, or from some part of yourself that won't let you be the person you want to be. There's just one question I have to ask you before I go back to my shop and pick up where I left off.'

'Yes?' Harrison asked coldly.

'Were you man enough to wear your butt plug today?'

'I can't believe you said that, Melanie,' Nathan laughed. 'I thought they were going to have to carry Harrison out of there on a stretcher!'

'I wouldn't know. I was too busy running for the door. I was sure the council members were going to stone me to death.'

'No need to worry about that. They'll change their minds once the truth sinks in. You're a moneymaker, my dear, whether you're working in the public or private domain.'

'Speaking of which, I should get back to the shop today,' Melanie said.

'Yes, you should. That's where you belong.'

They were standing beside Melanie's car. She dug through her purse, stalling for time as she pretended to hunt for her keys. She didn't feel ready to face Chimera yet, but she didn't want to go home, either. She didn't know what was waiting for her back at the carriage house. Maybe a note like the one that Paulette Winters had left on her door last month, offering a feeble excuse for kicking Melanie out.

'Sometimes I don't know if I *do* belong at Chimera. Or anywhere else around here,' Melanie admitted. 'I'm sure I blew it with Hannah. Serves me right for getting involved with a married couple.'

'Listen, why don't you go to the shop, make sure everything's in order, then go home and have a talk with Hannah and Ted? Don't let things go unresolved.'

'What if they don't want me to live there any more?'

'Then you can come and live with me. Of course, you'll be my full-time sex slave, but you won't mind that, I'm sure.'

Melanie swatted Nathan with her purse. 'I *would* mind that. Very much. You'll never turn me into a submissive.'

'But I'm having the time of my life trying.'

Nathan gave Melanie a knee-knocking kiss, his firm tongue weaving through her mouth with such passion that it left her breathless. As he let her come up for air, he stroked her bum, reviving the pain and sending a reverberation of yesterday's spanking echoing through her body.

'Don't ever stop trying,' Melanie said.

Driving away, she caught sight of Nathan in her rear-view mirror. He was standing where she'd left him, watching her. The longer she knew him, the more attractive she found him. He was big and gorgeous, strong and trustworthy, and best of all, he adored Melanie. She had hated to turn down his idea about the museum, but when push came to shove, Melanie wasn't the museum type. She didn't like to see precious objects displayed behind glass, shielded by alarms and protected by guards.

She liked living, vital things that she could hold in her hands, experience with all of her senses.

When Melanie arrived at Chimera, the shop was packed with customers. Apparently the demonstration hadn't discouraged business; if anything, the place looked busier than any holiday season that Melanie could remember. Walking through the front door, she felt like a different woman, as if the time she had spent away had altered her perspective, turning her into a customer instead of the shop's manager. With an expert eye, Melanie surveyed the interior, from the racks of vintage dress dripping with old lace and beads to the shiny new leather corsets. She saw the boldly painted nudes on the walls, contrasting with the delicate wreaths of dried flowers and herbs. Then of course there was the Alcove, now the heart of the shop, where countless erotic discoveries lay waiting for anyone who was adventurous enough to find them. Watching the crowds of customers, many of whom she didn't recognise, Melanie's pulse quickened.

This is my creation, Melanie thought. I imagined it, I made it real, and now, if I want to, I can leave it and move on.

Behind the counter, Pagan had already resumed her place and was ringing up one purchase after another. Luna was weaving her way through the shoppers, stopping here and there to answer questions. Assisting Pagan at the counter was a third girl, a statuesque blonde poured into a skintight red velvet jumpsuit. Pagan and Luna must have unofficially hired some extra help. From the number of men in the store, Melanie guessed that this new assistant was helping out quite a bit, indeed.

Melanie chuckled to herself. Before the girls could notice her, she turned and slipped out the door.

It was twilight by the time Melanie's car pulled up in front of the carriage house. The little white house with the peaked roof looked dark and empty, as did Ted and Hannah's place. Melanie saw no sign of Hannah's truck or Ted's car; the couple must have gone away. Melanie felt a rush of regret, wishing that she could have made the relationship work. If she were brutally honest with herself, she would have to admit that she wasn't good at long-term relationships. Sexual flings were her territory; as soon as she ventured out of the shallows of casual affection, she was lost.

Melanie's heart was heavy as she unlocked the door. She had just finished decorating the carriage house so that it was exactly to her taste: a cross between an eighteenth-century courtesan's boudoir and an underground New York nightclub. Now she was going to have to move again, before she'd even gotten settled.

Melanie stopped in her tracks. The room wasn't completely dark, as she had first thought. A double row of votive candles formed a pathway leading from her 'salon', as she called it, all the way up the stairs.

'Hello? Who's there?' she called.

The glowing trail of flames beckoned her to follow, but Melanie held back. She didn't want to enter the house if there were some psycho with a candle fetish waiting for her in the shadows. From upstairs, she heard soft, muffled laughter.

'Who's there?' she called again, but this time there was more curiosity than fear. Step by step, she moved towards the staircase that led to the loft where she slept. The candles cast an enchanted glow through the room, giving her familiar furniture otherworldly shapes. As she got closer to her goal, strains of music, barely audible, caught her attention. The scent of something wild and spicy and sweet drifted down the stairs. By the time she reached the top, Melanie was about to burst with excitement.

The transformation that had taken place in her loft

surpassed her expectations. She could hardly believe that she had ever slept in that bed, which was half-hidden under a canopy of trailing vines and roses. Interwoven with the leaves and flowers were hundreds of tiny, twinkling lights, which provided enough illumination for Melanie to see the brass incense burner, the source of the spicy fragrance, sitting on her nightstand. The nightstand itself was covered with rose blossoms, as was her vanity table. In the centre of a wreath of ivy on the vanity sat a bottle of champagne, uncorked so recently that frosty smoke was still drifting out of the bottle's mouth. The music drifting from her stereo was a recording of a string ensemble, playing a Renaissance love song. It was a scene straight out of *A Midsummer Night's Dream*, a scene that could only have been orchestrated by someone with a gift for the theatrical, someone like . . .

'Ted?' Melanie cried. 'Hannah? I know it's you. Come out!'

Like everything else in the room, the two figures who emerged from the shadows were as different from their ordinary selves as night and day. Hannah wore her hair in an abundant mane of spiral curls. A mask painted with golden glitter covered her eyes, and she wore a long white toga accented with wreaths of silk roses around her wrists, waist, and throat. Ted wore a gold mask, too, an elaborate creation shaped like the leering face of Pan. He was naked except for a wreath of silk laurel leaves around his waist, and his sleek muscles were painted with shimmering body paint. Both Ted and Hannah held glass flutes topped with champagne.

'Happy New Year,' Hannah giggled. 'Nathan called us last night and told us that you'd be coming home today. We thought we'd surprise you with a celebration.'

'It's not New Year's Eve yet,' Melanie said, though she was so delighted that she couldn't care less what day it was.

'But tonight marks a new start for the three of us,' said Ted. 'Right, Hannah?'

'That's right.' Hannah handed Melanie a glass of champagne. 'I'm sorry about that scene I made at the shop, Melanie. I wasn't fair to you – I changed the rules of the game. I want our relationship to be truly open now, the way it's supposed to be.'

'Are you sure about that?' Melanie asked. 'Do you really want me here?'

'That's why we did all this, to show you how much we want you.' Ted raised his glass. 'Let's seal it with a toast.'

'To new beginnings?' Hannah suggested.

'Sounds good to me,' said Melanie.

After that long, exhausting day, the alcohol went straight to Melanie's head. The buzz of the champagne made everything seem to glow around the edges, including Ted and Hannah. As the couple chatted about their plans for the coming year, Melanie sipped at her glass of bubbly elixir and listened.

'What about you, Melanie?' Ted asked. 'What new worlds are you going to conquer?'

'I'm not sure yet.' Melanie smiled. She didn't want to commit herself to anything more than a night of erotic pleasure.

'How are you feeling tonight?' Hannah asked. 'You've hardly said a word since you got here.'

'I feel distinctly overdressed. You two look like characters out of a Greek myth, and I'm still wrapped in my winter wool.'

'There's only one way to fix that, isn't there?'

Ted lifted the glass out of Melanie's hand, and Hannah helped her peel off her clothes. Together the couple moved her over to the bed and laid her down under the tent of vines and flowers. Ted and Hannah pulled their masks off so that they could kiss Melanie's lips, throat, and breasts as their hands roved over her skin. Their faces glowed under the glitter paint, and their eyes were rimmed with dramatic black arabesques. Hannah slid out of her toga and rubbed her large body against Melanie's slim one. Melanie felt as if she were being rocked on a warm sea of flesh. The glitter that covered Ted and Hannah had come off on her own skin; now she was sparkling, too.

Then Ted said something that almost ruined the moment.

'We heard that you were a bad girl in Boston, Melanie.'

The words 'bad girl' caught Melanie off guard. For a moment she didn't know how to react. She rolled the phrase around in her mind, testing its impact, then she realised that it had lost its power to hurt her. If people wanted to reject creativity and sexuality in favour of old fears and prejudices, that was their loss. Tonight Melanie was starting over, and in her new life, dusty taunts from the past couldn't touch her.

'I'm always a bad girl,' Melanie declared. 'And proud of it, too.'

'Well, tonight you'll get what's coming to you,' Hannah said.

Ted hooked his arm under Melanie's knees, pulled her legs up against her belly, and lightly spanked her bottom until it tingled with delicious anticipation. Hannah fondled Melanie's breasts, pinching the nipples just hard enough to set off delicious sparks of pain. The combined sensations of being cradled, caressed, and punished were already making Melanie want to come. Now her former teacher was parting her legs so that he could taste the sweet-and-sour wetness between, and Hannah was straddling Melanie's body, offering her bush to Melanie's mouth. Melanie lapped at Hannah's plump lower lips, savouring the salty tang mingled with the dry aftertaste of the champagne. While Ted's tongue wove through the whorls of Melanie's vulva, Melanie tightened her grip on Hannah's thighs and intensified her licking.

Hannah was the first to come, whimpering and bucking against Melanie's mouth. Melanie followed her soon after, succumbing to Ted's attentions. As she peaked, she felt that she was climaxing with all of her senses – sight, smell, touch, taste, sound – in the magical grove that Ted and Hannah had created for her. Then Ted was on top of her, inside her, while Hannah lay back and watched. Ted's thrusting sent more ripples of pleasure through Melanie's loins, and she wrapped her legs around his back and urged him to fuck her harder. Each time his cock hit her core, Melanie felt another aftershock of joy. Hannah lay back and watched, without a trace of jealousy on her face.

I'm so lucky, Melanie thought, just before she came again. But that's only because I deserve to be.

After Ted and Hannah had gone back to their house, Melanie lay on her velvet-upholstered fainting couch and watched the winter stars through the skylight in her roof. Tonight really did feel like the beginning of a new season in her life. She didn't know where she would be living this year, or where she would be working, or whom she would be sleeping with, but the uncertainty was more exciting than any agenda she could imagine.

Melanie picked up her glass and poured one last toast. She rummaged through her mind for something brilliant to say, some scintillating phrase that would capture her sense of anticipation, but nothing seemed quite right.

'To me,' she finally said, and swallowed the last of the champagne.

LOOK OUT FOR THE ALL-NEW BLACK LACE BOOKS – AVAILABLE NOW!

All books priced £6.99 in the UK. Please note publication dates apply to the UK only. For other territories, please contact your retailer.

MIXED SIGNALS
Anna Clare
ISBN O 352 33889 X

Adele Western knows what it's like to be an outsider. As a teenager she was teased mercilessly by the sixth-form girls for the size of her lips. Now twenty-six, we follow the ups and downs of her life and loves. There's the cultured restaurateur Paul, whose relationship with his working-class boyfriend raises eyebrows, not least because he is still having sex with his ex-wife. There's former chart-topper Suki, whose career has nosedived and who is venturing on a lesbian affair. Underlying everyone's story is a tale of ambiguous sexuality, and Adele is caught up in some very saucy antics. **The sexy *tour de force* of wild, colourful characters makes this a hugely enjoyable novel of modern sexual dilemmas.**

PACKING HEAT
Karina Moore
ISBN O 352 33356 1

When spoilt and pretty Californian Nadine has her allowance stopped by her rich Uncle Willem, she becomes desperate to maintain her expensive lifestyle. She joins forces with her lover, Mark, and together they conspire to steal a vast sum of cash from a flashy businessman and pin the blame on their target's girlfriend. The deed done, the sexual stakes rise as they make their escape. Naturally, their getaway doesn't go entirely to plan, and they are pursued across the desert and into the casinos of Las Vegas, where a showdown is inevitable. The clock is ticking for Nadine, Mark and the guys who are chasing them – but a Ferrari-driving blonde temptress is about to play them all for suckers. **Fast cars and even faster women in this modern pulp fiction classic.**

To be published in September 2004

CLUB CRÈME
Primula Bond
ISBN 0352 33907 1

Suki Summers gets a job as a housekeeper for a private gentlemen's club in London. Club Crème has been founded by the debonair Sir Simeon for chaps who want an elegant retreat where they can relax and indulge their taste for old-fashioned frolics. Her first impression is that the place is very stuffy, but it isn't long before she realises that anything goes, as long as it is behind closed doors where she is required to either keep watch or join in.

BONDED
Fleur Reynolds
ISBN 0352 33192 5

Sapphire Western is a beautiful young investment broker whose best friend Zinnia has recently married Jethro Clarke, one of the wealthiest and most lecherous men in Texas. Sapphire and Zinnia have a mutual friend, Aurelie de Bouys, whose life is no longer her own now that her scheming cousin Jeanine controls her desires and money. In a world where being rich is everything and being decadent is commonplace, Jeanine and her hedonistic associates still manage to shock and surprise.

Also available

THE BLACK LACE SEXY QUIZ BOOK
Maddie Saxon
ISBN O 352 33884 9
£6.99

- What sexual personality type are you?
- Have you ever faked it because that was easier than explaining what you wanted?
- What kind of fantasy figures turn you on – and does your partner know?
- What sexual signals are you giving out right now?

Today's image-conscious dating scene is a tough call. Our sexual expectations are cranked up to the max, and the sexes seem to have become highly critical of each other in terms of appearance and performance in the bedroom. But even though guys have ditched their nasty Y-fronts and girls are more babe-licious than ever, a huge number of us are still being let down sexually. Sex therapist Maddie Saxon thinks this is because we are finding it harder to relax and let our true sexual selves shine through.

The Black Lace Sexy Quiz Book will help you negotiate the minefield of modern relationships. Through a series of fun, revealing quizzes, you will be able to rate your sexual needs honestly and get what you really want from your partner. The quizzes will get you thinking about and discussing your desires in ways you haven't previously considered. Unlock the mysteries of your sexual psyche in this fun, revealing quiz book designed with today's sex-savvy girl in mind.

Black Lace Booklist

Information is correct at time of printing. To avoid disappointment check availability before ordering. Go to www.blacklace-books.co.uk. All books are priced £6.99 unless another price is given.

BLACK LACE BOOKS WITH A CONTEMPORARY SETTING

☐ SHAMELESS Stella Black	ISBN 0 352 33485 1	£5.99
☐ INTENSE BLUE Lyn Wood	ISBN 0 352 33496 7	£5.99
☐ A SPORTING CHANCE Susie Raymond	ISBN 0 352 33501 7	£5.99
☐ TAKING LIBERTIES Susie Raymond	ISBN 0 352 33357 X	£5.99
☐ A SCANDALOUS AFFAIR Holly Graham	ISBN 0 352 33523 8	£5.99
☐ THE NAKED FLAME Crystalle Valentino	ISBN 0 352 33528 9	£5.99
☐ ON THE EDGE Laura Hamilton	ISBN 0 352 33534 3	£5.99
☐ LURED BY LUST Tania Picarda	ISBN 0 352 33533 5	£5.99
☐ THE HOTTEST PLACE Tabitha Flyte	ISBN 0 352 33536 X	£5.99
☐ THE NINETY DAYS OF GENEVIEVE Lucinda Carrington	ISBN 0 352 33070 8	£5.99
☐ DREAMING SPIRES Juliet Hastings	ISBN 0 352 33584 X	
☐ THE TRANSFORMATION Natasha Rostova	ISBN 0 352 33311 1	
☐ SIN.NET Helena Ravenscroft	ISBN 0 352 33598 X	
☐ TWO WEEKS IN TANGIER Annabel Lee	ISBN 0 352 33599 8	
☐ HIGHLAND FLING Jane Justine	ISBN 0 352 33616 1	
☐ PLAYING HARD Tina Troy	ISBN 0 352 33617 X	
☐ SYMPHONY X Jasmine Stone	ISBN 0 352 33629 3	
☐ SUMMER FEVER Anna Ricci	ISBN 0 352 33625 0	
☐ CONTINUUM Portia Da Costa	ISBN 0 352 33120 8	
☐ OPENING ACTS Suki Cunningham	ISBN 0 352 33630 7	
☐ FULL STEAM AHEAD Tabitha Flyte	ISBN 0 352 33637 4	
☐ A SECRET PLACE Ella Broussard	ISBN 0 352 33307 3	
☐ GAME FOR ANYTHING Lyn Wood	ISBN 0 352 33639 0	
☐ CHEAP TRICK Astrid Fox	ISBN 0 352 33640 4	
☐ THE GIFT OF SHAME Sara Hope-Walker	ISBN 0 352 32935 1	
☐ COMING UP ROSES Crystalle Valentino	ISBN 0 352 33658 7	
☐ GOING TOO FAR Laura Hamilton	ISBN 0 352 33657 9	

☐ HOP GOSSIP Savannah Smythe   ISBNO 352 33880 6
☐ GOING DEEP Kimberly Dean   ISBNO 352 33876 8

BLACK LACE BOOKS WITH AN HISTORICAL SETTING

☐ PRIMAL SKIN Leona Benkt Rhys   ISBN O 352 33500 9 £5.99
☐ DEVIL'S FIRE Melissa MacNeal   ISBN O 352 33527 0 £5.99
☐ DARKER THAN LOVE Kristina Lloyd   ISBN O 352 33279 4
☐ THE CAPTIVATION Natasha Rostova   ISBN O 352 33234 4
☐ MINX Megan Blythe   ISBN O 352 33638 2
☐ DEMON'S DARE Melissa MacNeal   ISBN O 352 33683 8
☐ DIVINE TORMENT Janine Ashbless   ISBN O 352 33719 2
☐ SATAN'S ANGEL Melissa MacNeal   ISBN O 352 33726 5
☐ THE INTIMATE EYE Georgia Angelis   ISBN O 352 33004 X
☐ OPAL DARKNESS Cleo Cordell   ISBN O 352 33033 3
☐ SILKEN CHAINS Jodi Nicol   ISBN O 352 33143 7
☐ ACE OF HEARTS Lisette Allen   ISBN O 352 33059 7
☐ THE LION LOVER Mercedes Kelly   ISBN O 352 33162 3
☐ THE AMULET Lisette Allen   ISBN O 352 33019 8
☐ WHITE ROSE ENSNARED Juliet Hastings   ISBN O 352 33052 X
☐ UNHALLOWED RITES Martine Marquand   ISBN O 352 33222 0
☐ LA BASQUAISE Angel Strand   ISBN O 352 32988 2
☐ THE HAND OF AMUN Juliet Hastings   ISBN O 352 33144 5
☐ THE SENSES BEJEWELLED Cleo Cordell   ISBN O 352 32904 1

BLACK LACE ANTHOLOGIES

☐ WICKED WORDS Various   ISBN O 352 33363 4
☐ MORE WICKED WORDS Various   ISBN O 352 33487 8
☐ WICKED WORDS 3 Various   ISBN O 352 33522 X
☐ WICKED WORDS 4 Various   ISBN O 352 33603 X
☐ WICKED WORDS 9 Various   ISBN O 352 33860 1
☐ WICKED WORDS 10 Various   ISBN O 352 33893 8
☐ THE BEST OF BLACK LACE 2 Various   ISBN O 352 33718 4

BLACK LACE NON-FICTION

- ☐ THE BLACK LACE BOOK OF WOMEN'S SEXUAL FANTASIES Ed. Kerri Sharp   ISBN 0 352 33793 1   £6.99
- ☐ THE BLACK LACE SEXY QUIZ BOOK Maddie Saxon   ISBN 0 352 33884 9   £6.99

To find out the latest information about Black Lace titles, check out the website: www.blacklace-books.co.uk or send for a booklist with complete synopses by writing to:

Black Lace Booklist, Virgin Books Ltd
Thames Wharf Studios
Rainville Road
London W6 9HA

Please include an SAE of decent size. Please note only British stamps are valid.

Our privacy policy
We will not disclose information you supply us to any other parties. We will not disclose any information which identifies you personally to any person without your express consent.

From time to time we may send out information about Black Lace books and special offers. Please tick here if you do <u>not</u> wish to receive Black Lace information.   ☐

Please send me the books I have ticked above.

Name ....

Address ....

....

....

....

Post Code ....

Send to: Virgin Books Cash Sales, Thames Wharf Studios, Rainville Road, London W6 9HA.

US customers: for prices and details of how to order books for delivery by mail, call 1-800-343-4499.

Please enclose a cheque or postal order, made payable to Virgin Books Ltd, to the value of the books you have ordered plus postage and packing costs as follows:

UK and BFPO – £1.00 for the first book, 50p for each subsequent book.

Overseas (including Republic of Ireland) – £2.00 for the first book, £1.00 for each subsequent book.

If you would prefer to pay by VISA, ACCESS/MASTERCARD, DINERS CLUB, AMEX or SWITCH, please write your card number and expiry date here:

....

Signature ....

Please allow up to 28 days for delivery.